Timothy and the Transgalactic Towel™

A Silverline™ Books Production
A Division Of
Shadowline™ image®

TIMOTHY and the TRANSGALACTIC TOWEL
ISBN: 978-1-60706-021-5

Ages 9-12

Published by Silverline Books/Image Comics, Inc. Office of publication: 2134 Allston Way, Second Floor, Berkeley, California 94704. Copyright © 2009 MIKE BULLOCK. All rights reserved. TIMOTHY and the TRANSGALACTIC TOWEL™ (including all prominent characters featured herein), its logo and all character likenesses are trademarks of MIKE BULLOCK, unless otherwise noted. Image Comics® and its logos are registered trademarks of Image Comics, Inc. Silverline Books and its logos are ™ and © 2008 Jim Valentino. All names, characters, events and locales in this publication are entirely fictional. Any resemblance to actual persons (living or dead), events or places, without satiric intent, is coincidental. No part of this publication may be reproduced or transmitted, in any form or by any means (except for short excerpts for review purposes) without the express written permission of Mr. BULLOCK

PRINTED IN SOUTH KOREA   First Printing, August, 2009

International Rights Representative:
Christine Jensen (christine@gfloystudio.com)

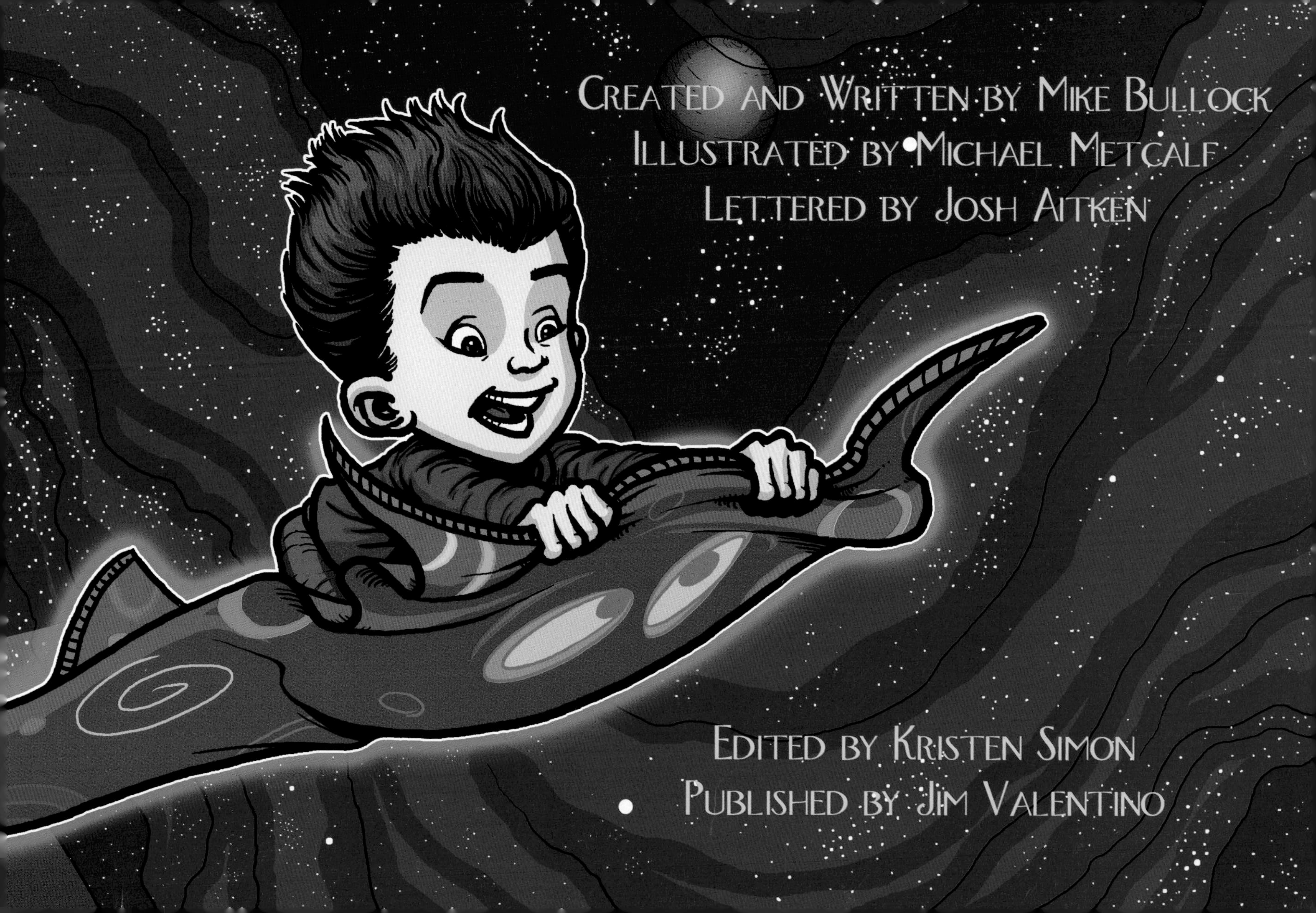

Created and Written by Mike Bullock
Illustrated by Michael Metcalf
Lettered by Josh Aitken

Edited by Kristen Simon
Published by Jim Valentino

FOR ANYONE WHO HAS EVER DREAMED...

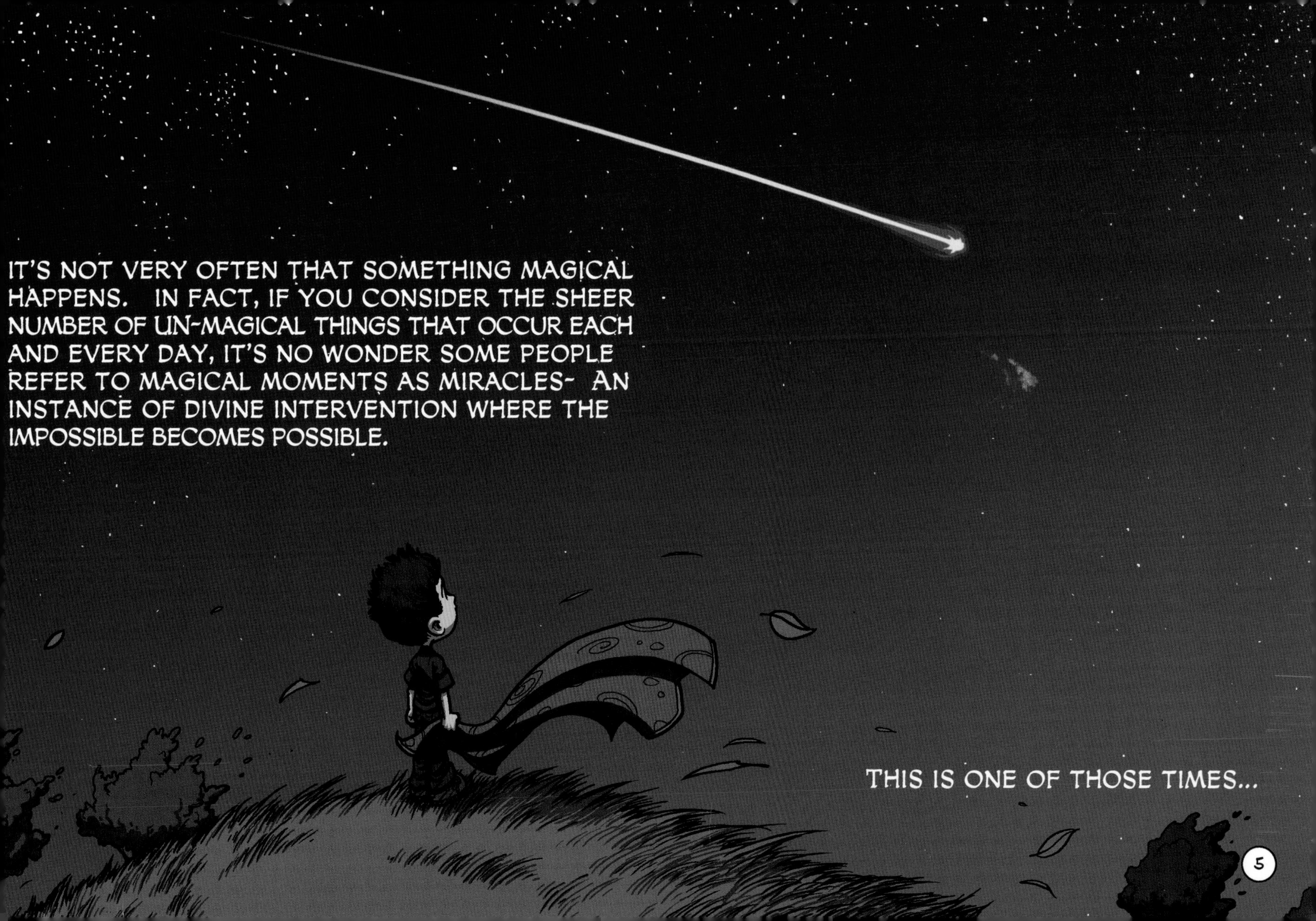
IT'S NOT VERY OFTEN THAT SOMETHING MAGICAL HAPPENS. IN FACT, IF YOU CONSIDER THE SHEER NUMBER OF UN-MAGICAL THINGS THAT OCCUR EACH AND EVERY DAY, IT'S NO WONDER SOME PEOPLE REFER TO MAGICAL MOMENTS AS MIRACLES- AN INSTANCE OF DIVINE INTERVENTION WHERE THE IMPOSSIBLE BECOMES POSSIBLE.
THIS IS ONE OF THOSE TIMES...

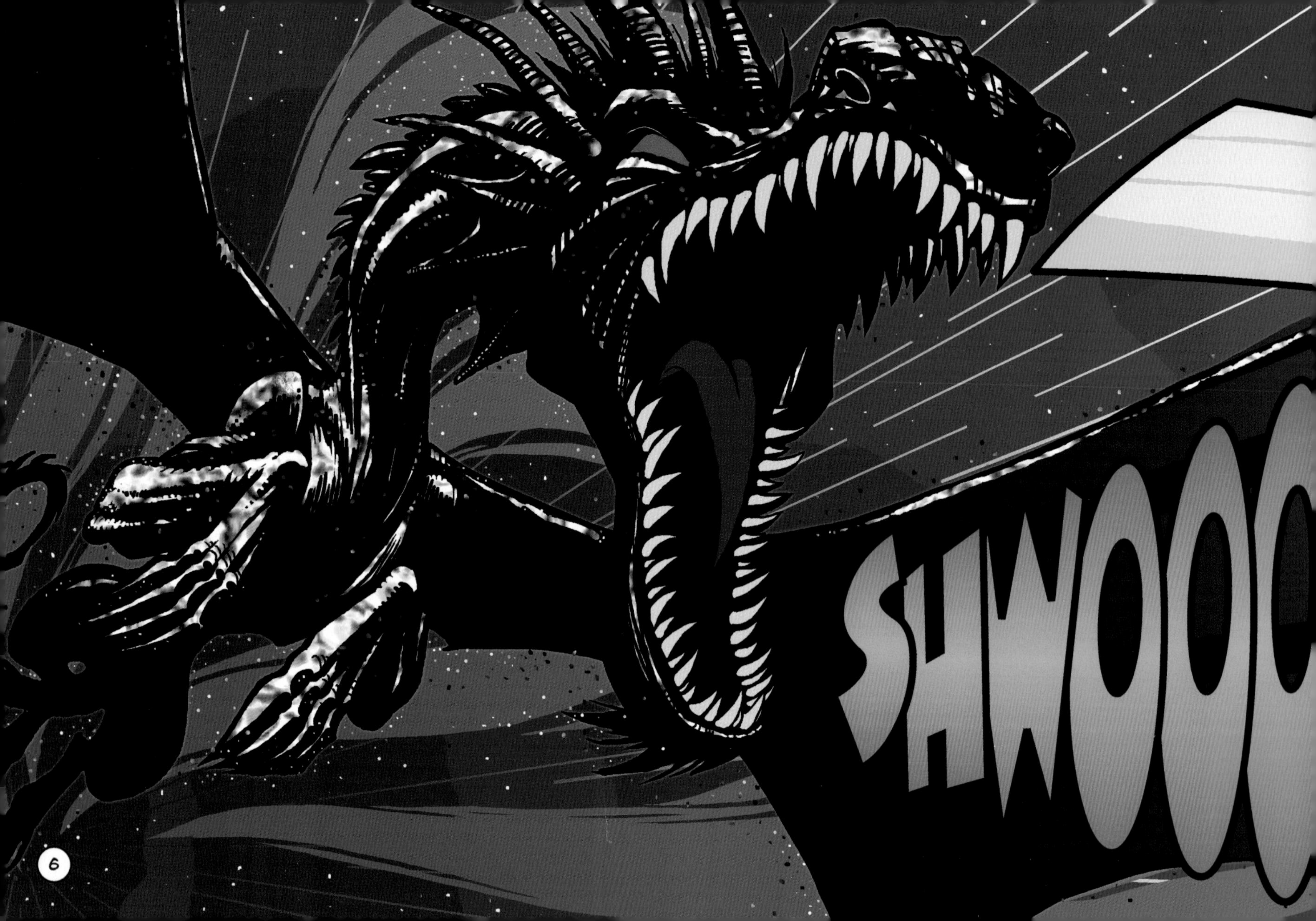
SHWOOO

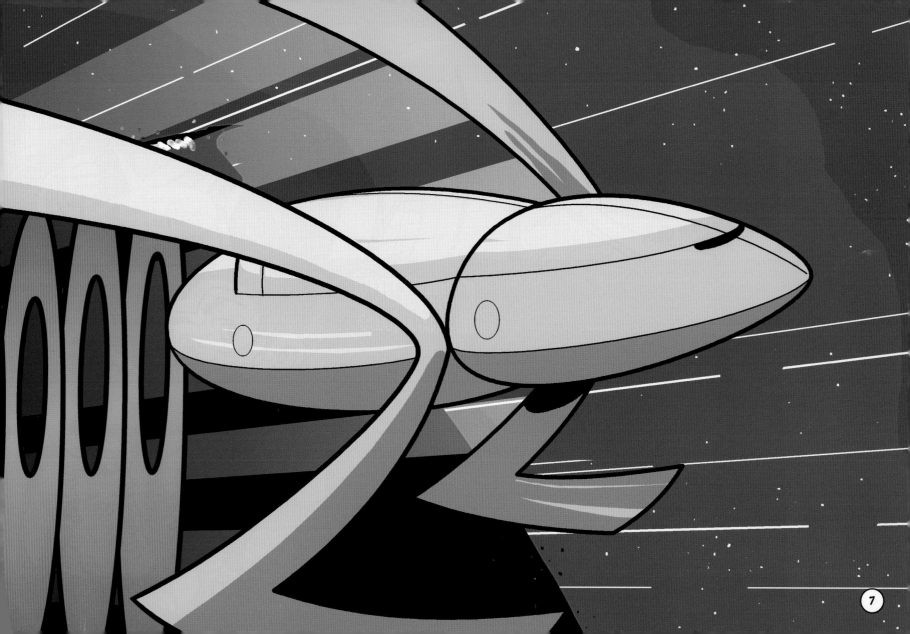

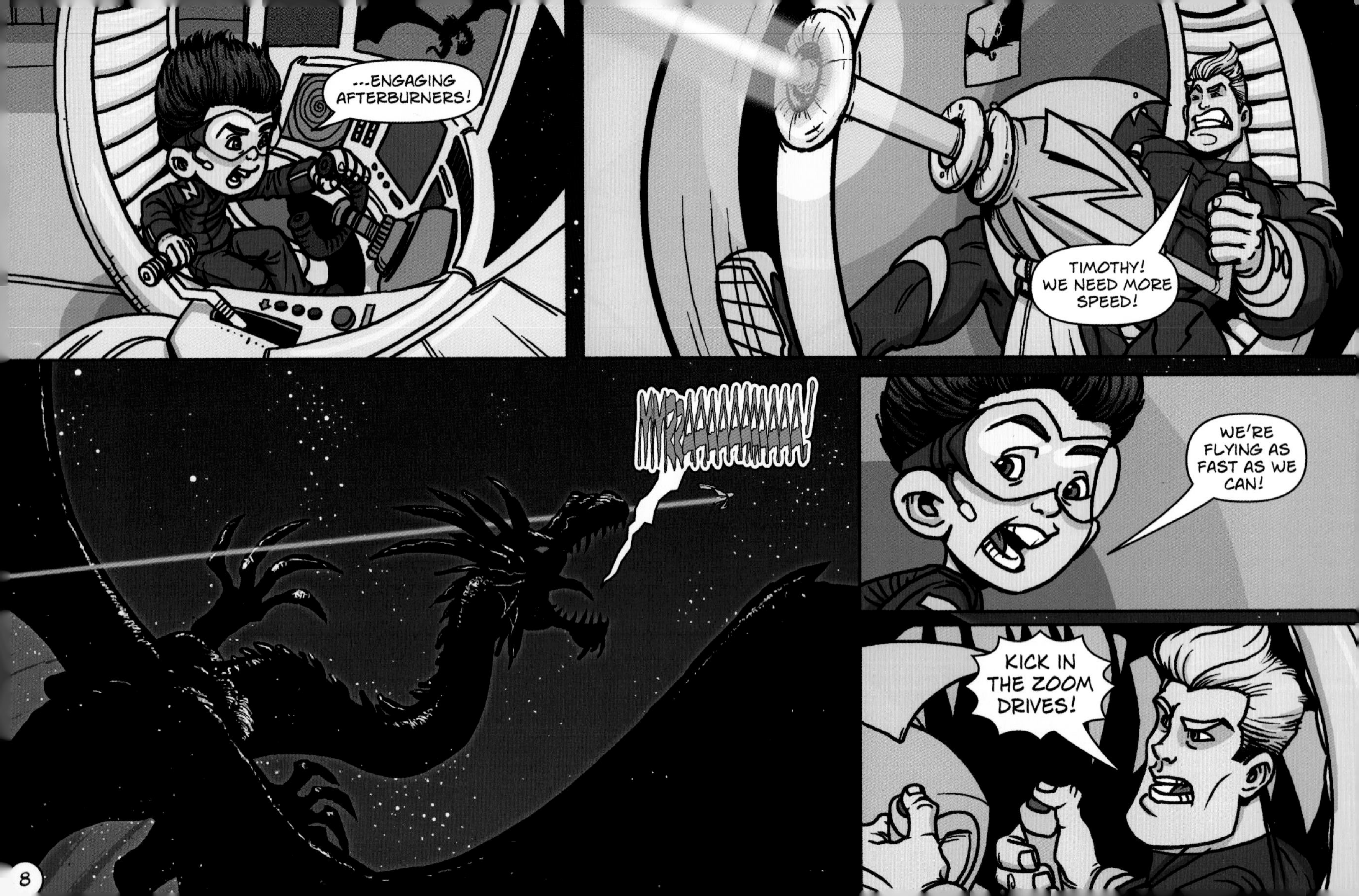

...ENGAGING AFTERBURNERS!
TIMOTHY! WE NEED MORE SPEED!
MYRRAAAAAAAAAAA!
WE'RE FLYING AS FAST AS WE CAN!
KICK IN THE ZOOM DRIVES!

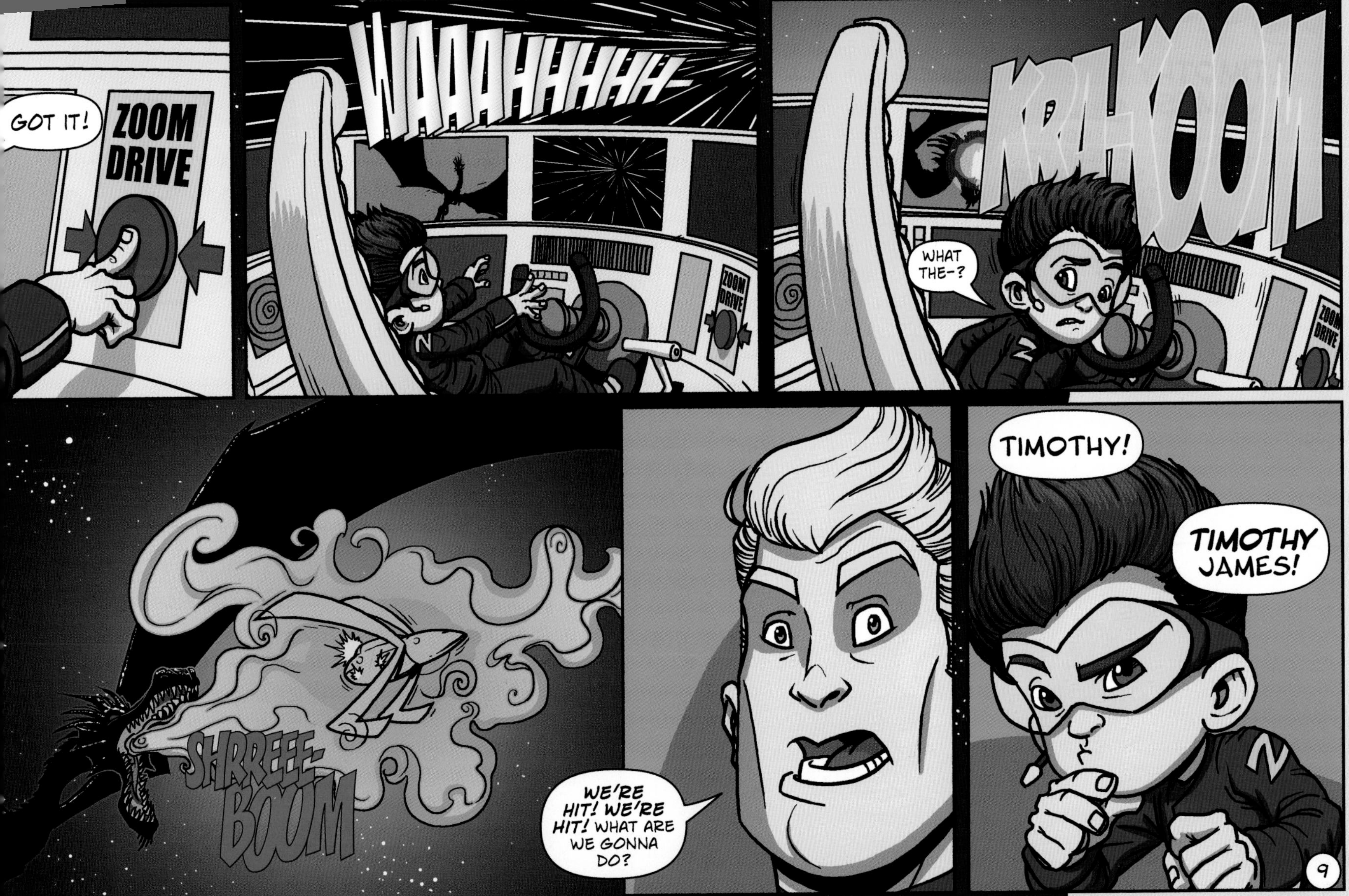
GOT IT!
ZOOM DRIVE
WAAAHHHHH-
KRA-KOOM
WHAT THE-?
SHRREEE-BOOM
WE'RE HIT! WE'RE HIT! WHAT ARE WE GONNA DO?
TIMOTHY!
TIMOTHY JAMES!

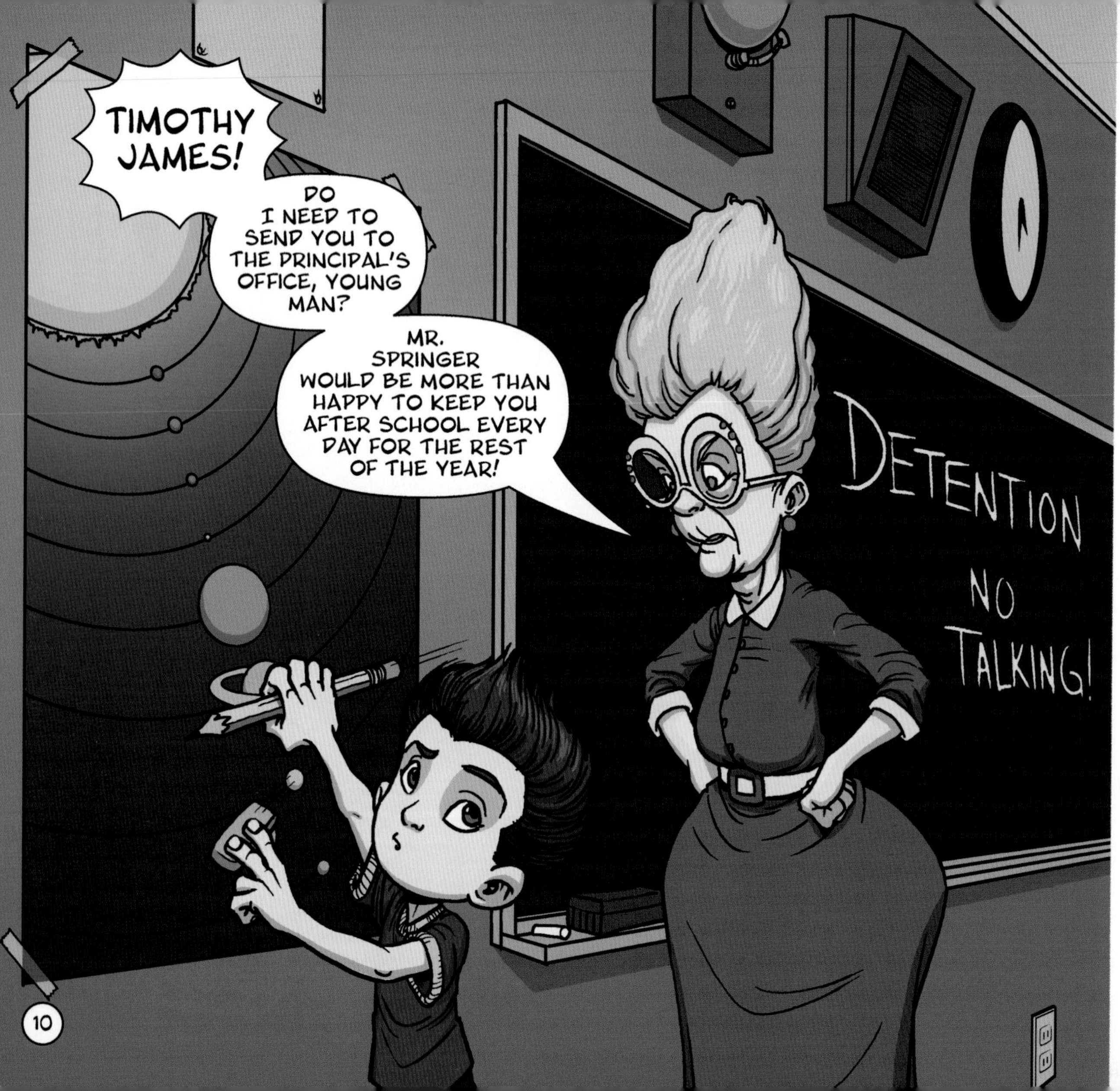

TIMOTHY JAMES!
DO I NEED TO SEND YOU TO THE PRINCIPAL'S OFFICE, YOUNG MAN?
MR. SPRINGER WOULD BE MORE THAN HAPPY TO KEEP YOU AFTER SCHOOL EVERY DAY FOR THE REST OF THE YEAR!
DETENTION
NO TALKING!

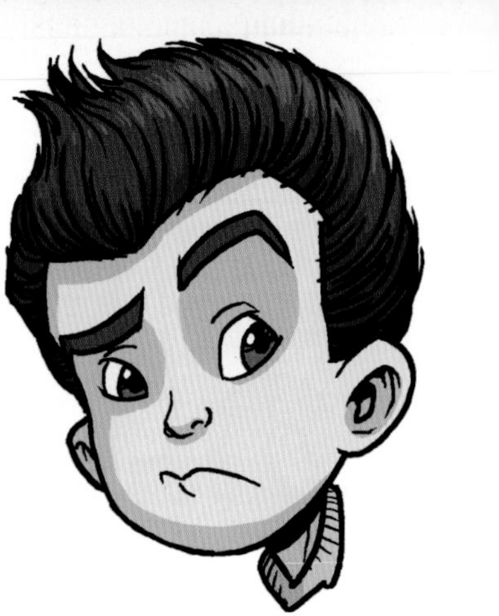

"PRINCIPAL'S OFFICE"?

WHY CAN'T SHE EVER SEND
TO ***TIGGERON'S MOON*** O
THE ***VALLEY OF DOOM***? W
DOES IT ALWAYS HAVE TO B
THE ***PRINCIPAL'S OFFICE***?

NOTHING FUN EVER HAPPENS
THERE. JUST ***BORING*** OLD
STUFF. MR. SPRINGER IS S
LAME I THINK HIS OFFICE I
ACTUALLY WHERE FUN GOES
DIE.

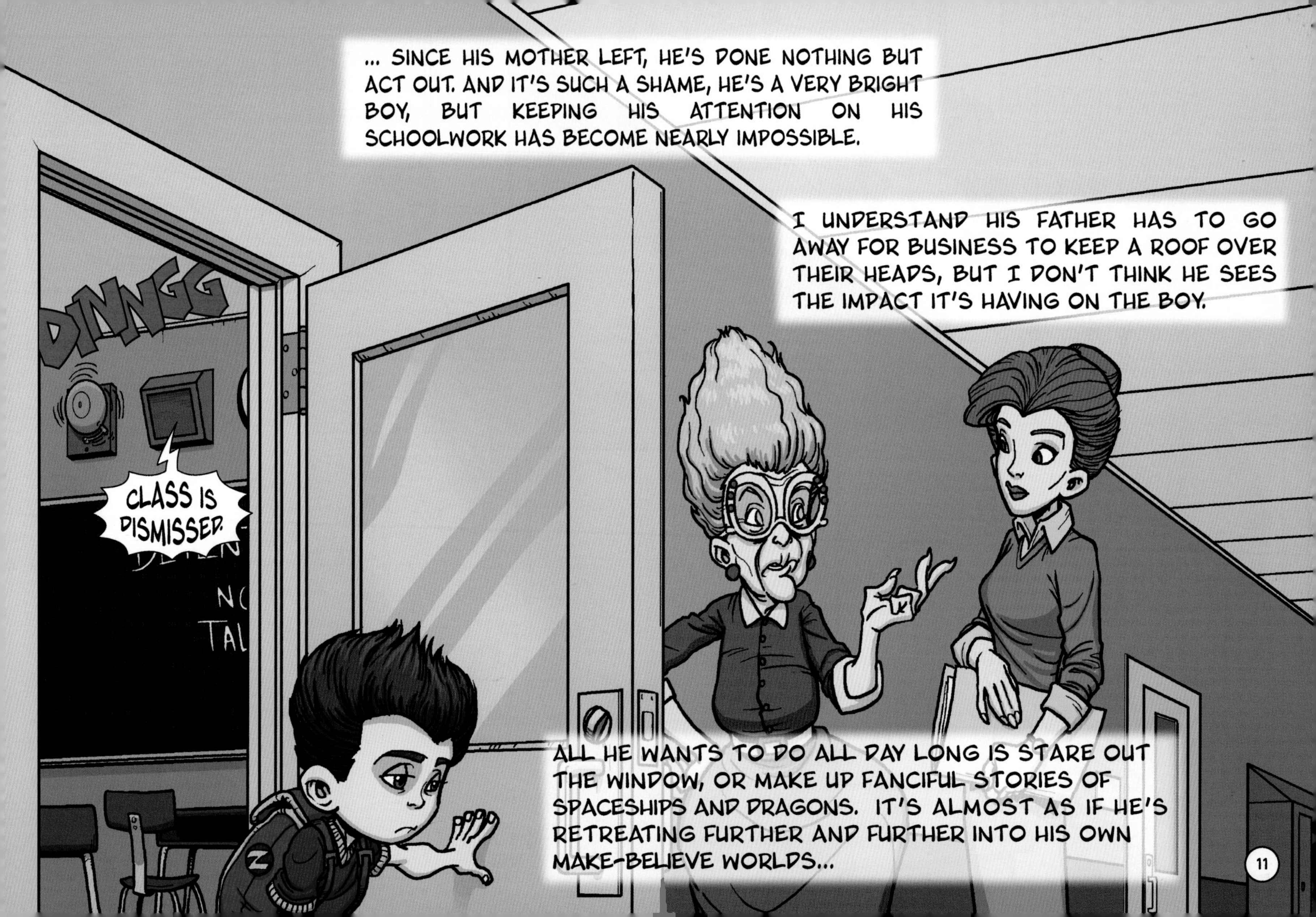
... SINCE HIS MOTHER LEFT, HE'S DONE NOTHING BUT ACT OUT. AND IT'S SUCH A SHAME, HE'S A VERY BRIGHT BOY, BUT KEEPING HIS ATTENTION ON HIS SCHOOLWORK HAS BECOME NEARLY IMPOSSIBLE.
DINNGG
CLASS IS DISMISSED.
I UNDERSTAND HIS FATHER HAS TO GO AWAY FOR BUSINESS TO KEEP A ROOF OVER THEIR HEADS, BUT I DON'T THINK HE SEES THE IMPACT IT'S HAVING ON THE BOY.
ALL HE WANTS TO DO ALL DAY LONG IS STARE OUT THE WINDOW, OR MAKE UP FANCIFUL STORIES OF SPACESHIPS AND DRAGONS. IT'S ALMOST AS IF HE'S RETREATING FURTHER AND FURTHER INTO HIS OWN MAKE-BELIEVE WORLDS...

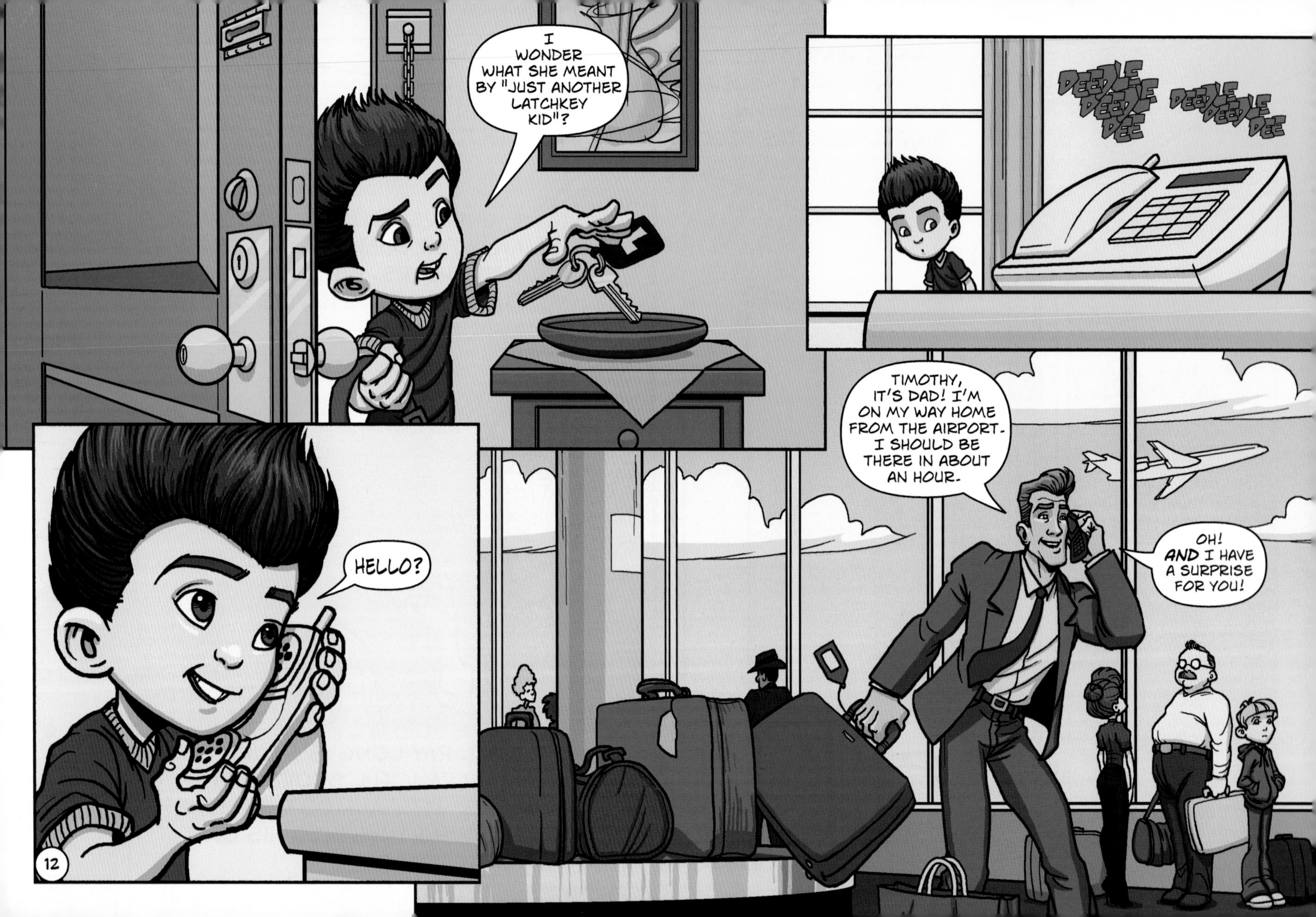
I WONDER WHAT SHE MEANT BY "JUST ANOTHER LATCHKEY KID"?
DEEDLE DEEDLE DEE DEEDLE DEEDLE DEE
HELLO?
TIMOTHY, IT'S DAD! I'M ON MY WAY HOME FROM THE AIRPORT. I SHOULD BE THERE IN ABOUT AN HOUR.
OH! AND I HAVE A SURPRISE FOR YOU!

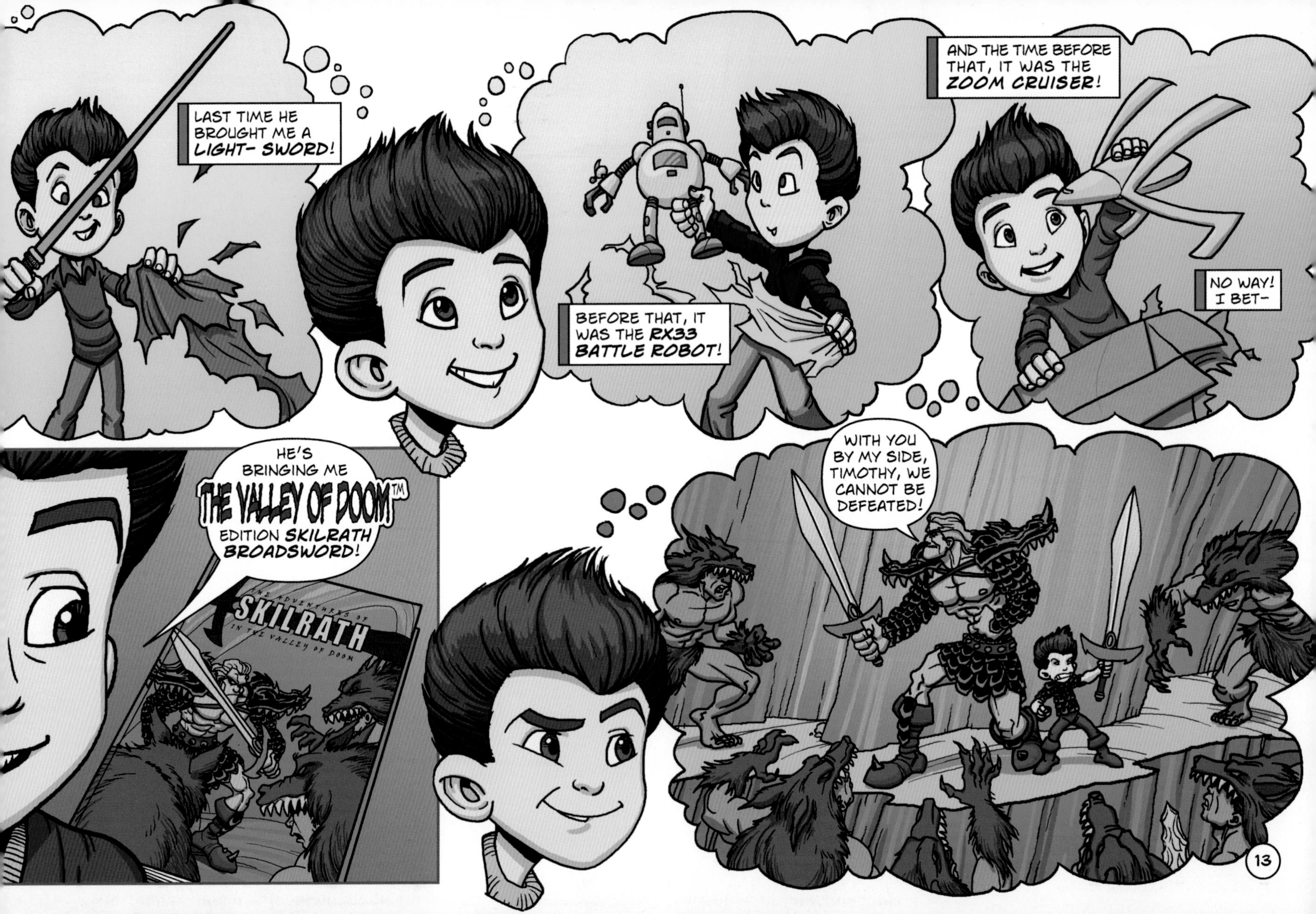

LAST TIME HE BROUGHT ME A LIGHT- SWORD!
BEFORE THAT, IT WAS THE RX33 BATTLE ROBOT!
AND THE TIME BEFORE THAT, IT WAS THE ZOOM CRUISER!
NO WAY! I BET-
HE'S BRINGING ME THE VALLEY OF DOOM™ EDITION SKILRATH BROADSWORD!
THE ADVENTURES OF SKILRATH IN THE VALLEY OF DOOM
WITH YOU BY MY SIDE, TIMOTHY, WE CANNOT BE DEFEATED!

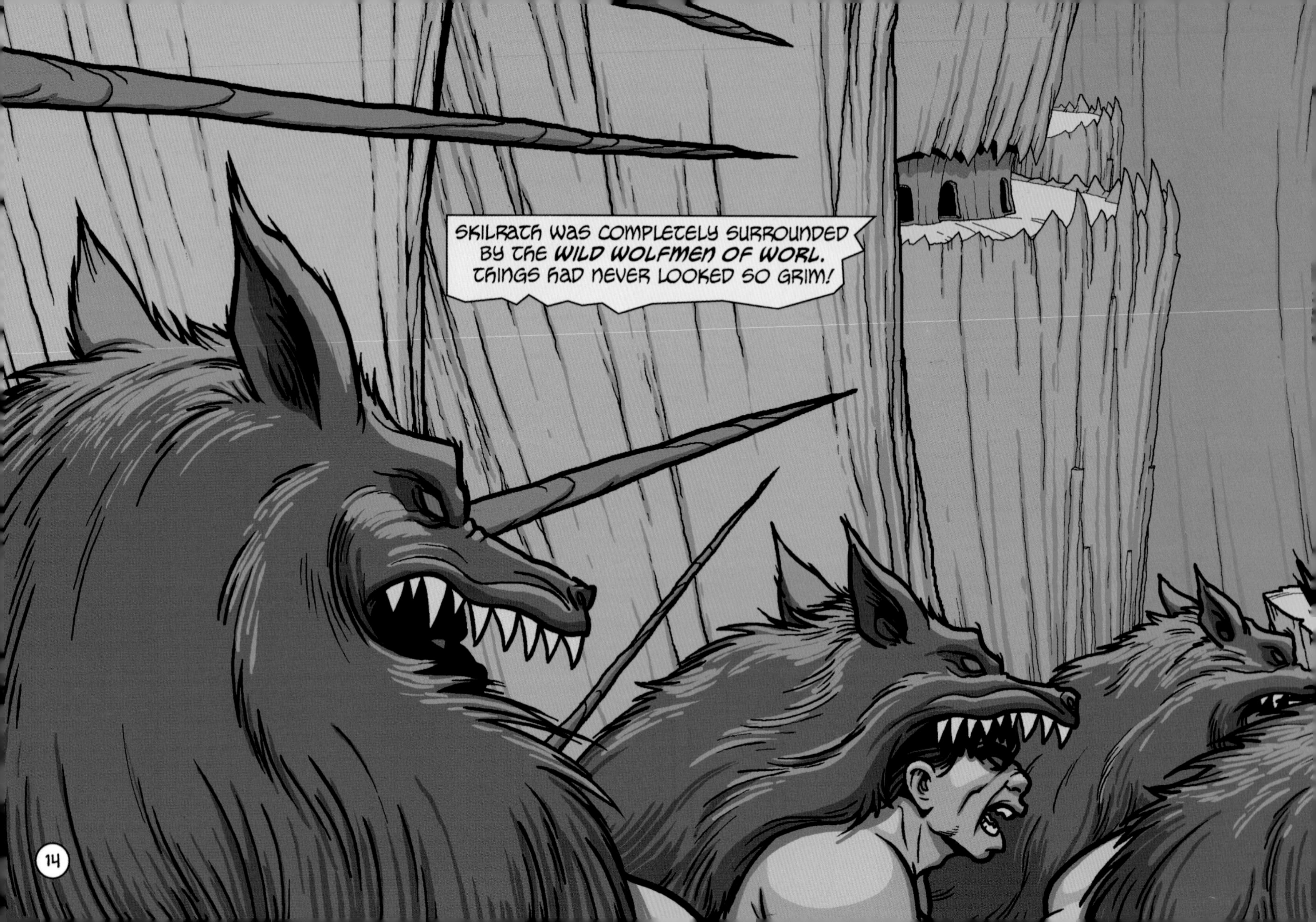
SKILRATH WAS COMPLETELY SURROUNDED BY THE WILD WOLFMEN OF WORL. THINGS HAD NEVER LOOKED SO GRIM!

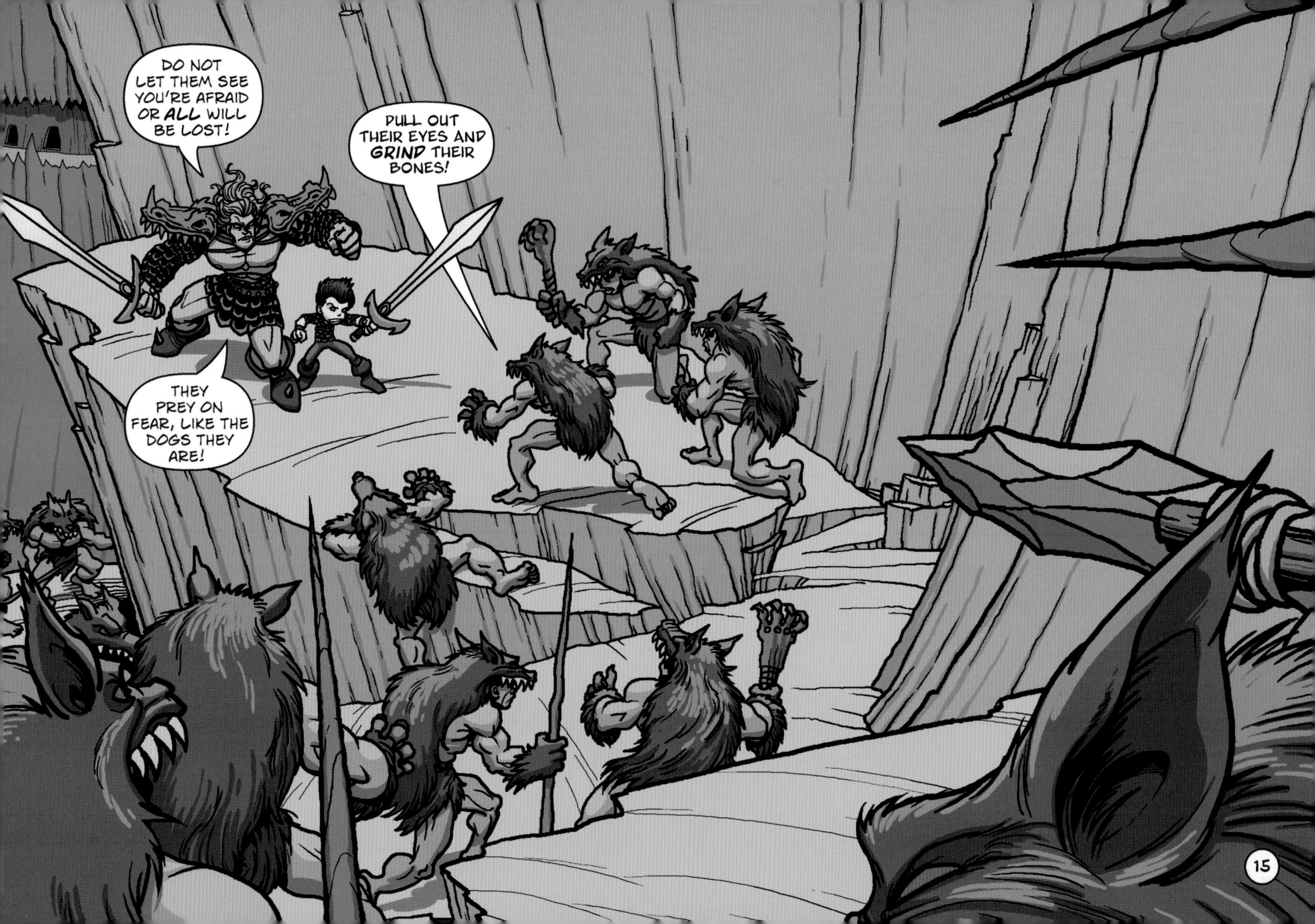
DO NOT LET THEM SEE YOU'RE AFRAID OR ALL WILL BE LOST!
THEY PREY ON FEAR, LIKE THE DOGS THEY ARE!
PULL OUT THEIR EYES AND GRIND THEIR BONES!

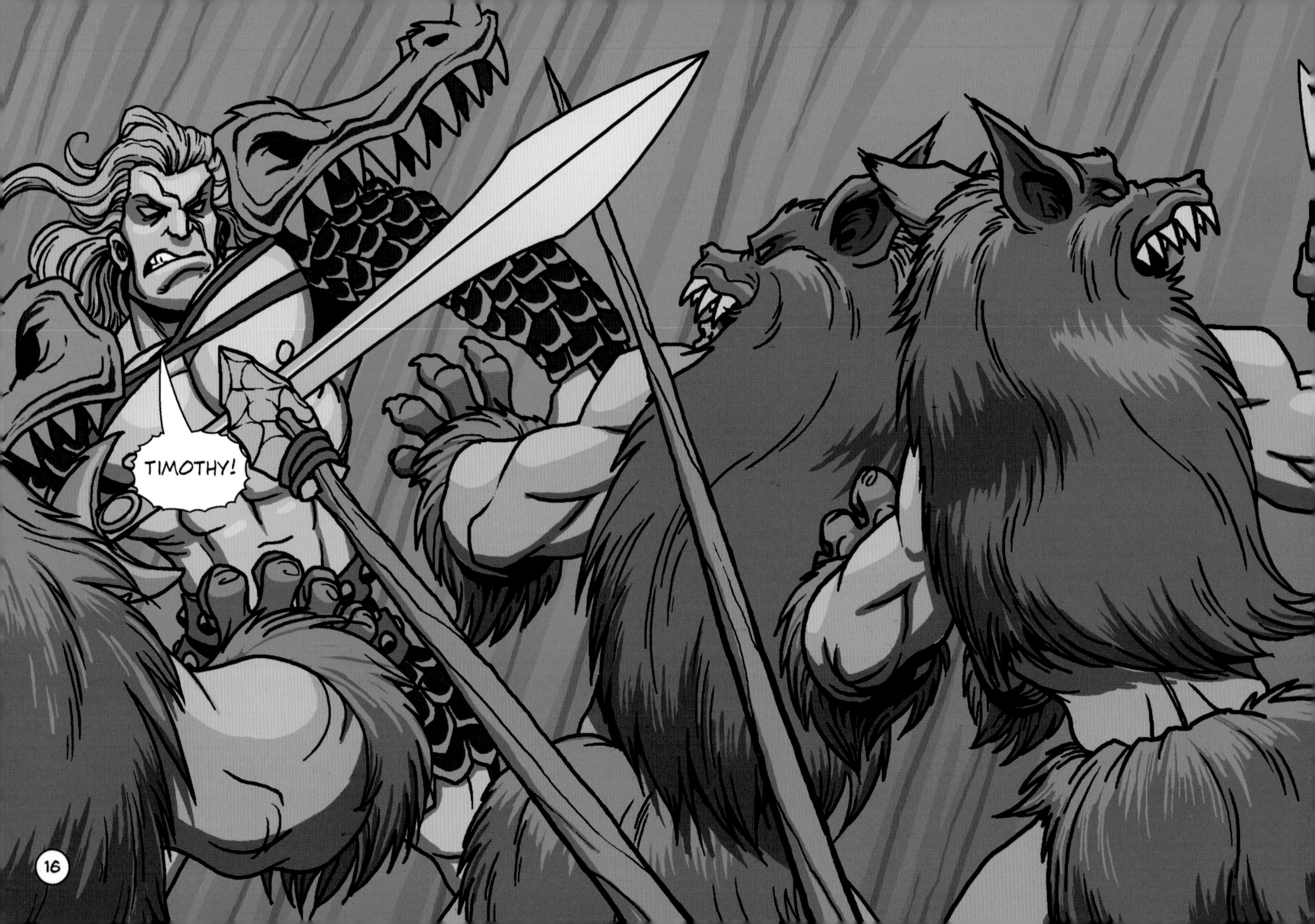
TIMOTHY!

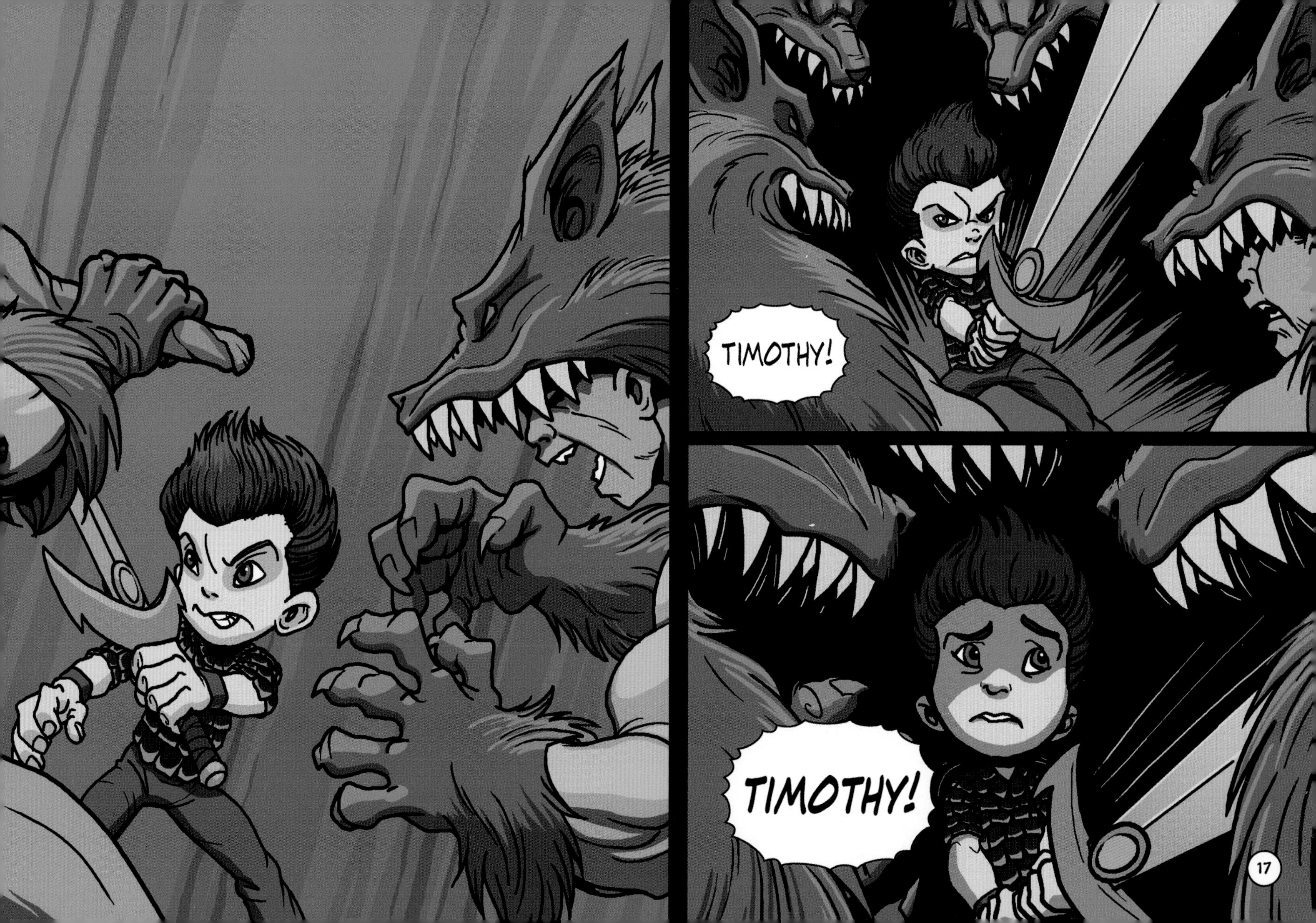
TIMOTHY!
TIMOTHY!

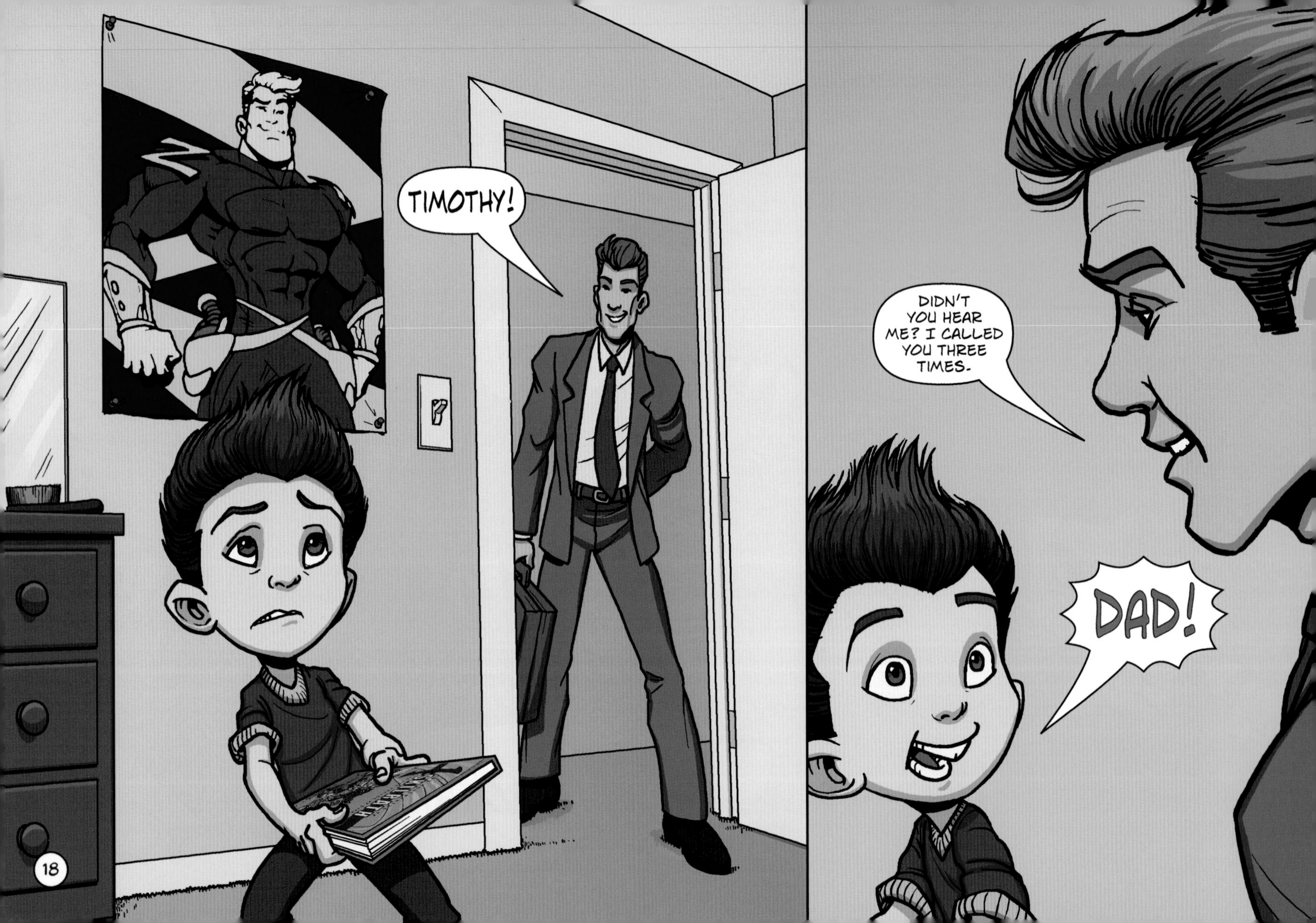
TIMOTHY!
DIDN'T YOU HEAR ME? I CALLED YOU THREE TIMES.
DAD!

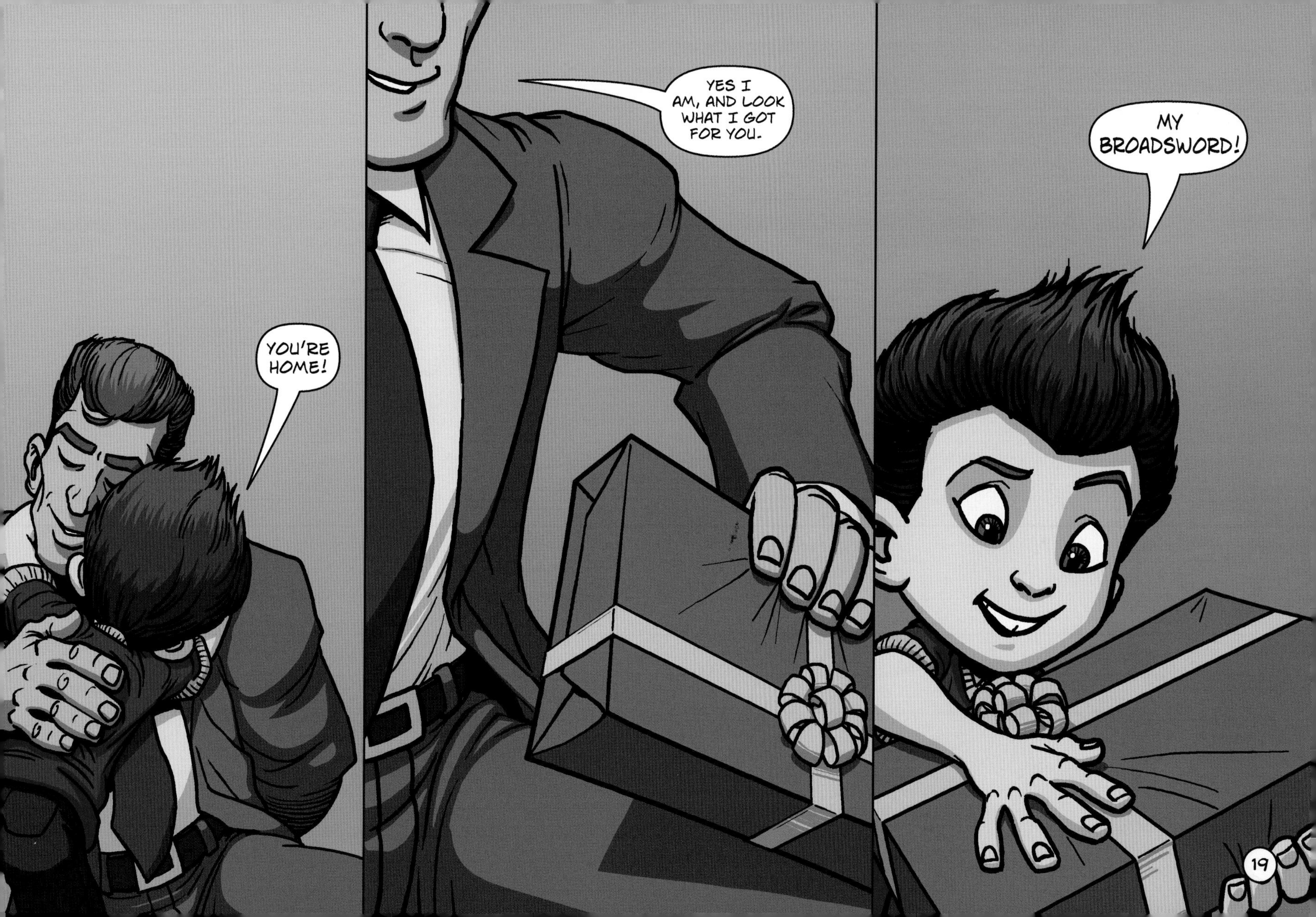
YOU'RE HOME!
YES I AM, AND LOOK WHAT I GOT FOR YOU.
MY BROADSWORD!

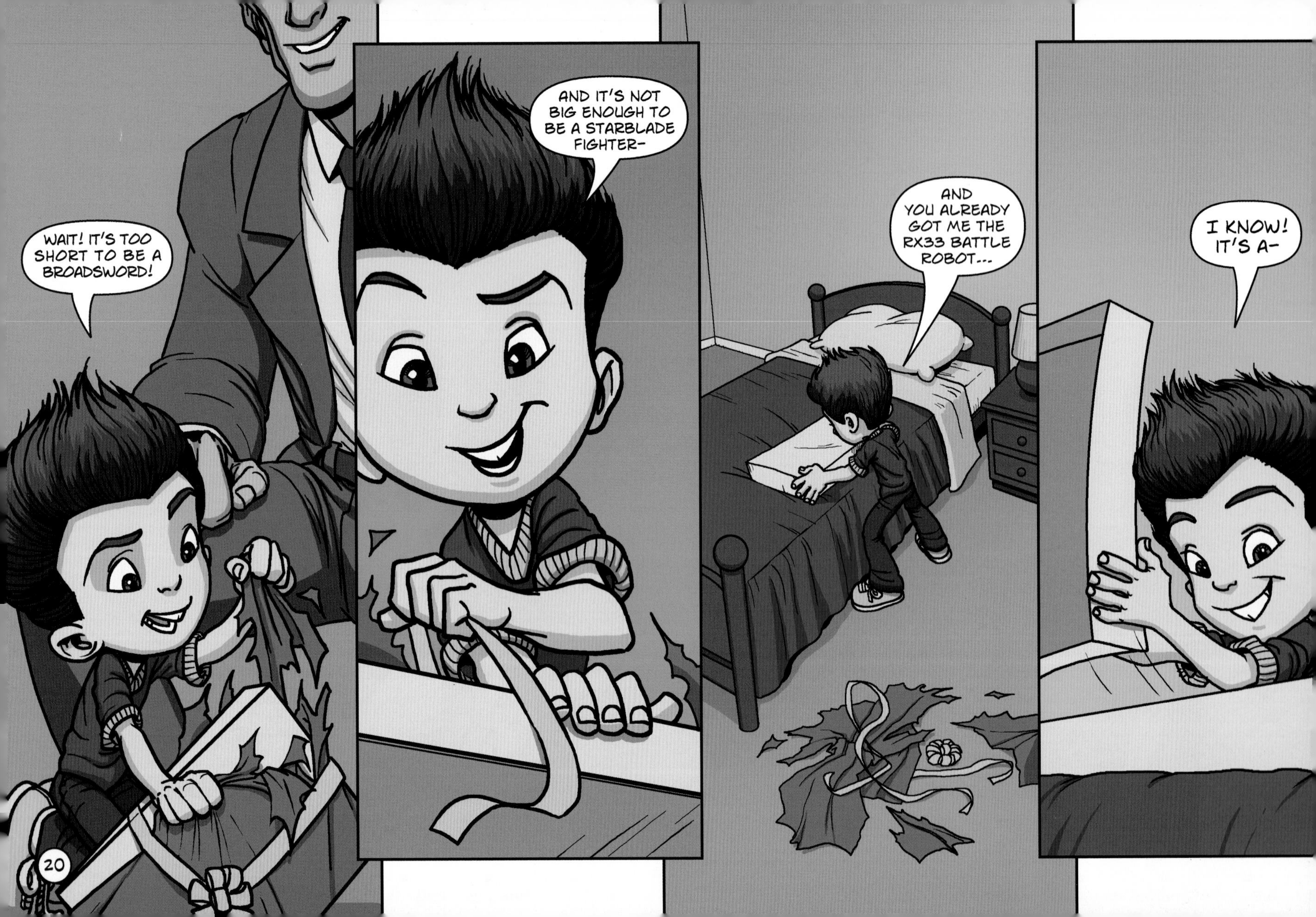
WAIT! IT'S TOO SHORT TO BE A BROADSWORD!
AND IT'S NOT BIG ENOUGH TO BE A STARBLADE FIGHTER-
AND YOU ALREADY GOT ME THE RX33 BATTLE ROBOT...
I KNOW! IT'S A-

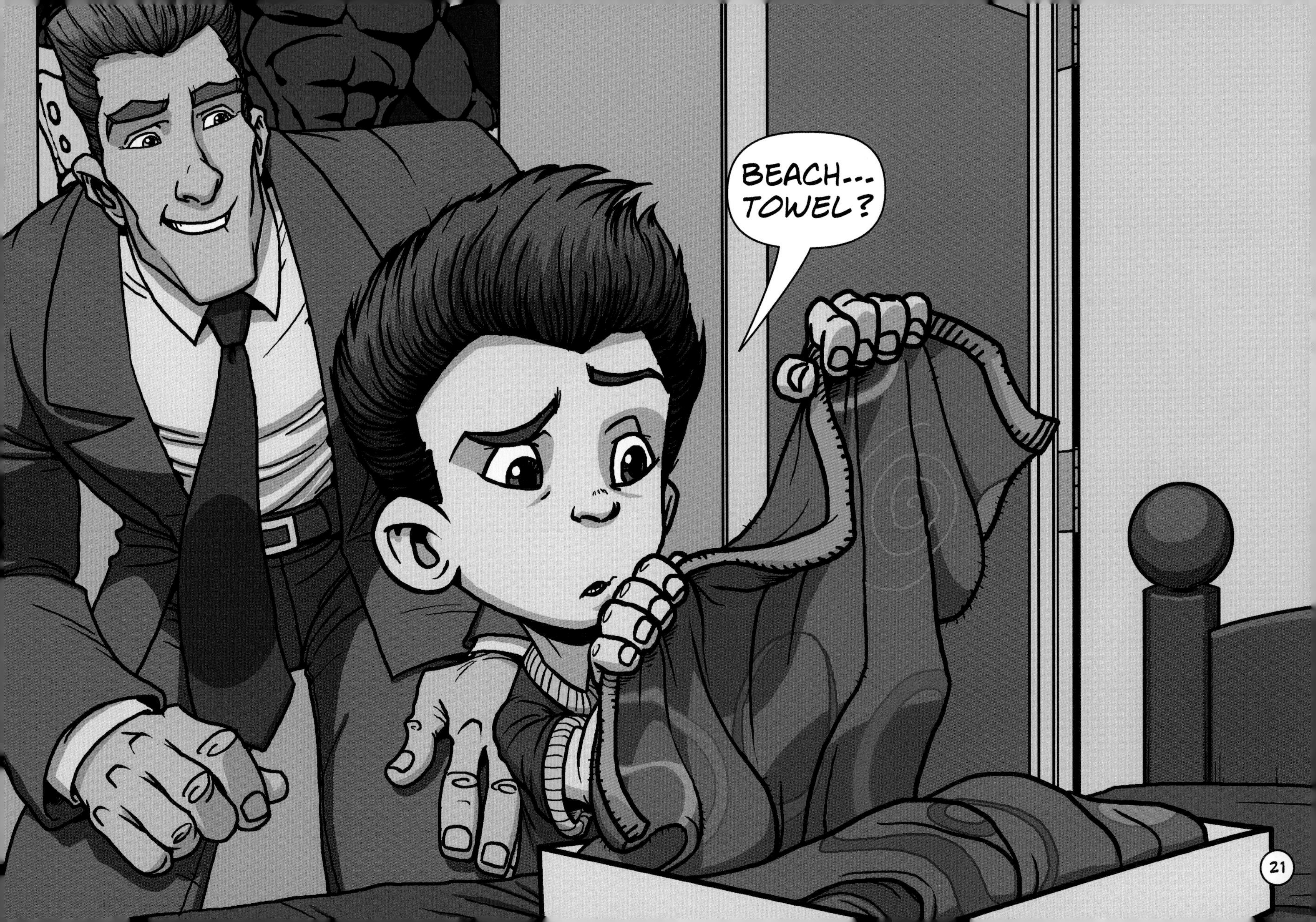
BEACH...
TOWEL?

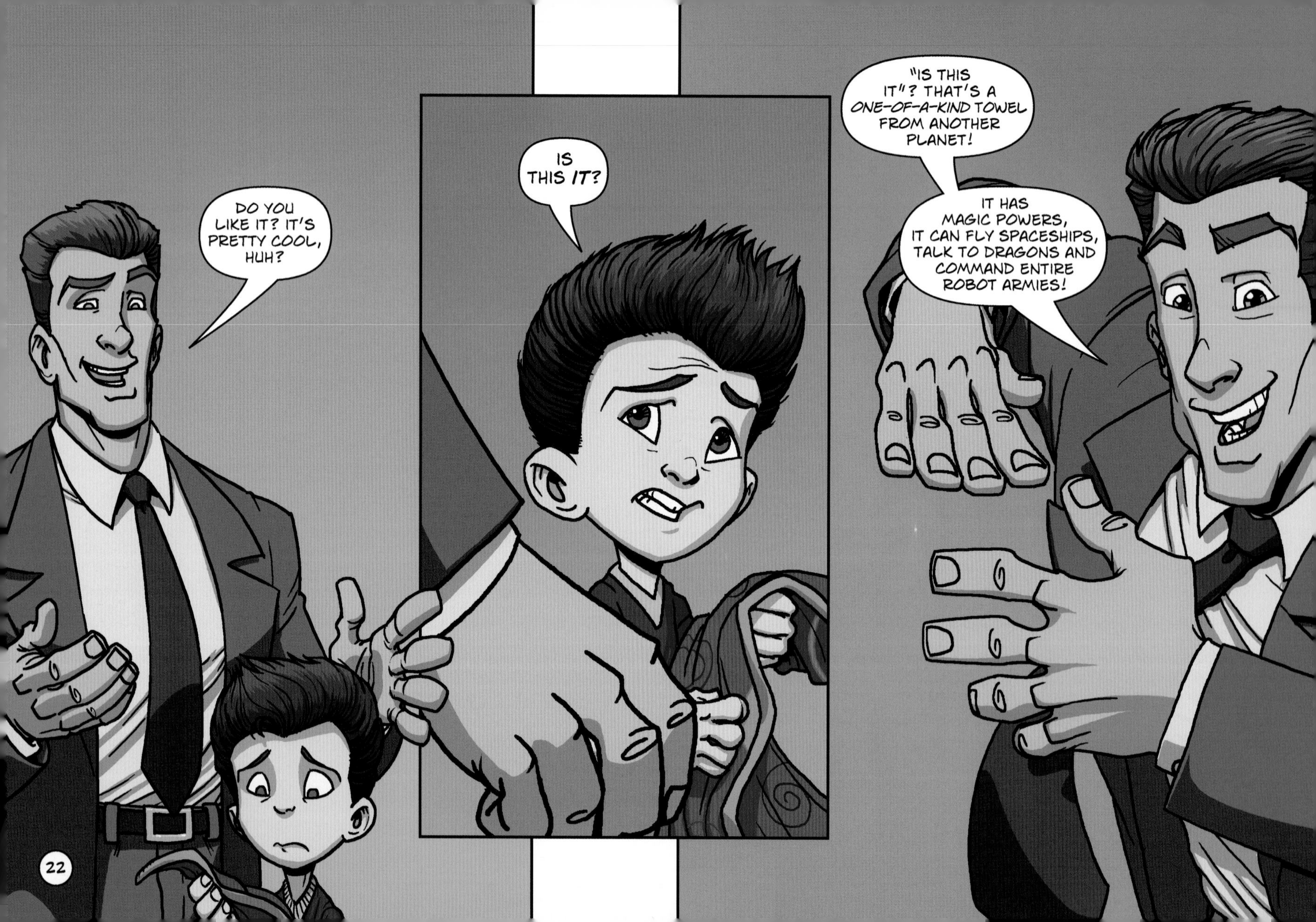
DO YOU LIKE IT? IT'S PRETTY COOL, HUH?
IS THIS *IT*?
"IS THIS IT"? THAT'S A *ONE-OF-A-KIND* TOWEL FROM ANOTHER PLANET!
IT HAS MAGIC POWERS, IT CAN FLY SPACESHIPS, TALK TO DRAGONS AND COMMAND ENTIRE ROBOT ARMIES!

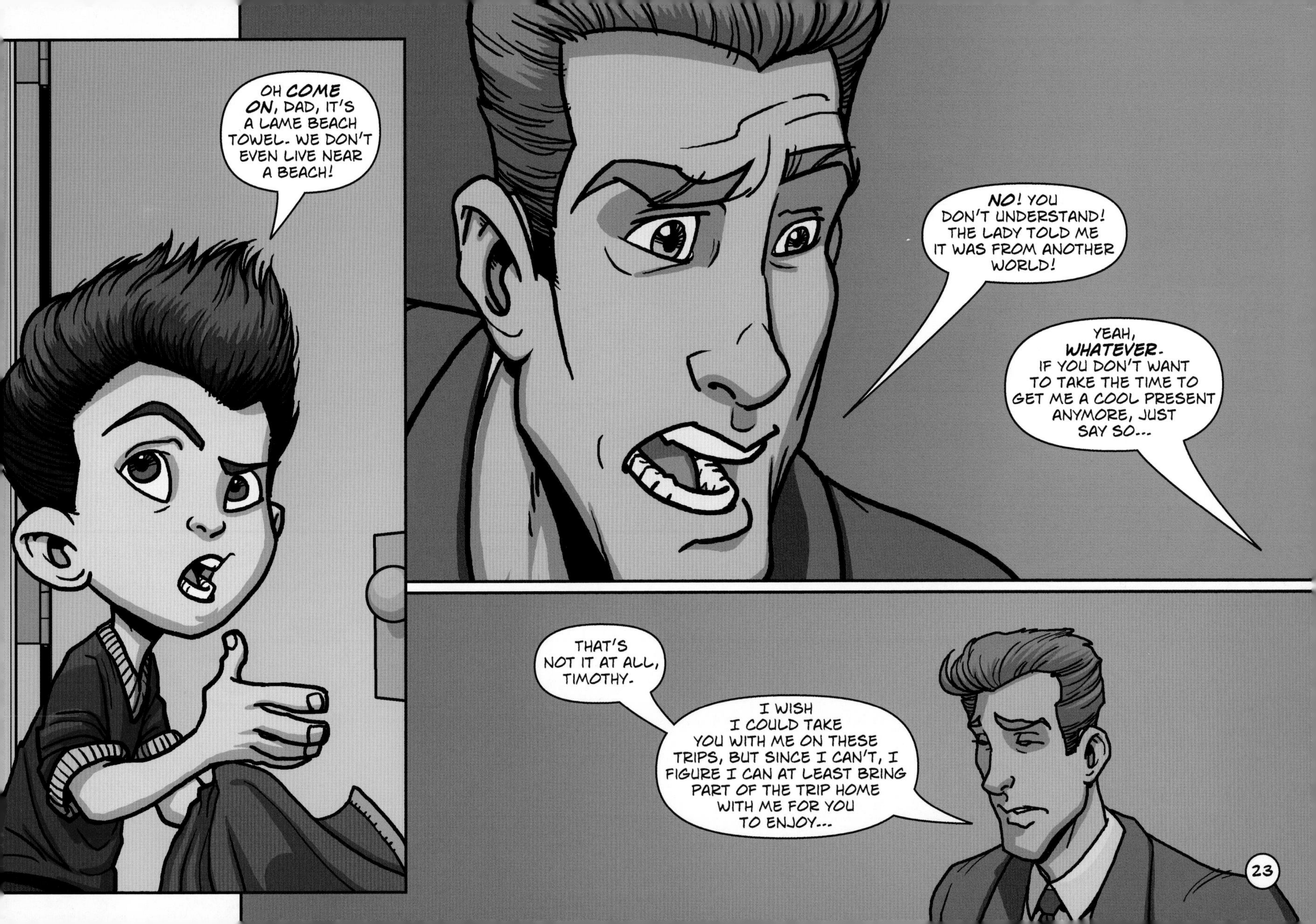
OH COME ON, DAD, IT'S A LAME BEACH TOWEL. WE DON'T EVEN LIVE NEAR A BEACH!
NO! YOU DON'T UNDERSTAND! THE LADY TOLD ME IT WAS FROM ANOTHER WORLD!
YEAH, WHATEVER. IF YOU DON'T WANT TO TAKE THE TIME TO GET ME A COOL PRESENT ANYMORE, JUST SAY SO...
THAT'S NOT IT AT ALL, TIMOTHY.
I WISH I COULD TAKE YOU WITH ME ON THESE TRIPS, BUT SINCE I CAN'T, I FIGURE I CAN AT LEAST BRING PART OF THE TRIP HOME WITH ME FOR YOU TO ENJOY...

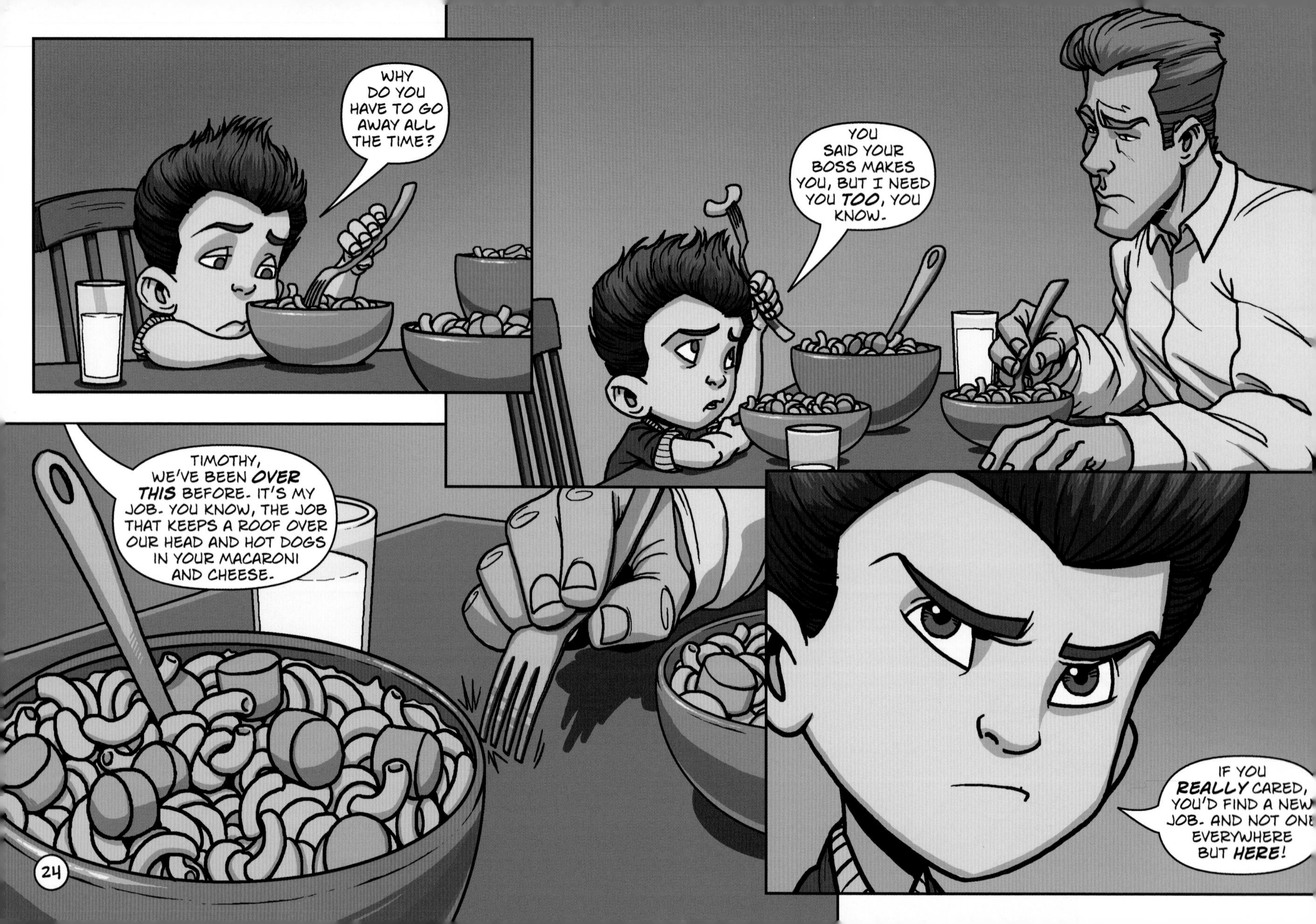
WHY DO YOU HAVE TO GO AWAY ALL THE TIME?
YOU SAID YOUR BOSS MAKES YOU, BUT I NEED YOU **TOO**, YOU KNOW.
TIMOTHY, WE'VE BEEN **OVER THIS** BEFORE. IT'S MY JOB. YOU KNOW, THE JOB THAT KEEPS A ROOF OVER OUR HEAD AND HOT DOGS IN YOUR MACARONI AND CHEESE.
IF YOU **REALLY** CARED, YOU'D FIND A NEW JOB. AND NOT ONE EVERYWHERE BUT **HERE**!

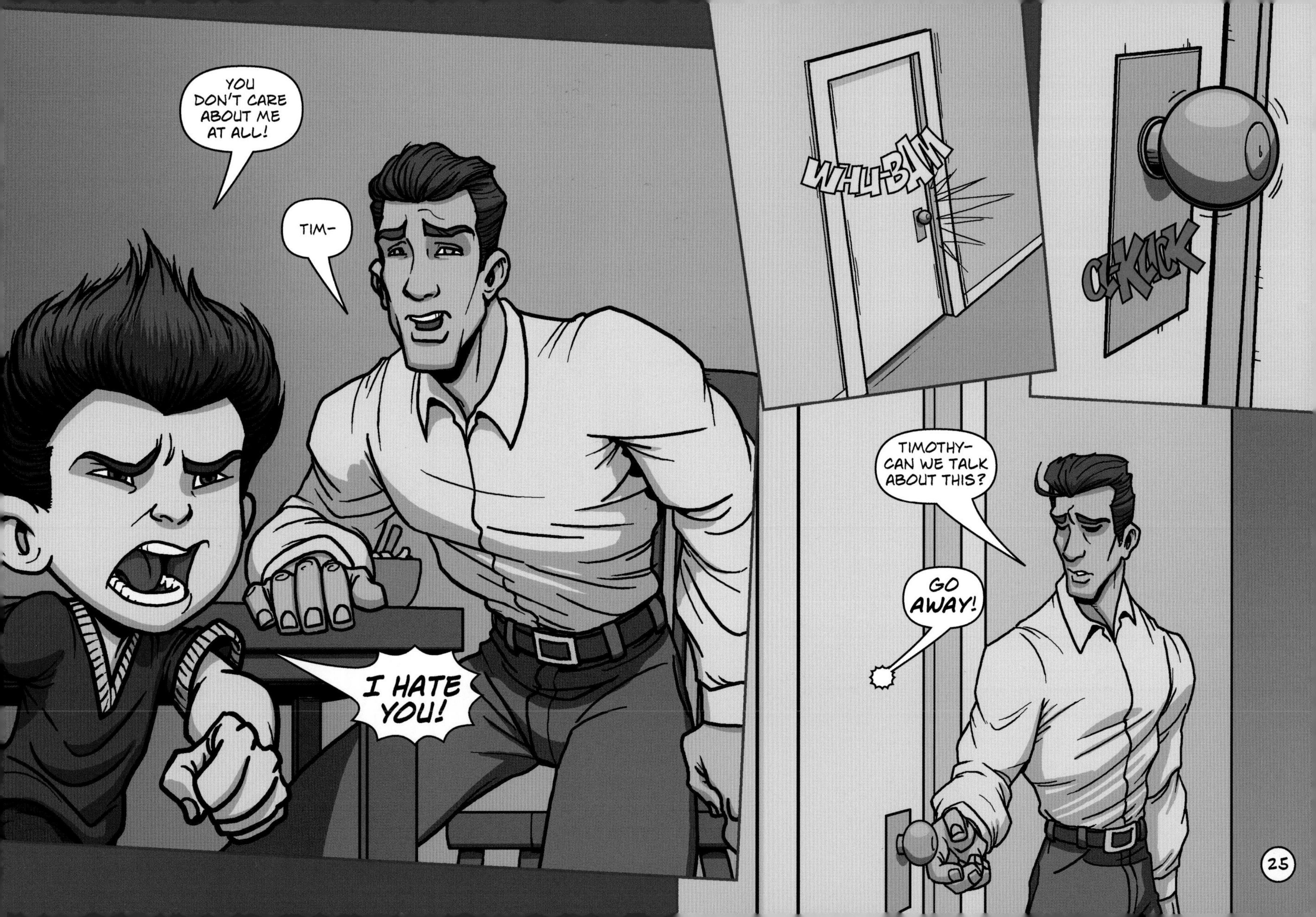
YOU DON'T CARE ABOUT ME AT ALL!
TIM-
I HATE YOU!
WHU-BAM
CL-KLICK
TIMOTHY-CAN WE TALK ABOUT THIS?
GO AWAY!

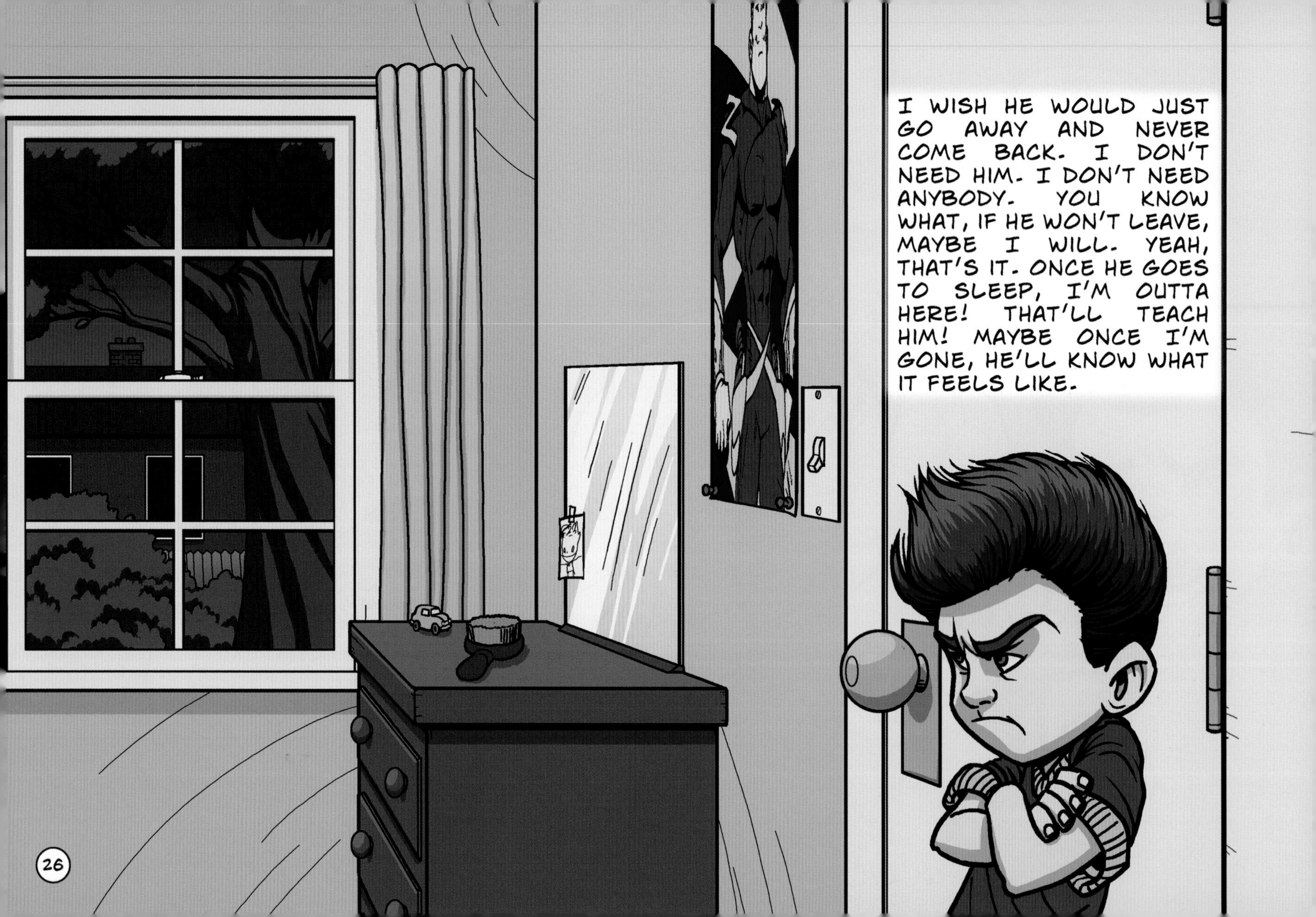
I WISH HE WOULD JUST GO AWAY AND NEVER COME BACK. I DON'T NEED HIM. I DON'T NEED ANYBODY. YOU KNOW WHAT, IF HE WON'T LEAVE, MAYBE I WILL. YEAH, THAT'S IT. ONCE HE GOES TO SLEEP, I'M OUTTA HERE! THAT'LL TEACH HIM! MAYBE ONCE I'M GONE, HE'LL KNOW WHAT IT FEELS LIKE.

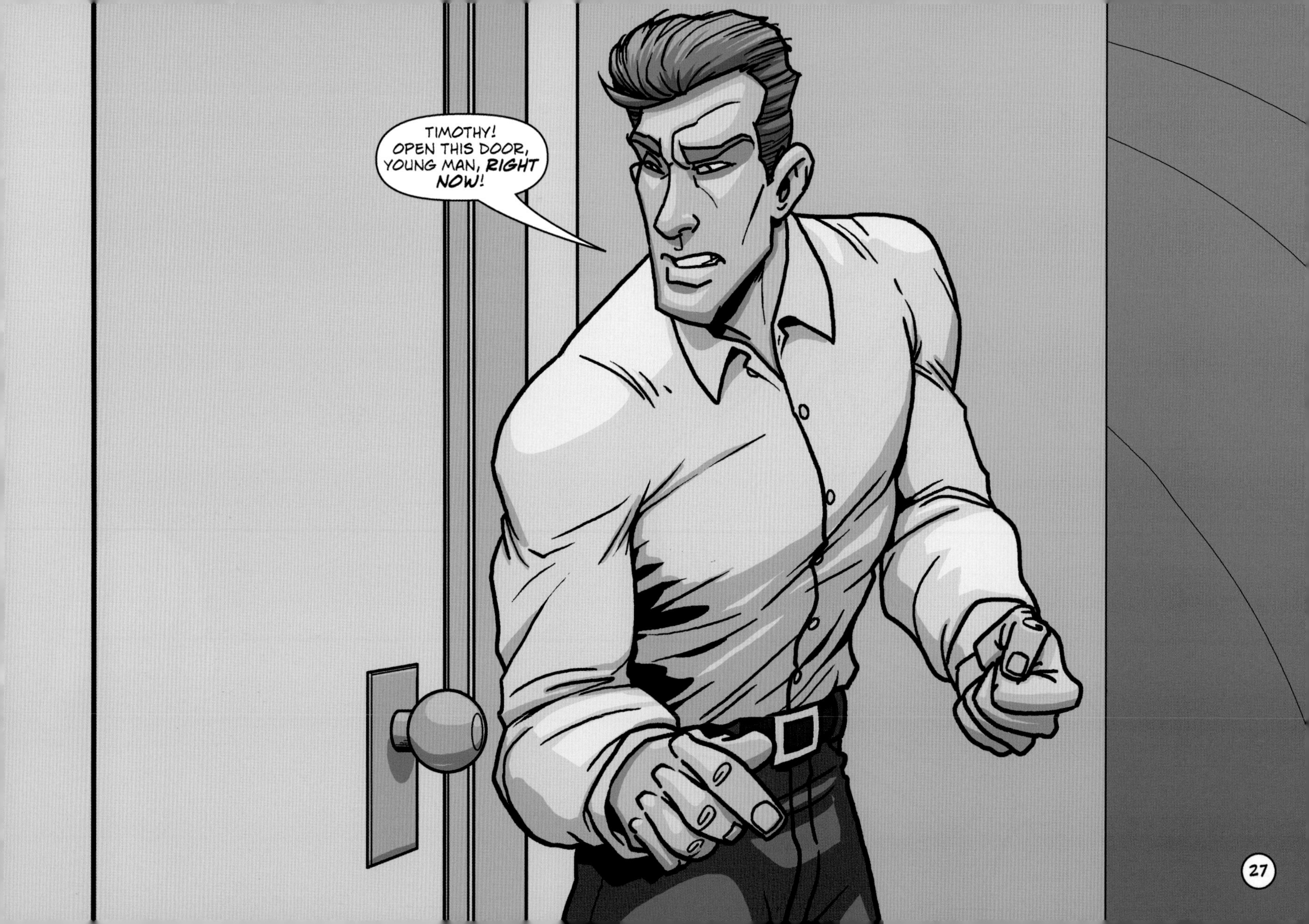
TIMOTHY! OPEN THIS DOOR, YOUNG MAN, RIGHT NOW!

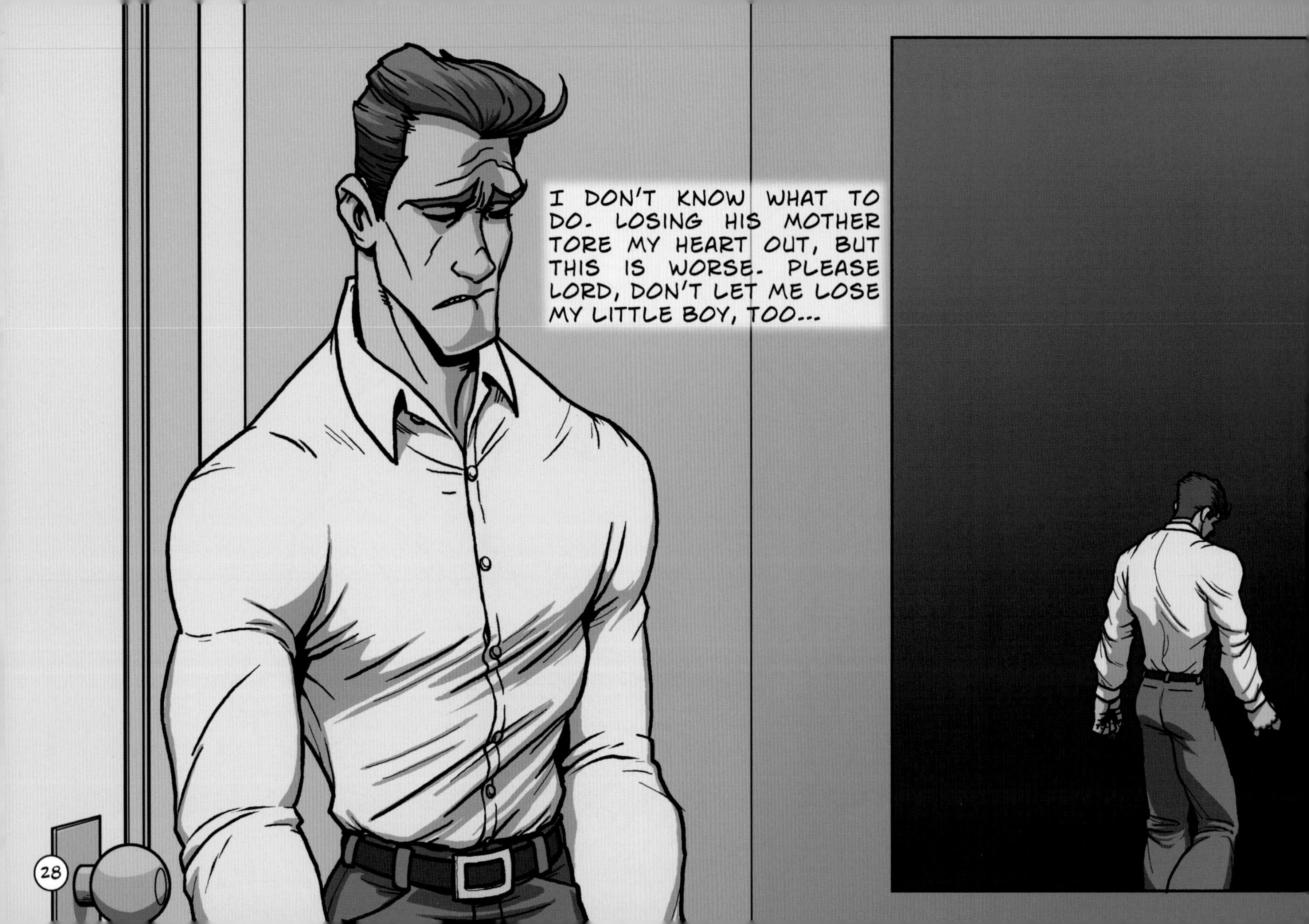
I DON'T KNOW WHAT TO DO. LOSING HIS MOTHER TORE MY HEART OUT, BUT THIS IS WORSE. PLEASE LORD, DON'T LET ME LOSE MY LITTLE BOY, TOO...

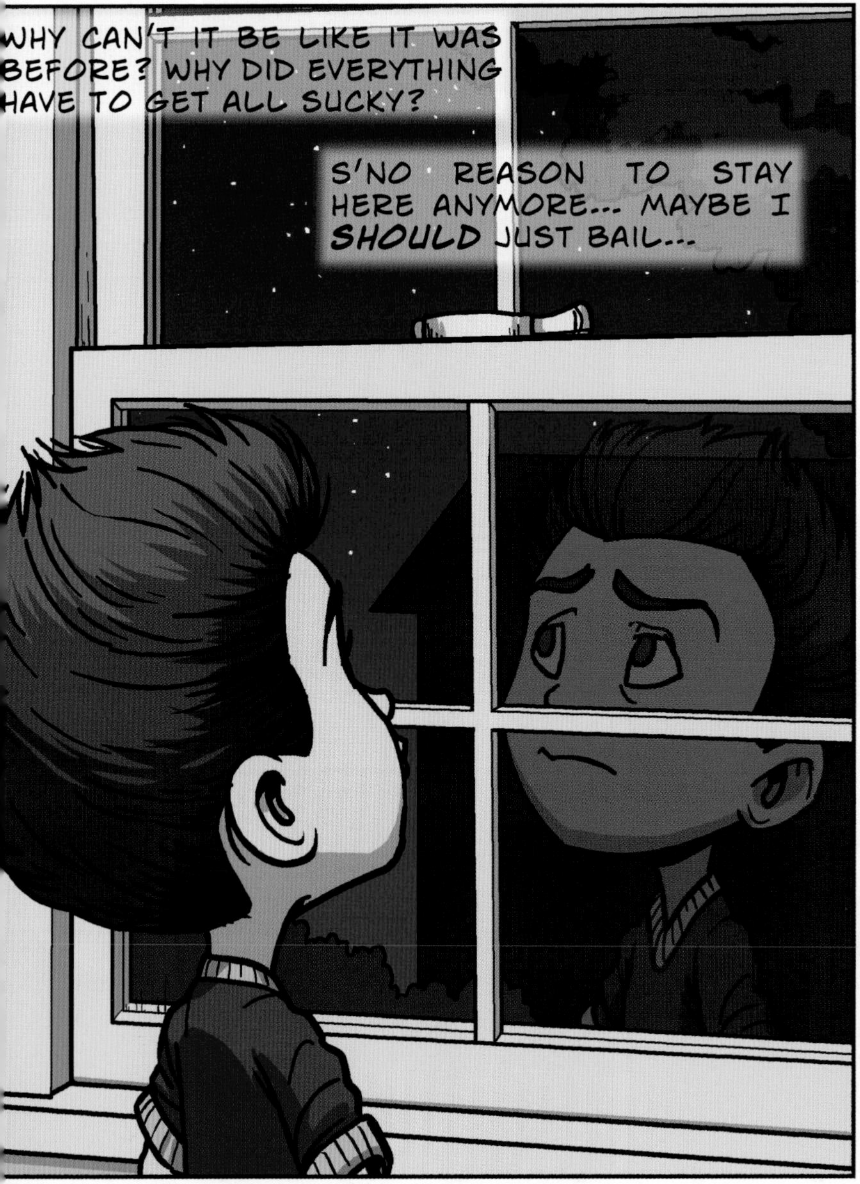
WHY CAN'T IT BE LIKE IT WAS BEFORE? WHY DID EVERYTHING HAVE TO GET ALL SUCKY?
S'NO REASON TO STAY HERE ANYMORE... MAYBE I SHOULD JUST BAIL...

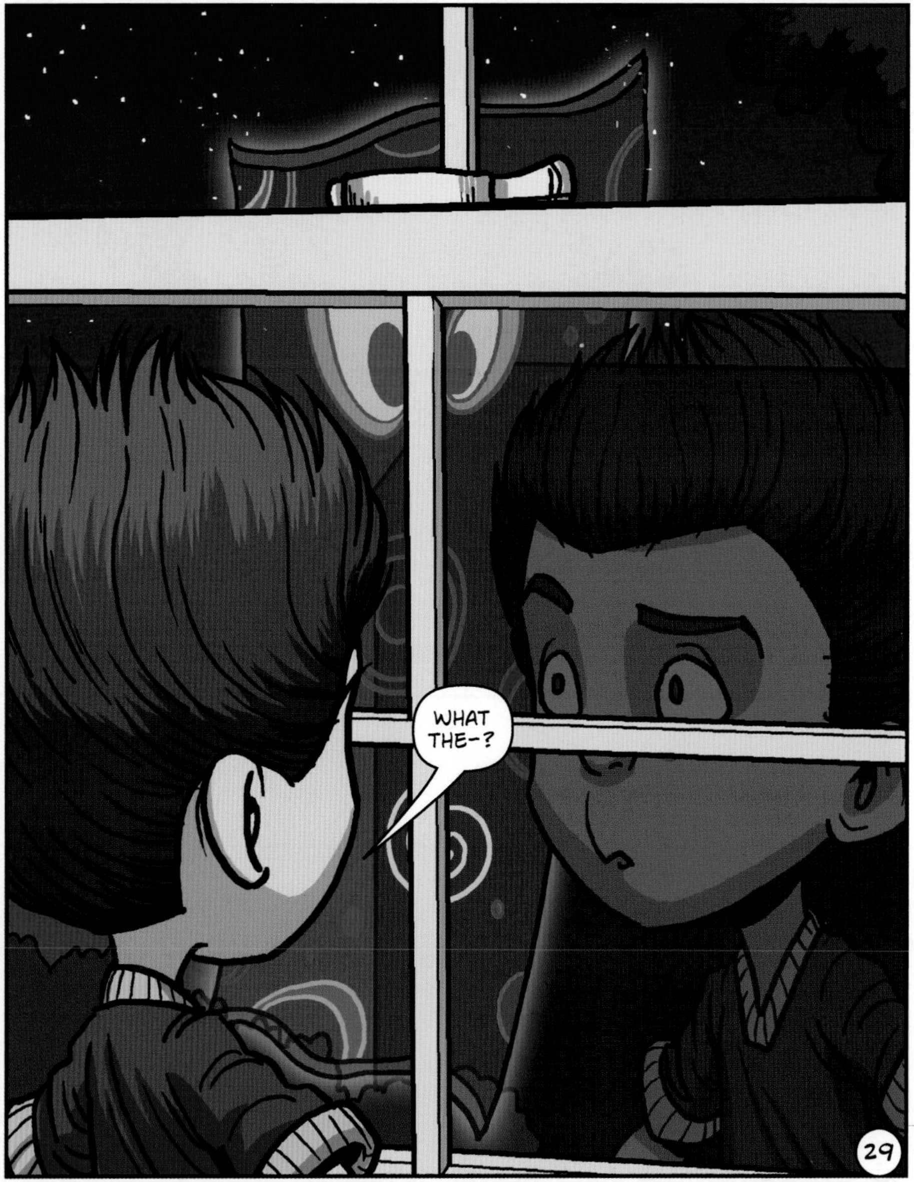
WHAT THE-?

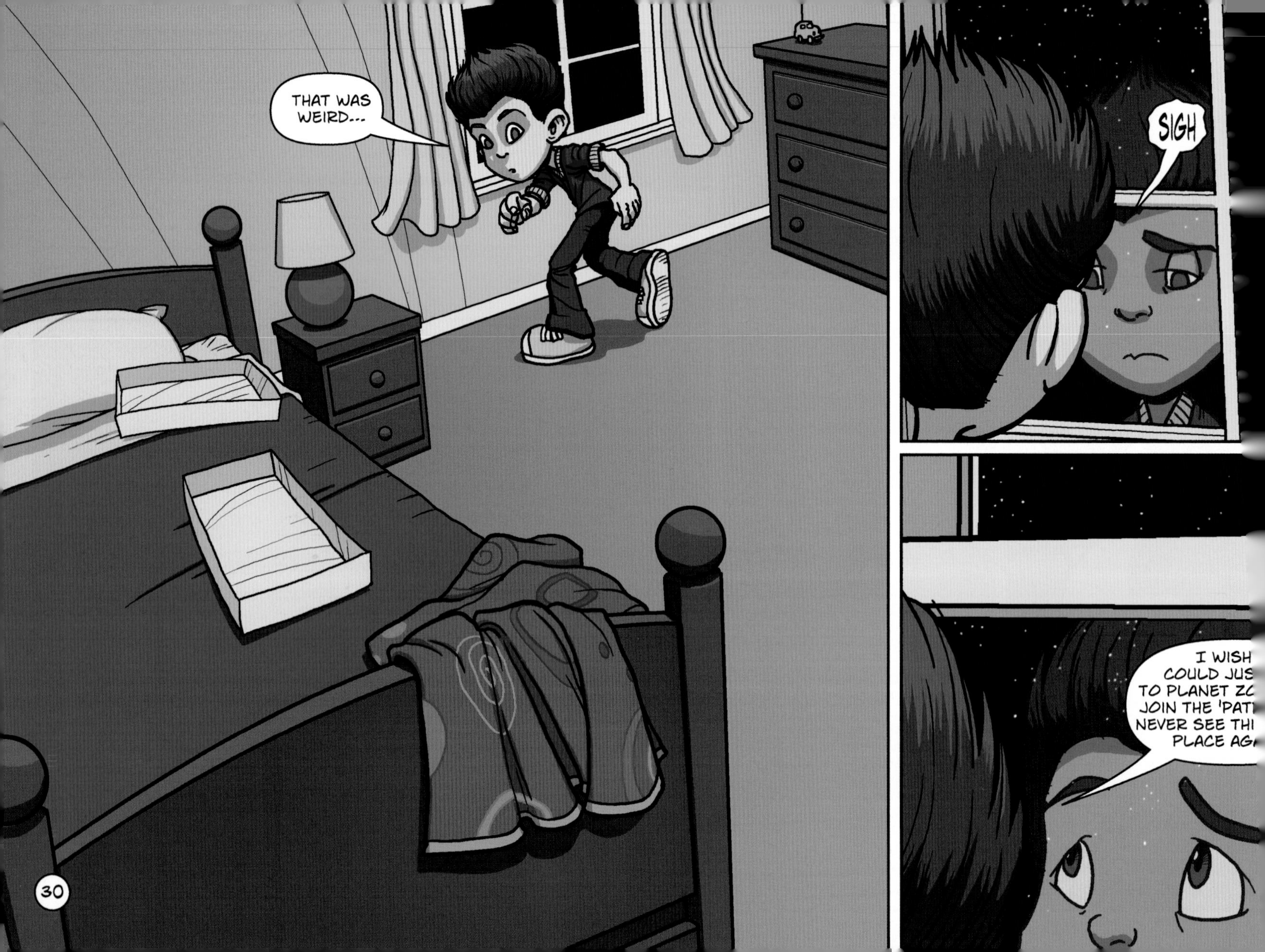
THAT WAS WEIRD...
SIGH
I WISH COULD JUS TO PLANET ZO JOIN THE 'PAT NEVER SEE THI PLACE AG

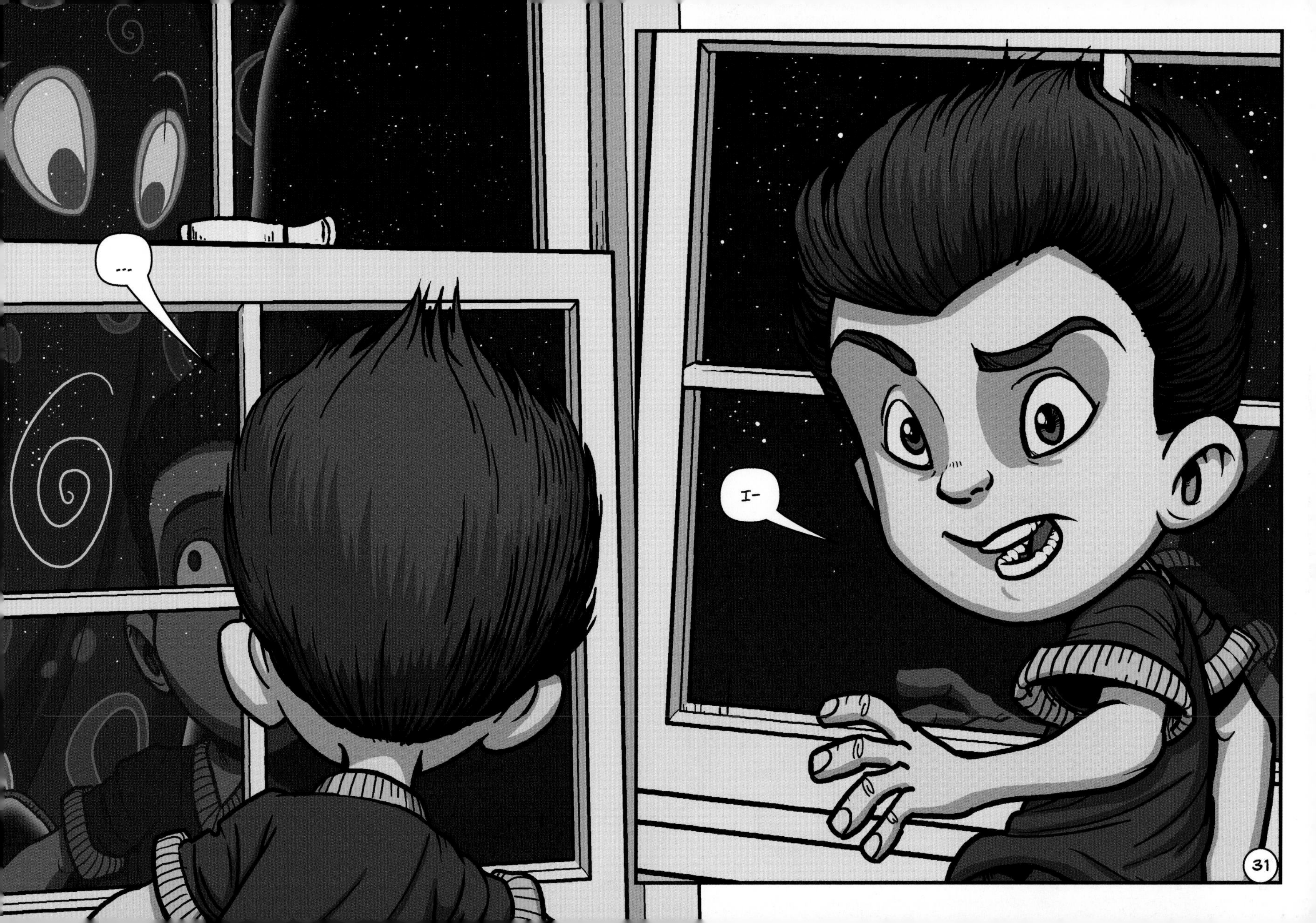
...
I-

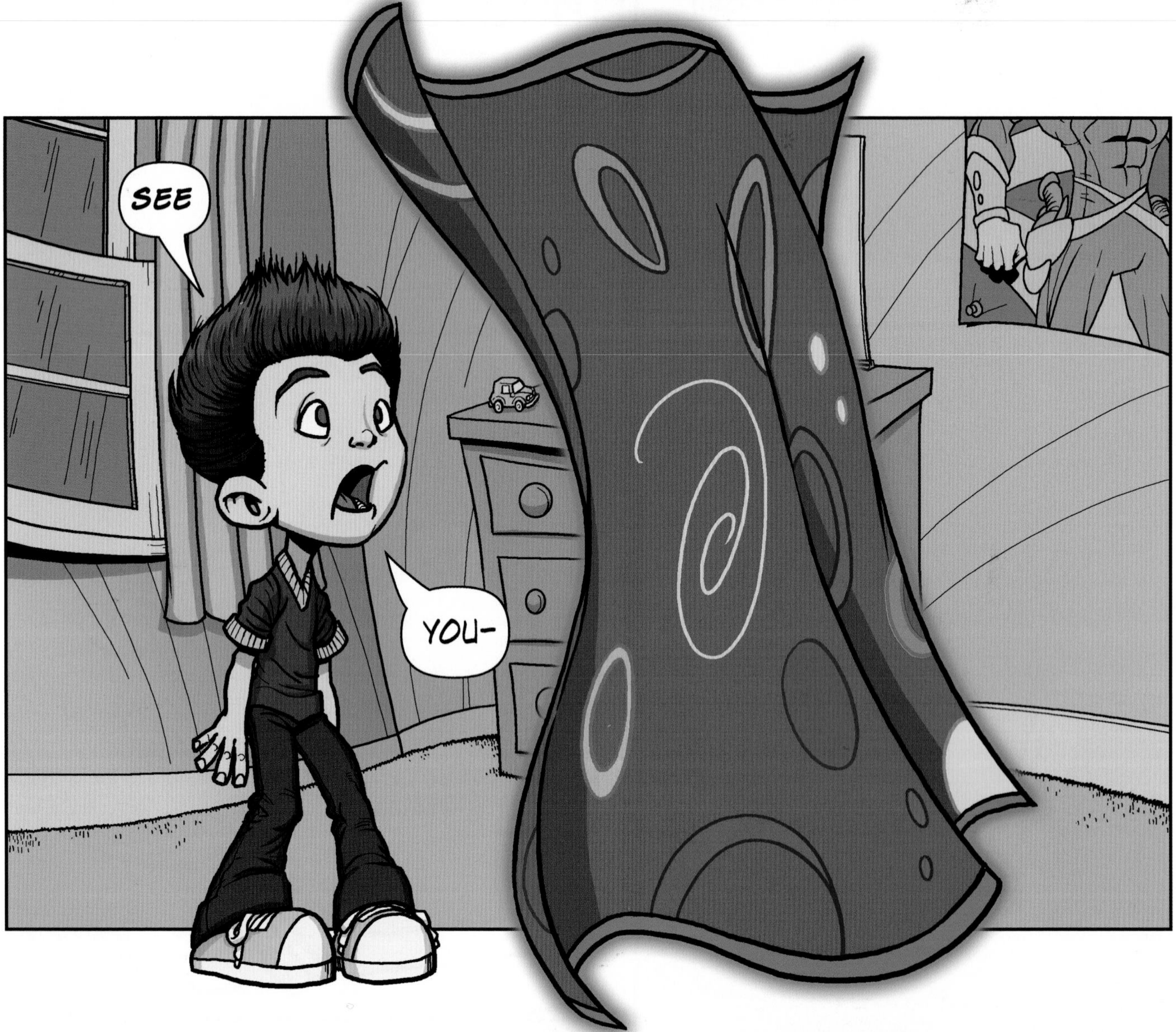
SEE
YOU-

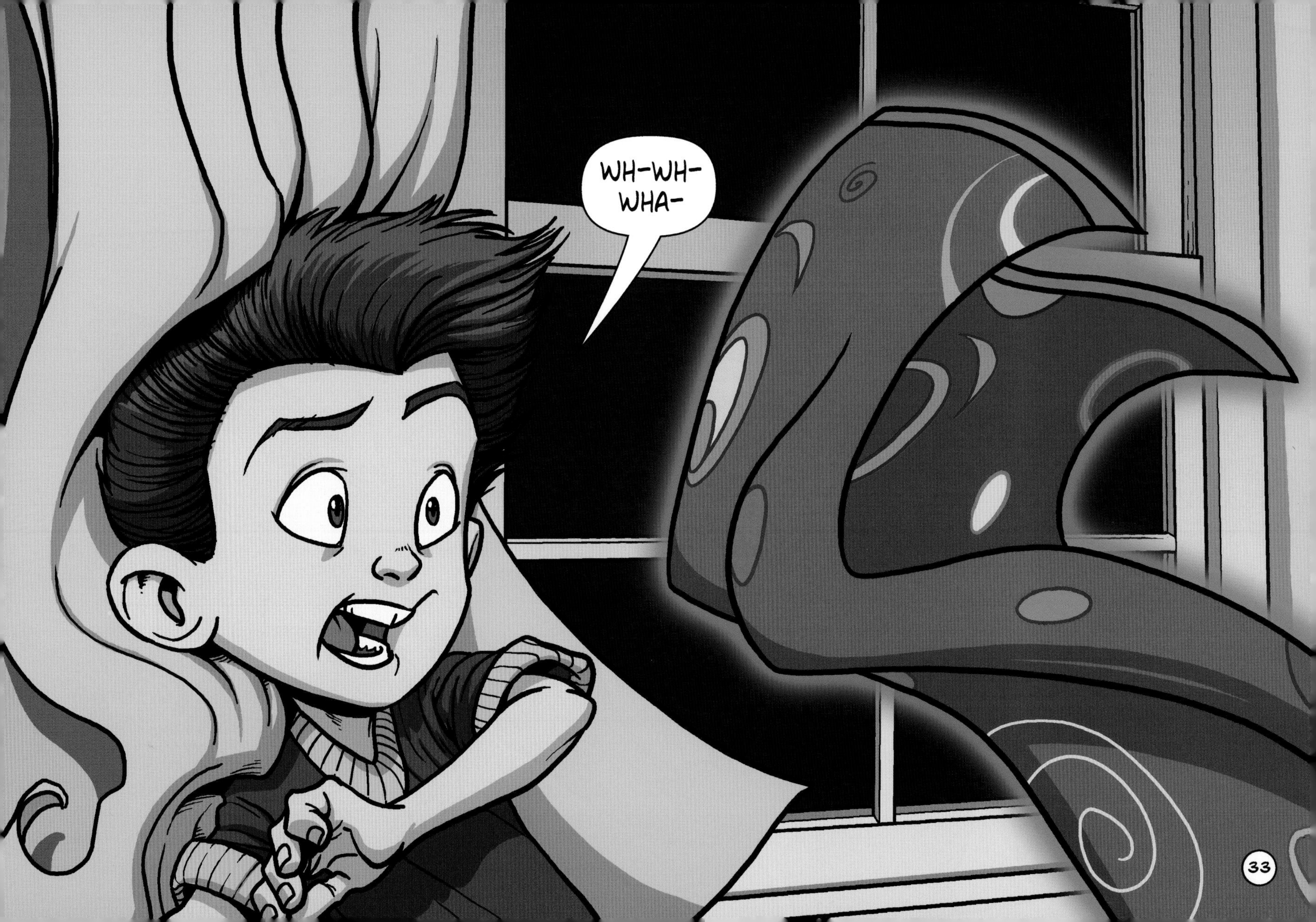
WH-WH-
WHA-

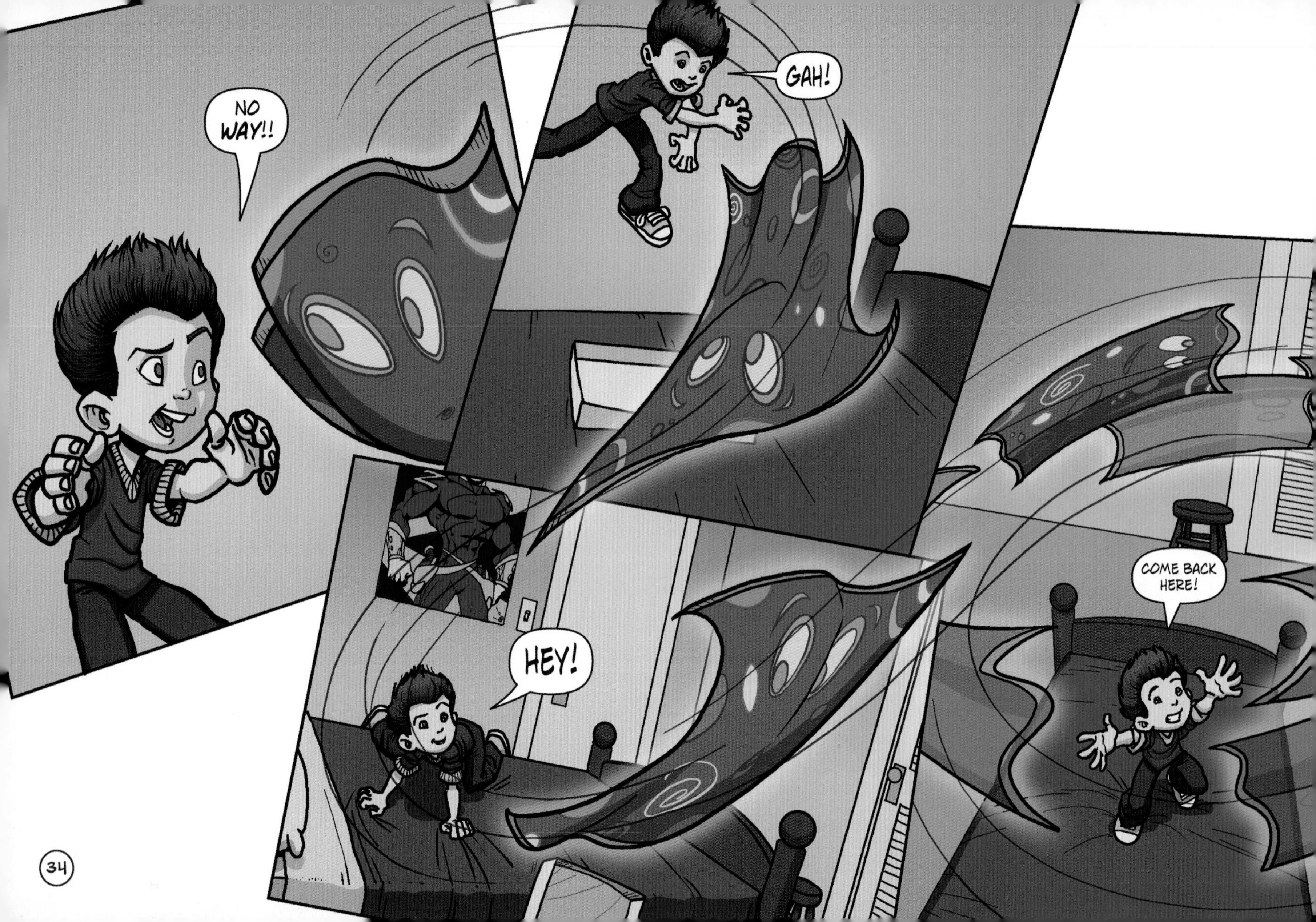
NO WAY!!
GAH!
HEY!
COME BACK HERE!

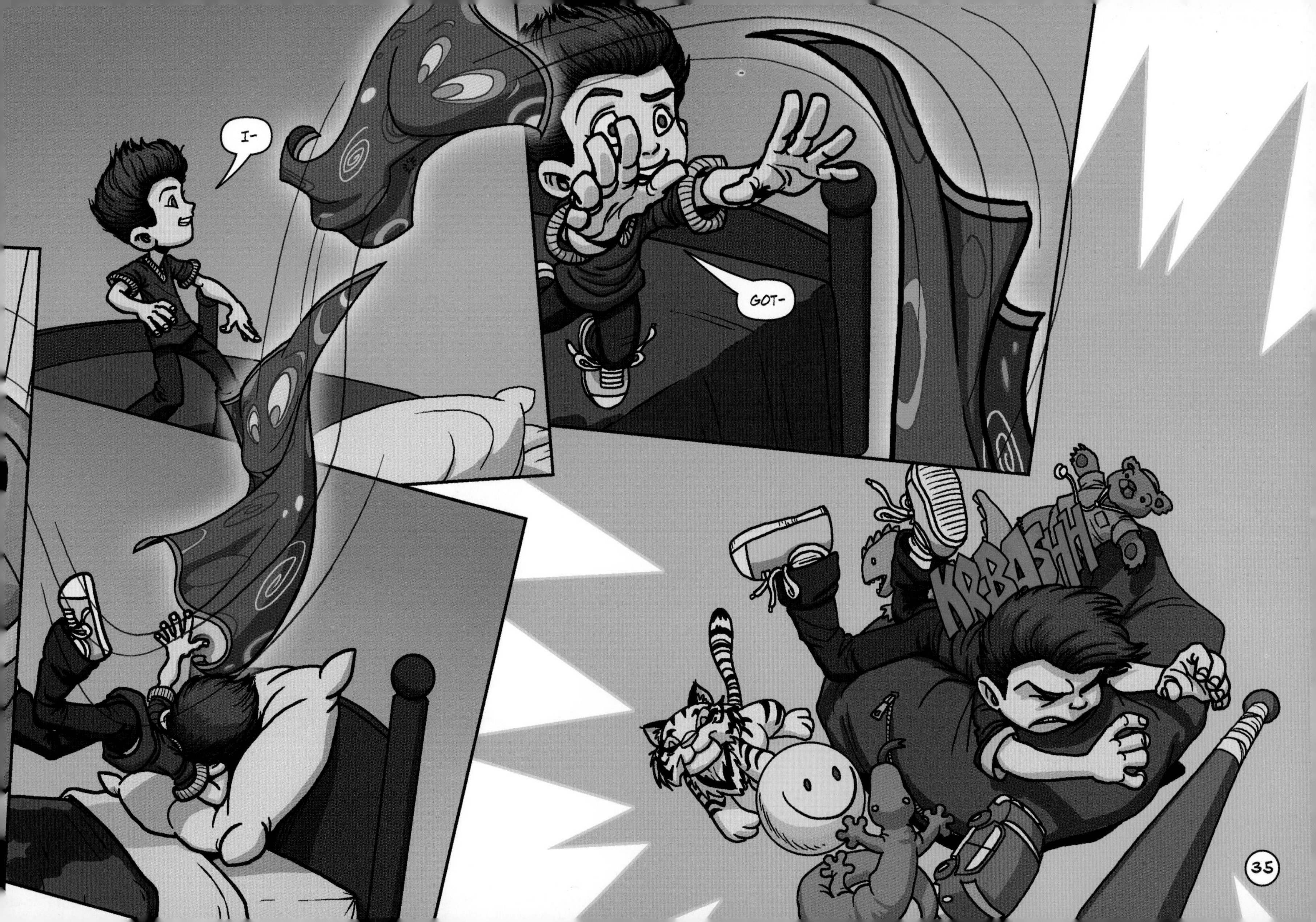
I-
GOT-
KRBASHH!

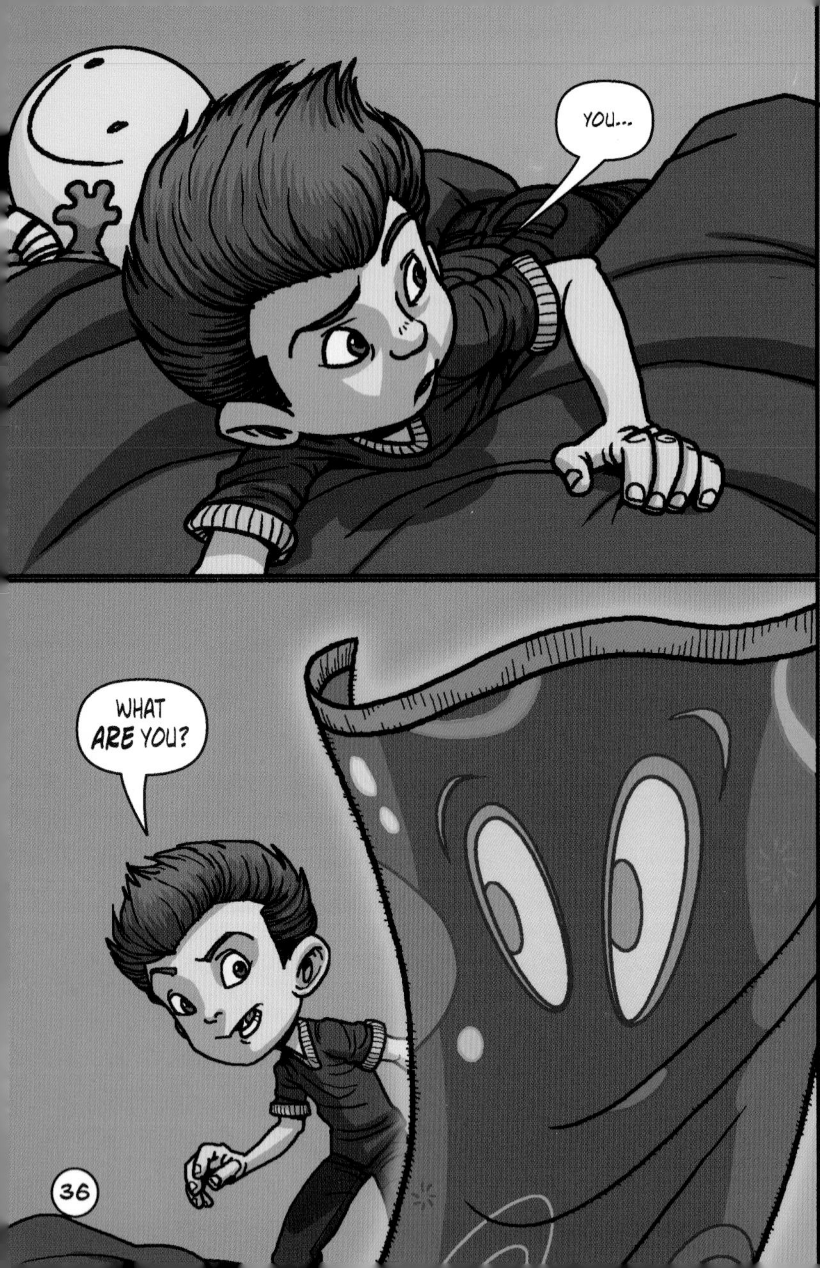
YOU...
WHAT ARE YOU?

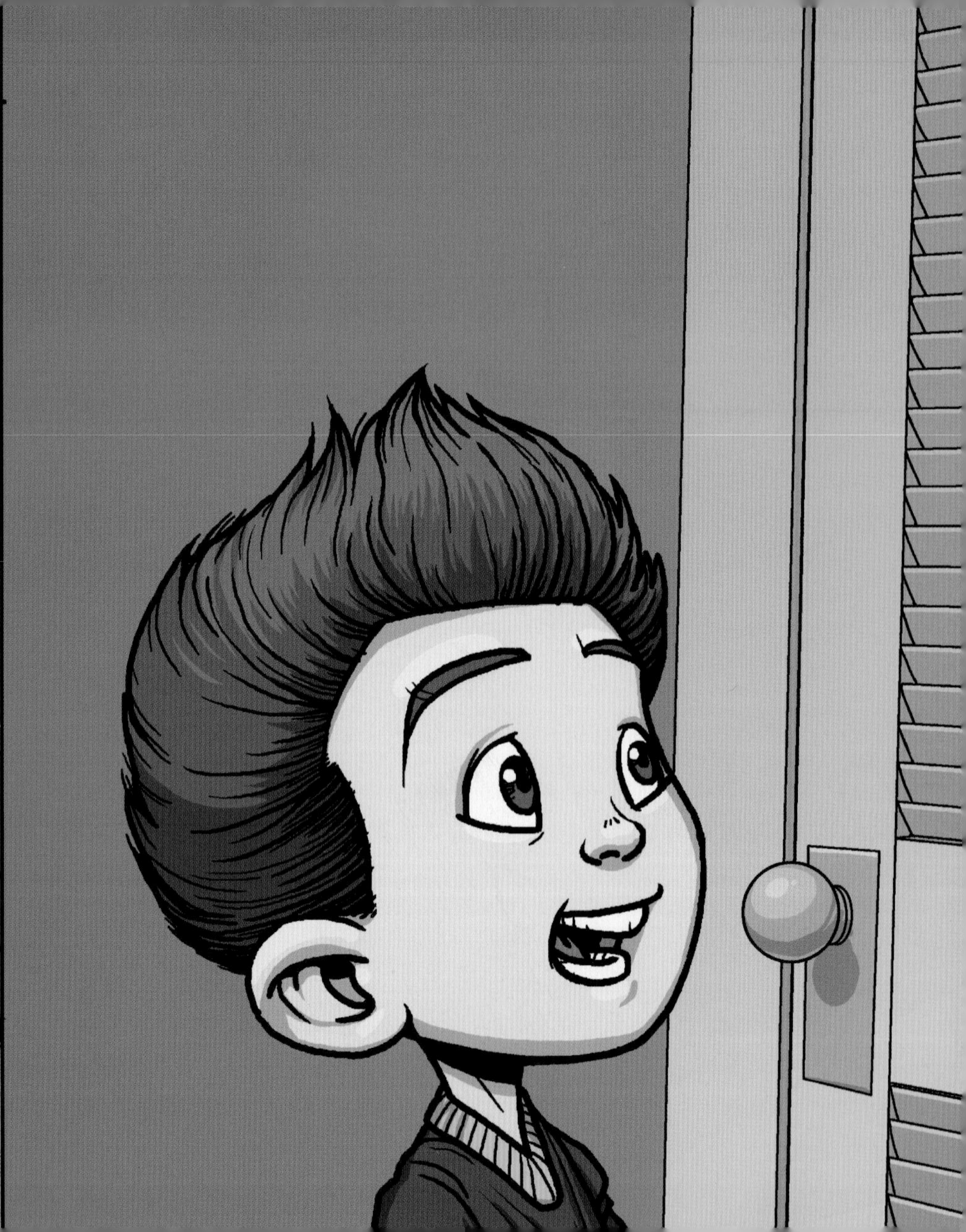

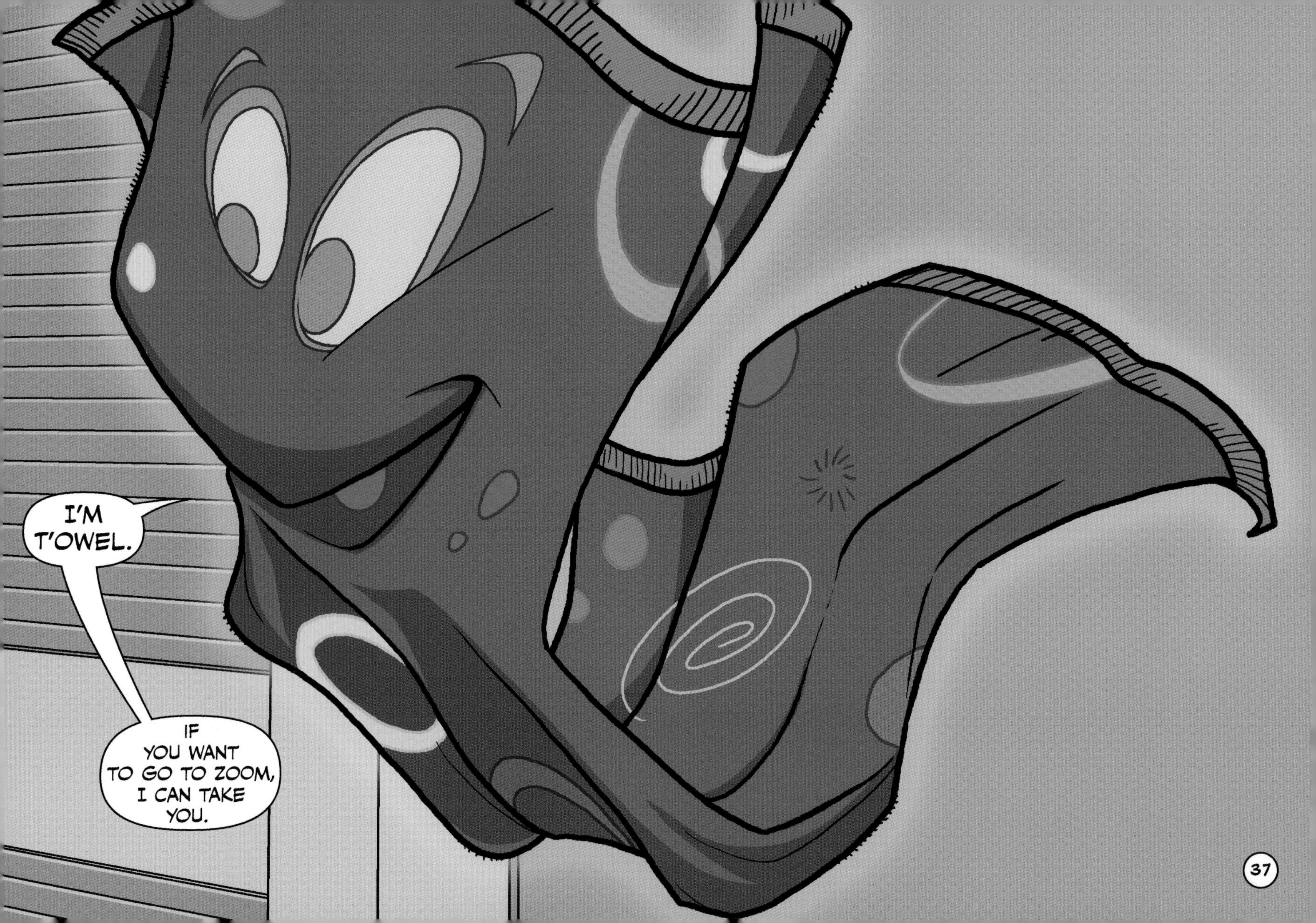
I'M T'OWEL.
IF YOU WANT TO GO TO ZOOM, I CAN TAKE YOU.

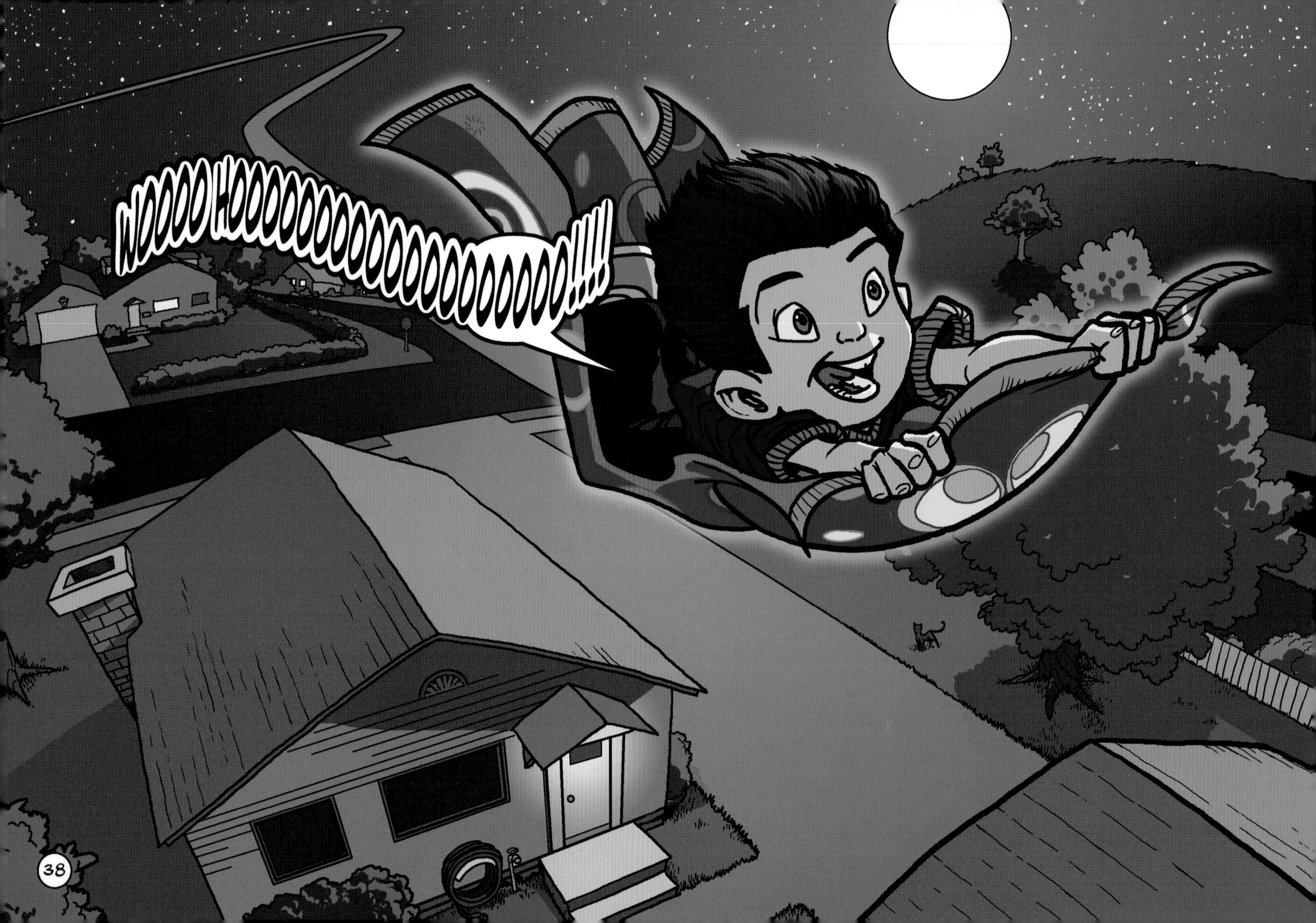
WOOO HOOOOOOOOOOOOOOOOOOOO!!!!

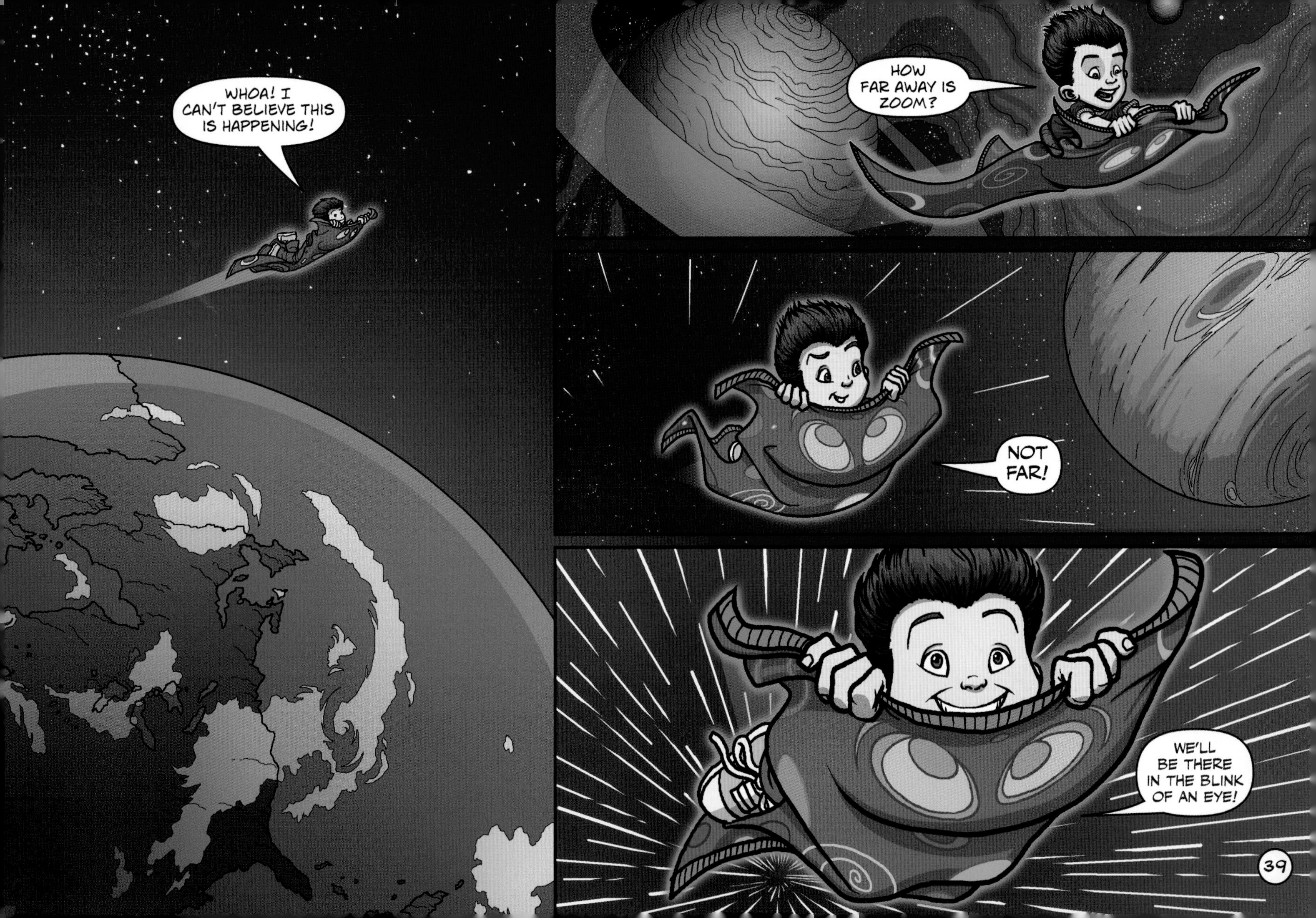
WHOA! I CAN'T BELIEVE THIS IS HAPPENING!
HOW FAR AWAY IS ZOOM?
NOT FAR!
WE'LL BE THERE IN THE BLINK OF AN EYE!

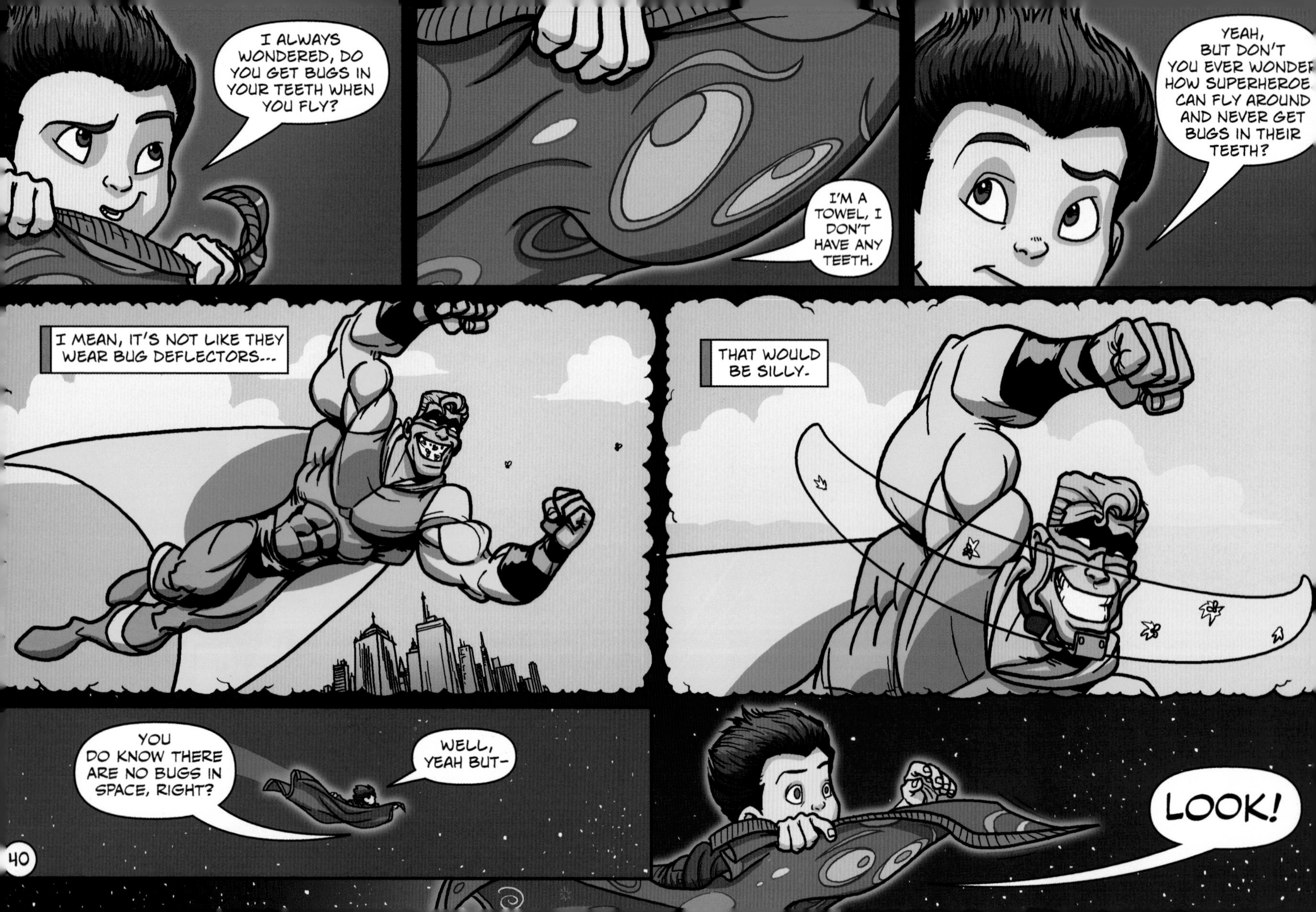

I ALWAYS WONDERED, DO YOU GET BUGS IN YOUR TEETH WHEN YOU FLY?
I'M A TOWEL, I DON'T HAVE ANY TEETH.
YEAH, BUT DON'T YOU EVER WONDER HOW SUPERHEROES CAN FLY AROUND AND NEVER GET BUGS IN THEIR TEETH?
I MEAN, IT'S NOT LIKE THEY WEAR BUG DEFLECTORS...
THAT WOULD BE SILLY.
YOU DO KNOW THERE ARE NO BUGS IN SPACE, RIGHT?
WELL, YEAH BUT-
LOOK!

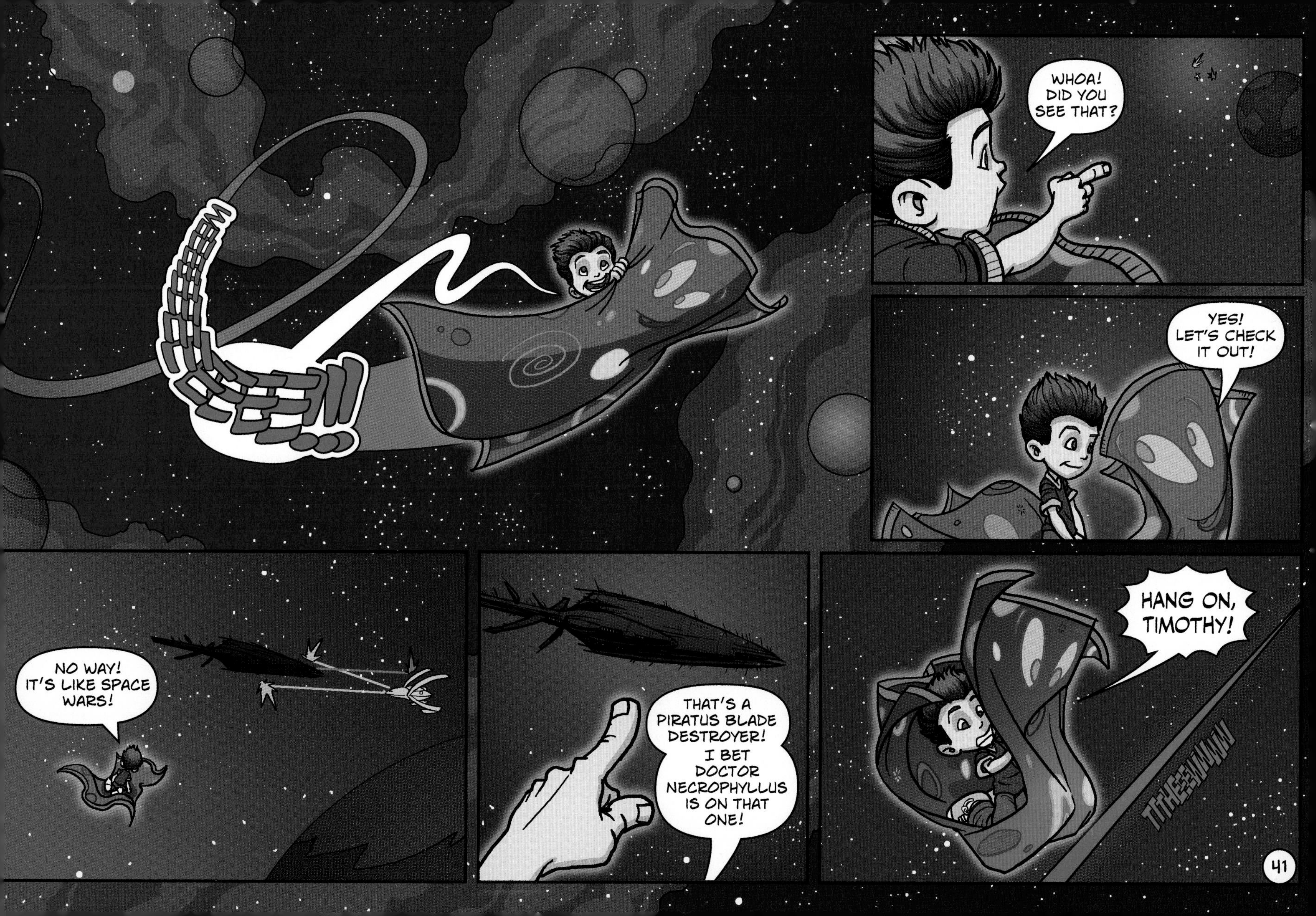
WHOA! DID YOU SEE THAT?
YES! LET'S CHECK IT OUT!
NO WAY! IT'S LIKE SPACE WARS!
THAT'S A PIRATUS BLADE DESTROYER!
I BET DOCTOR NECROPHYLLUS IS ON THAT ONE!
HANG ON, TIMOTHY!

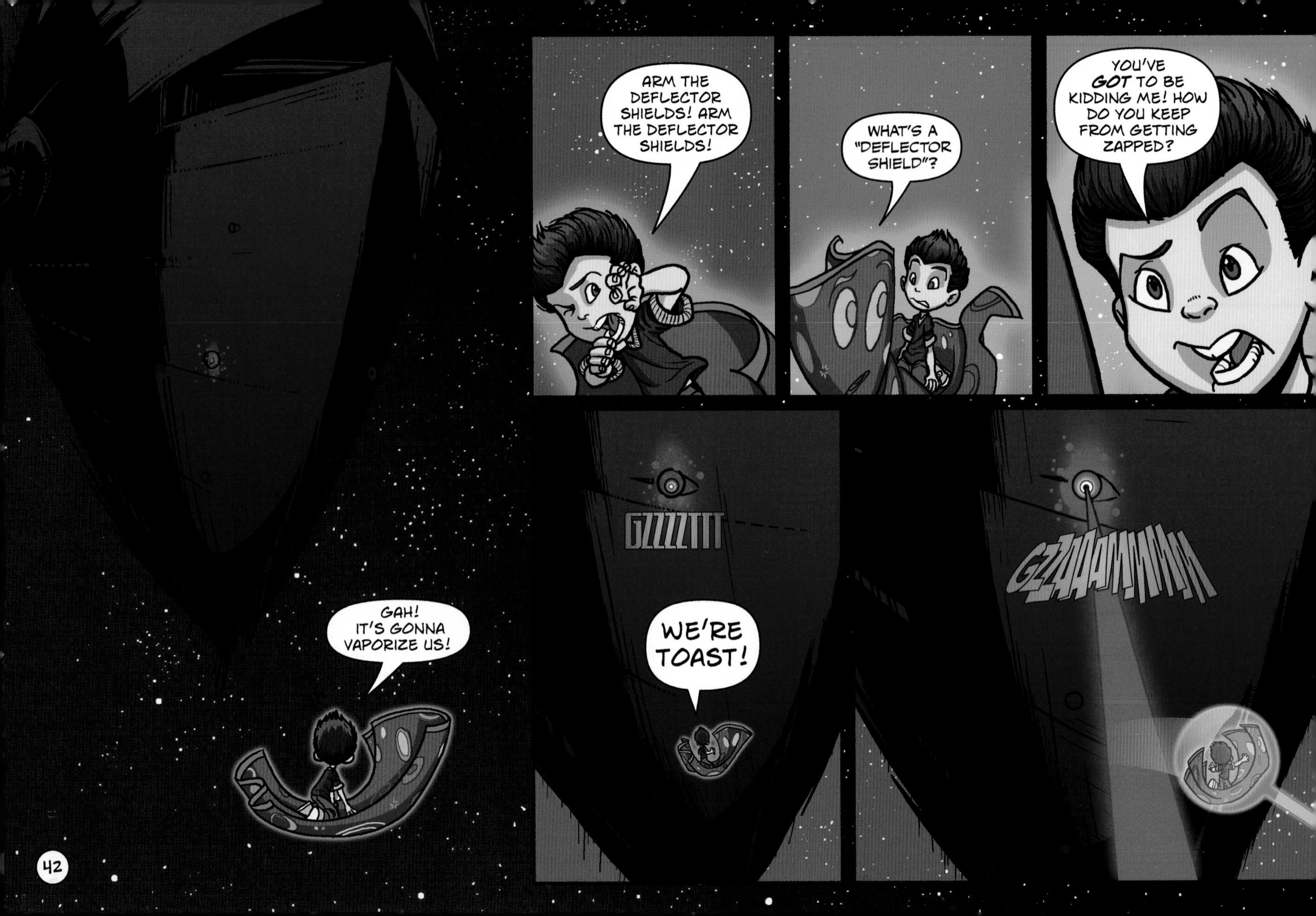
GAH! IT'S GONNA VAPORIZE US!
ARM THE DEFLECTOR SHIELDS! ARM THE DEFLECTOR SHIELDS!
WHAT'S A "DEFLECTOR SHIELD"?
YOU'VE **GOT** TO BE KIDDING ME! HOW DO YOU KEEP FROM GETTING ZAPPED?
GZZZZTTT
WE'RE TOAST!
GZZAAMMMMM

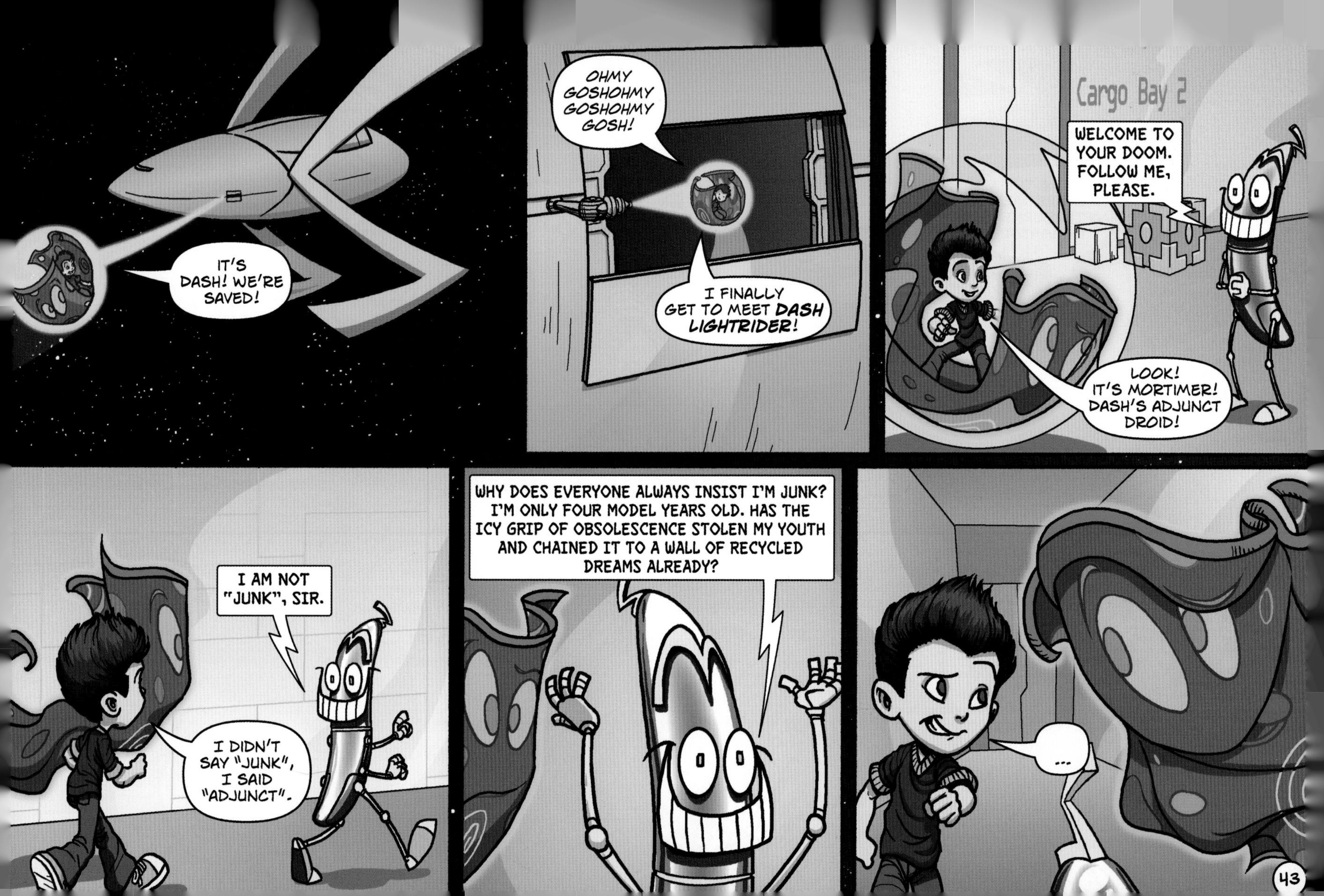
IT'S DASH! WE'RE SAVED!
OHMY GOSHOHMY GOSHOHMY GOSH!
I FINALLY GET TO MEET DASH LIGHTRIDER!
Cargo Bay 2
WELCOME TO YOUR DOOM. FOLLOW ME, PLEASE.
LOOK! IT'S MORTIMER! DASH'S ADJUNCT DROID!
I AM NOT "JUNK", SIR.
I DIDN'T SAY "JUNK", I SAID "ADJUNCT".
WHY DOES EVERYONE ALWAYS INSIST I'M JUNK? I'M ONLY FOUR MODEL YEARS OLD. HAS THE ICY GRIP OF OBSOLESCENCE STOLEN MY YOUTH AND CHAINED IT TO A WALL OF RECYCLED DREAMS ALREADY?
...

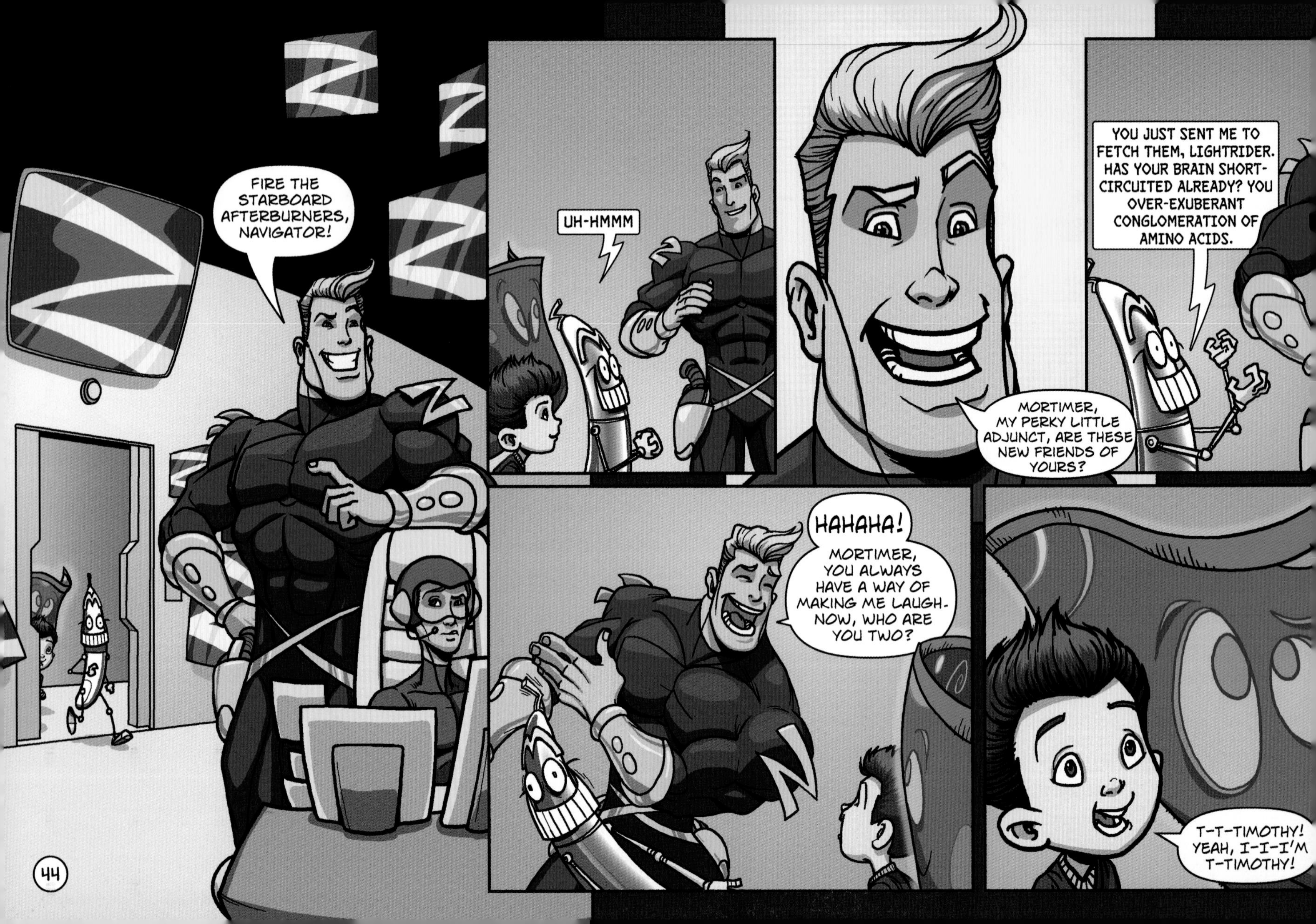
FIRE THE STARBOARD AFTERBURNERS, NAVIGATOR!
UH-HMMM
MORTIMER, MY PERKY LITTLE ADJUNCT, ARE THESE NEW FRIENDS OF YOURS?
YOU JUST SENT ME TO FETCH THEM, LIGHTRIDER. HAS YOUR BRAIN SHORT-CIRCUITED ALREADY? YOU OVER-EXUBERANT CONGLOMERATION OF AMINO ACIDS.
HAHAHA!
MORTIMER, YOU ALWAYS HAVE A WAY OF MAKING ME LAUGH. NOW, WHO ARE YOU TWO?
T-T-TIMOTHY! YEAH, I-I-I'M T-TIMOTHY!

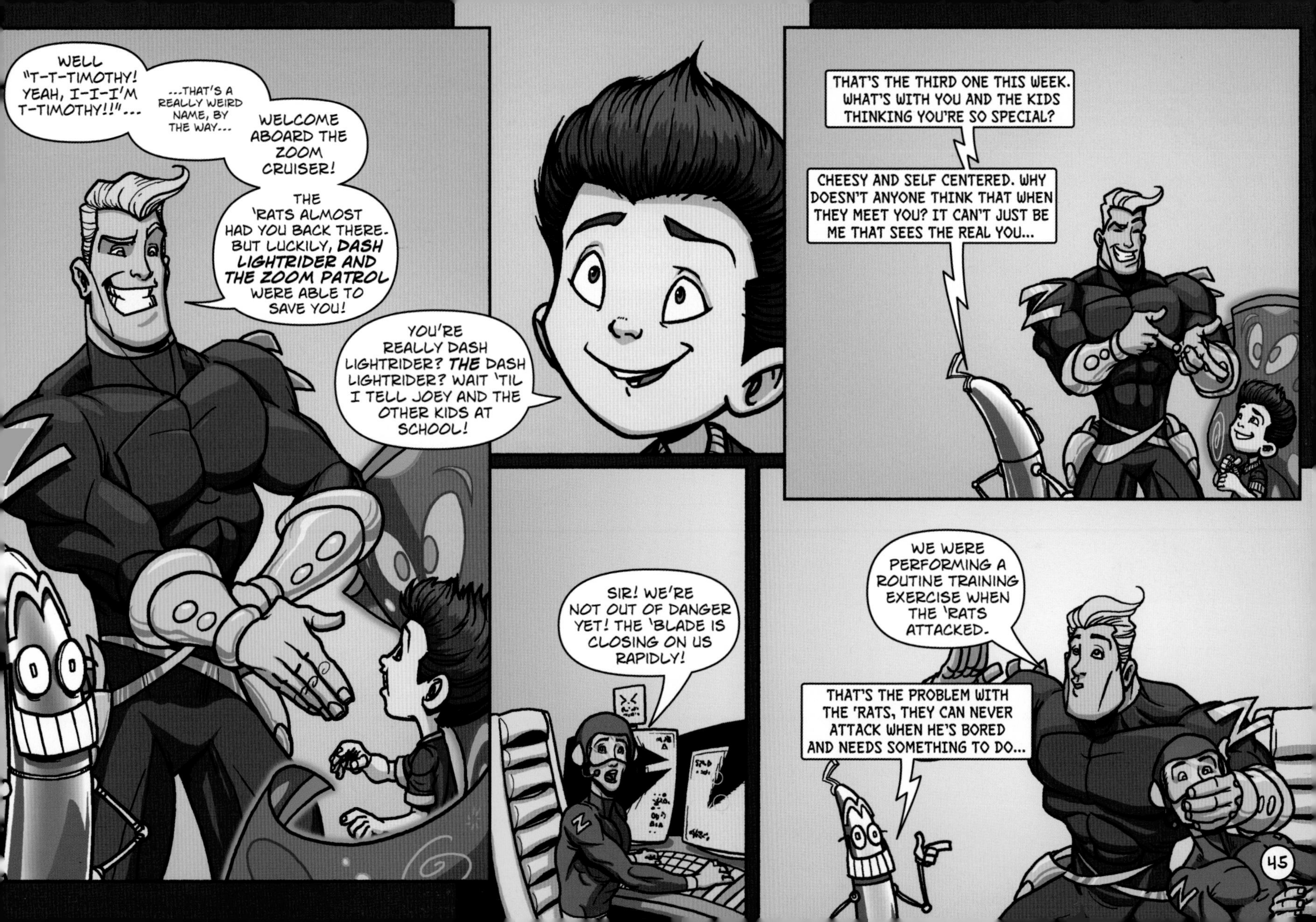
WELL "T-T-TIMOTHY! YEAH, I-I-I'M T-TIMOTHY!!"...
...THAT'S A REALLY WEIRD NAME, BY THE WAY...
WELCOME ABOARD THE ZOOM CRUISER!
THE 'RATS ALMOST HAD YOU BACK THERE. BUT LUCKILY, DASH LIGHTRIDER AND THE ZOOM PATROL WERE ABLE TO SAVE YOU!
YOU'RE REALLY DASH LIGHTRIDER? THE DASH LIGHTRIDER? WAIT 'TIL I TELL JOEY AND THE OTHER KIDS AT SCHOOL!
THAT'S THE THIRD ONE THIS WEEK. WHAT'S WITH YOU AND THE KIDS THINKING YOU'RE SO SPECIAL?
CHEESY AND SELF CENTERED. WHY DOESN'T ANYONE THINK THAT WHEN THEY MEET YOU? IT CAN'T JUST BE ME THAT SEES THE REAL YOU...
SIR! WE'RE NOT OUT OF DANGER YET! THE 'BLADE IS CLOSING ON US RAPIDLY!
WE WERE PERFORMING A ROUTINE TRAINING EXERCISE WHEN THE 'RATS ATTACKED.
THAT'S THE PROBLEM WITH THE 'RATS, THEY CAN NEVER ATTACK WHEN HE'S BORED AND NEEDS SOMETHING TO DO...

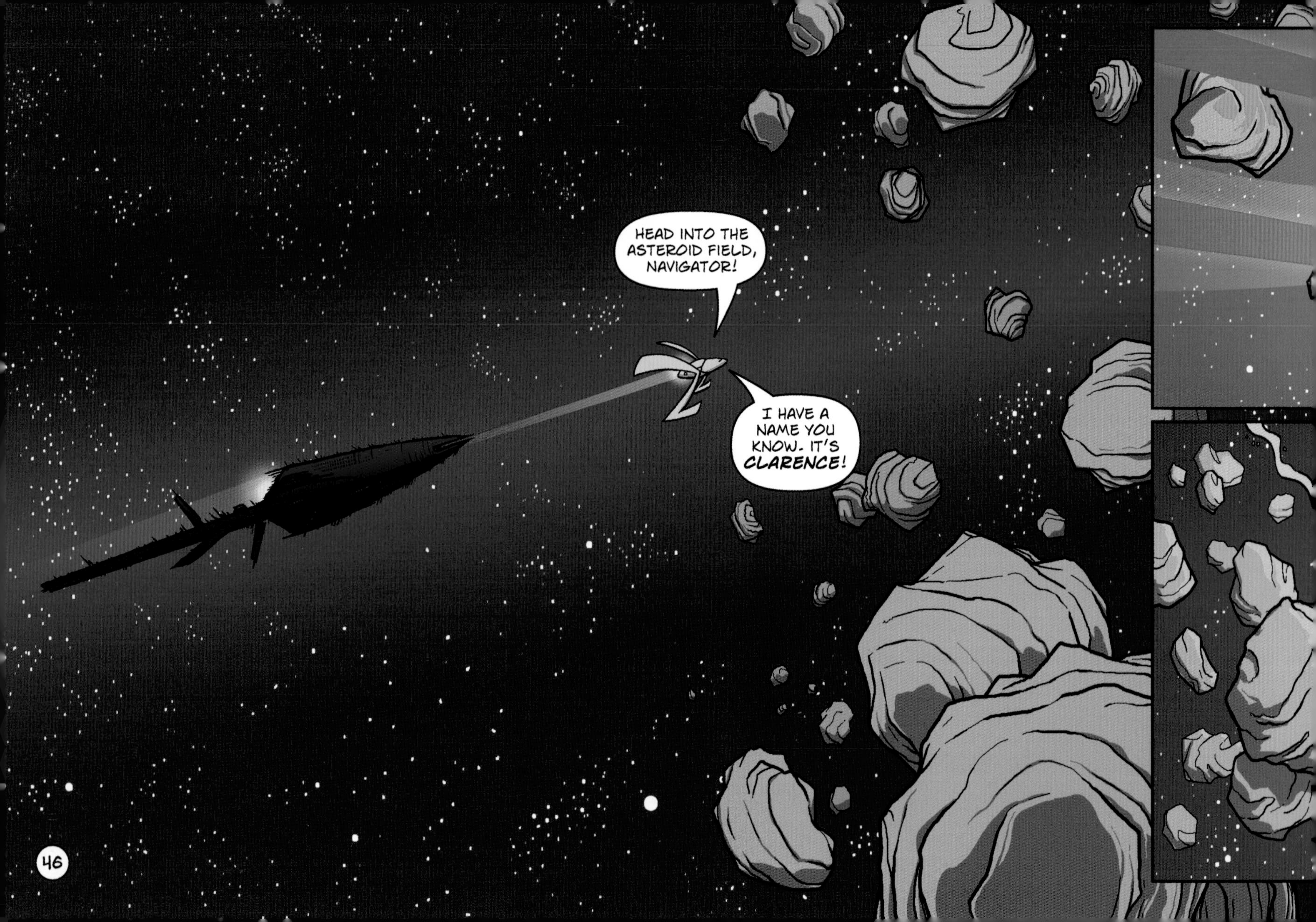
HEAD INTO THE ASTEROID FIELD, NAVIGATOR!
I HAVE A NAME YOU KNOW. IT'S CLARENCE!

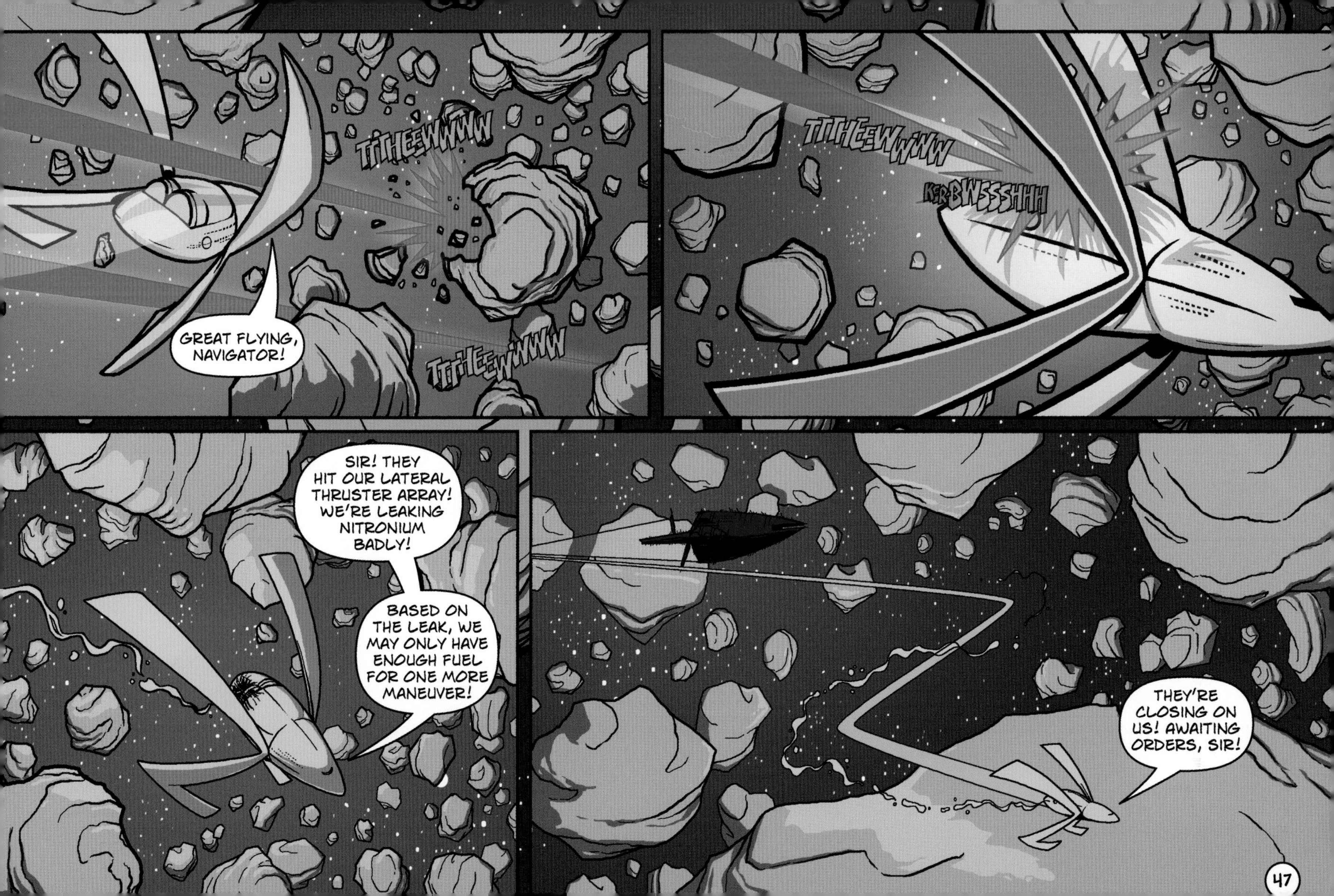
TTTHEEWWWW
GREAT FLYING, NAVIGATOR!
TTTHEEWWWW
TTTHEEWWWW
KER-BWSSSHHH
SIR! THEY HIT OUR LATERAL THRUSTER ARRAY! WE'RE LEAKING NITRONIUM BADLY!
BASED ON THE LEAK, WE MAY ONLY HAVE ENOUGH FUEL FOR ONE MORE MANEUVER!
THEY'RE CLOSING ON US! AWAITING ORDERS, SIR!

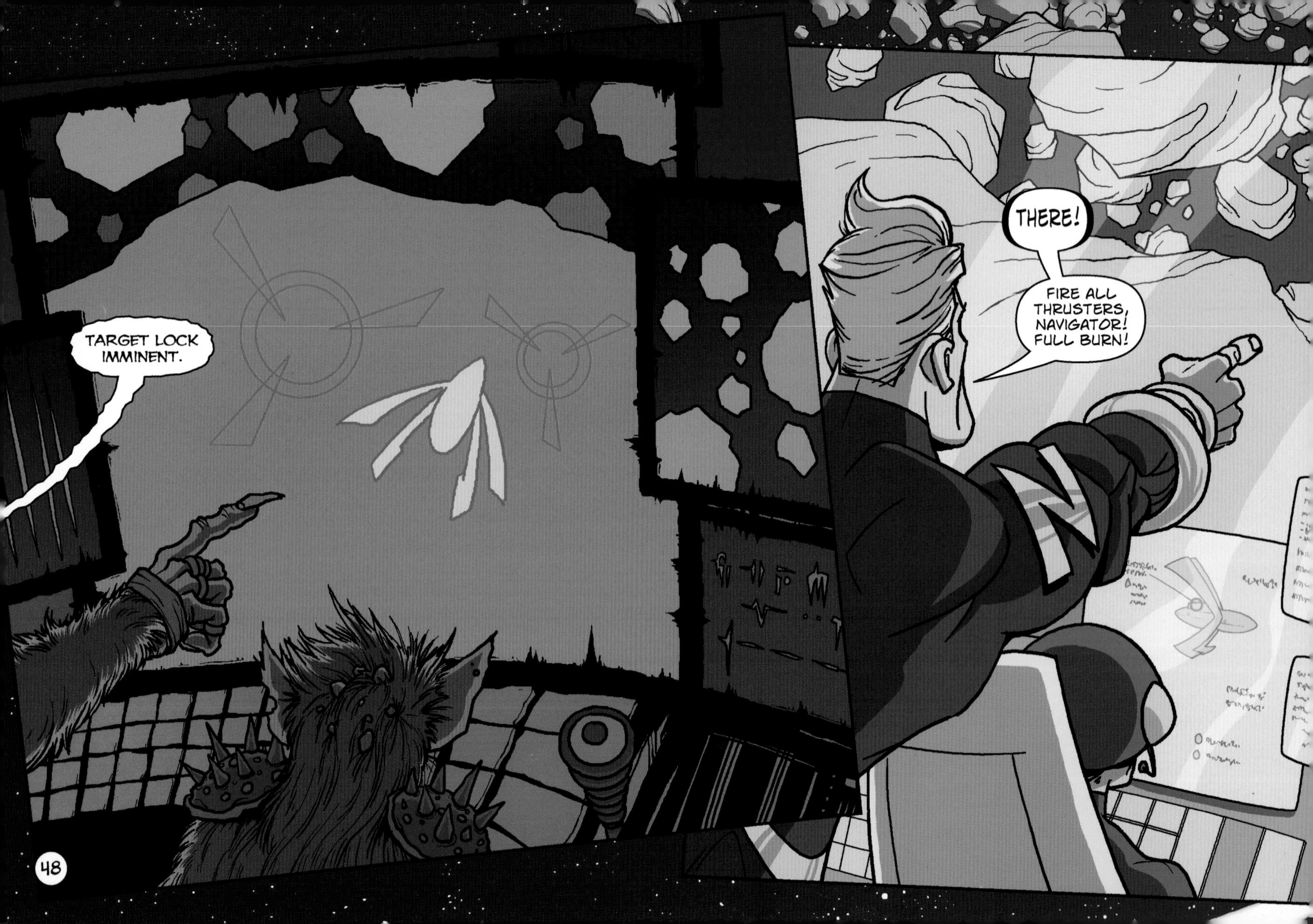
TARGET LOCK IMMINENT.
THERE!
FIRE ALL THRUSTERS, NAVIGATOR! FULL BURN!

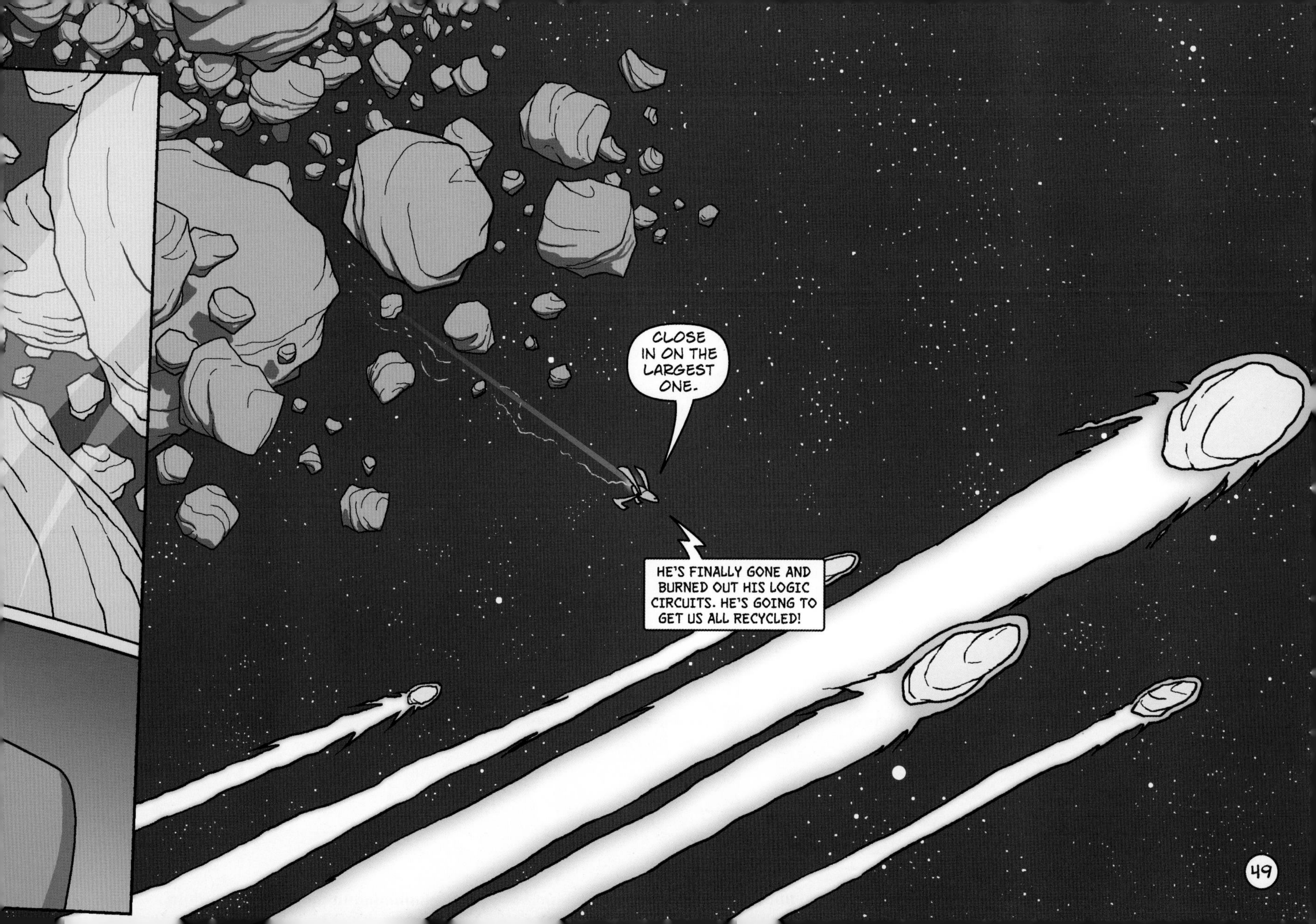
CLOSE IN ON THE LARGEST ONE.
HE'S FINALLY GONE AND BURNED OUT HIS LOGIC CIRCUITS. HE'S GOING TO GET US ALL RECYCLED!

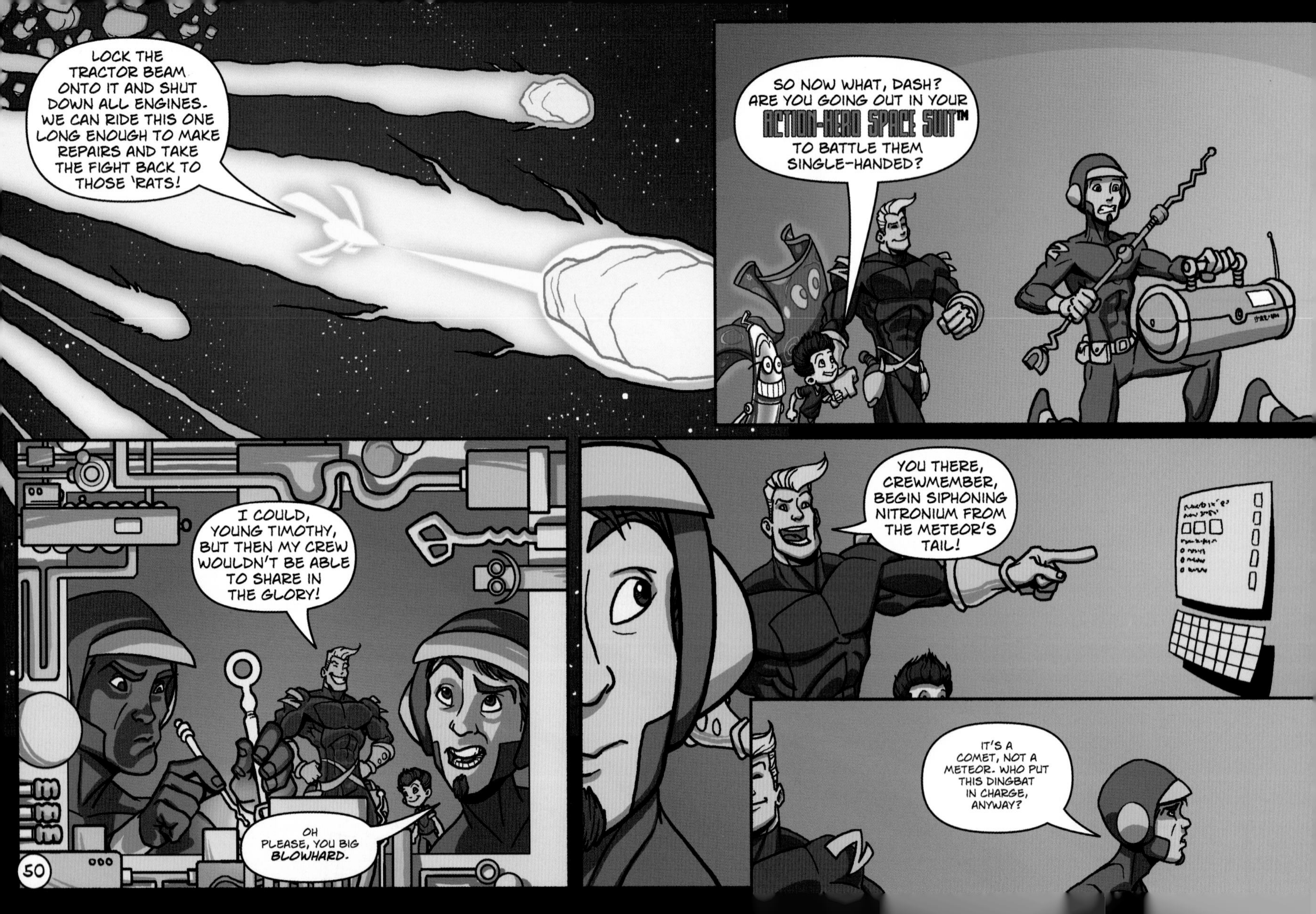
LOCK THE TRACTOR BEAM ONTO IT AND SHUT DOWN ALL ENGINES. WE CAN RIDE THIS ONE LONG ENOUGH TO MAKE REPAIRS AND TAKE THE FIGHT BACK TO THOSE 'RATS!
SO NOW WHAT, DASH? ARE YOU GOING OUT IN YOUR ACTION-HERO SPACE SUIT™ TO BATTLE THEM SINGLE-HANDED?
I COULD, YOUNG TIMOTHY, BUT THEN MY CREW WOULDN'T BE ABLE TO SHARE IN THE GLORY!
OH PLEASE, YOU BIG BLOWHARD.
YOU THERE, CREWMEMBER, BEGIN SIPHONING NITRONIUM FROM THE METEOR'S TAIL!
IT'S A COMET, NOT A METEOR. WHO PUT THIS DINGBAT IN CHARGE, ANYWAY?

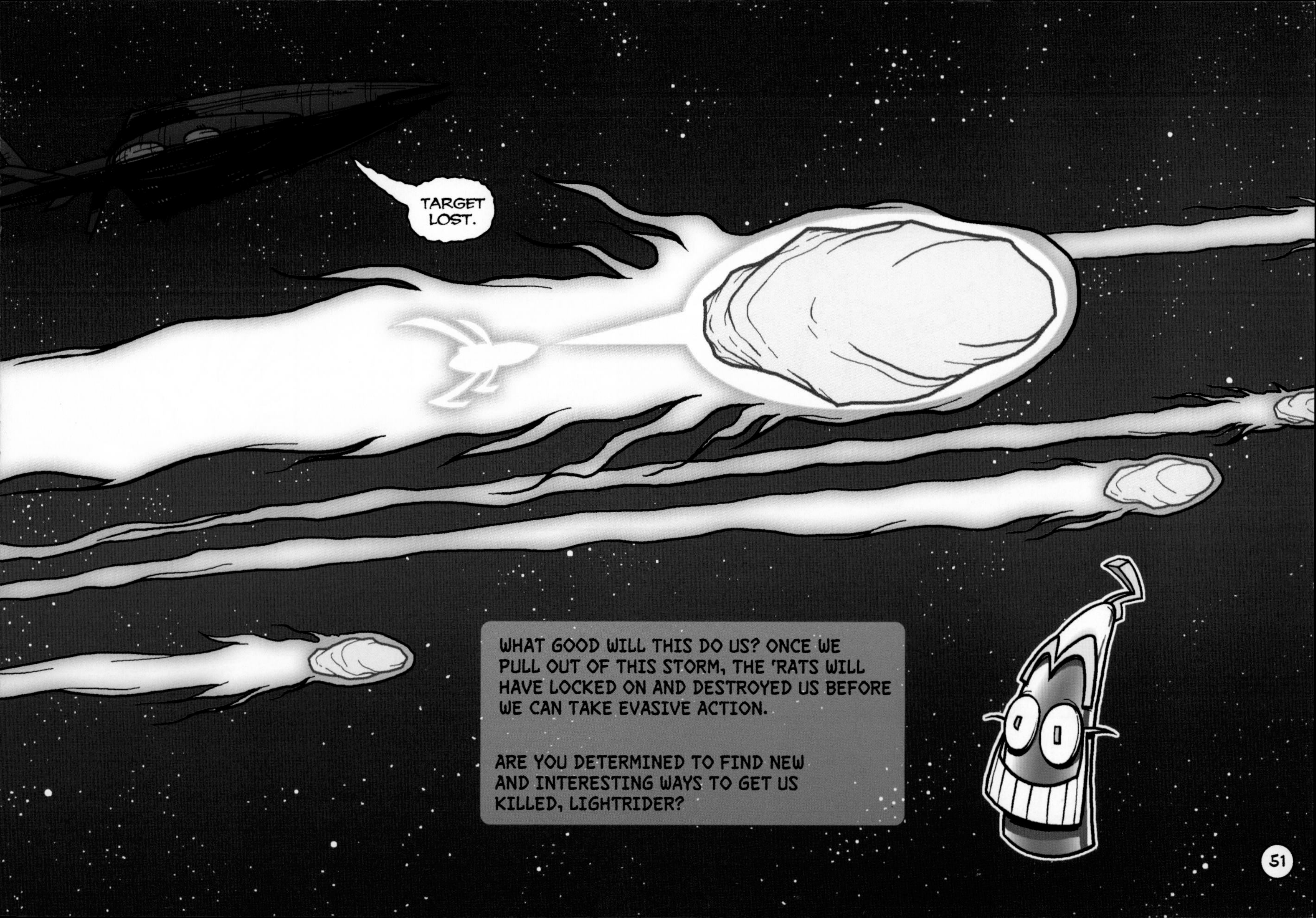
TARGET LOST.
WHAT GOOD WILL THIS DO US? ONCE WE PULL OUT OF THIS STORM, THE 'RATS WILL HAVE LOCKED ON AND DESTROYED US BEFORE WE CAN TAKE EVASIVE ACTION.
ARE YOU DETERMINED TO FIND NEW AND INTERESTING WAYS TO GET US KILLED, LIGHTRIDER?

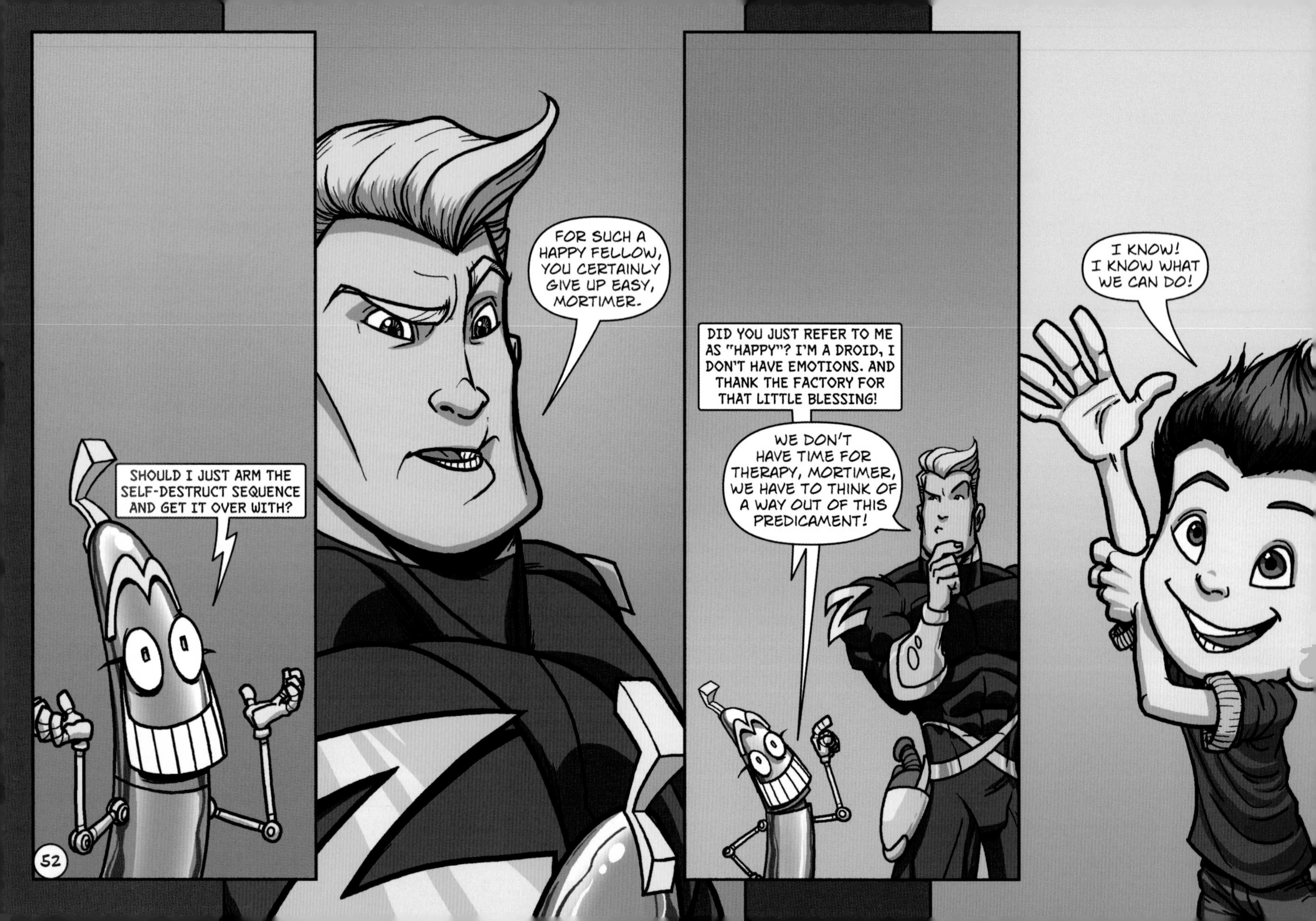
SHOULD I JUST ARM THE SELF-DESTRUCT SEQUENCE AND GET IT OVER WITH?
FOR SUCH A HAPPY FELLOW, YOU CERTAINLY GIVE UP EASY, MORTIMER.
DID YOU JUST REFER TO ME AS "HAPPY"? I'M A DROID, I DON'T HAVE EMOTIONS. AND THANK THE FACTORY FOR THAT LITTLE BLESSING!
WE DON'T HAVE TIME FOR THERAPY, MORTIMER, WE HAVE TO THINK OF A WAY OUT OF THIS PREDICAMENT!
I KNOW! I KNOW WHAT WE CAN DO!

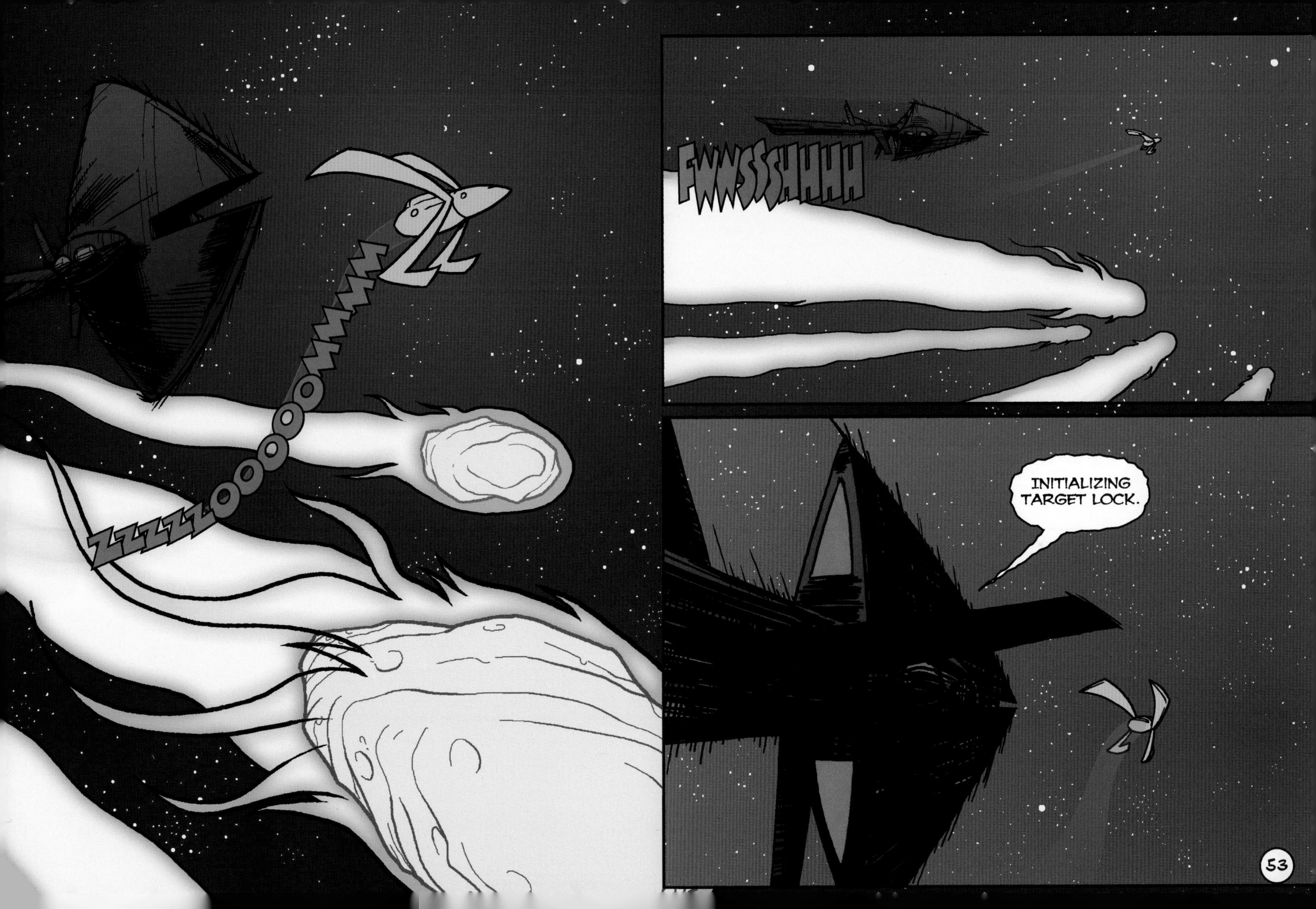
ZZZZZZOOOOOOOOMMMMMM
FWWSSSHHHH
INITIALIZING TARGET LOCK.

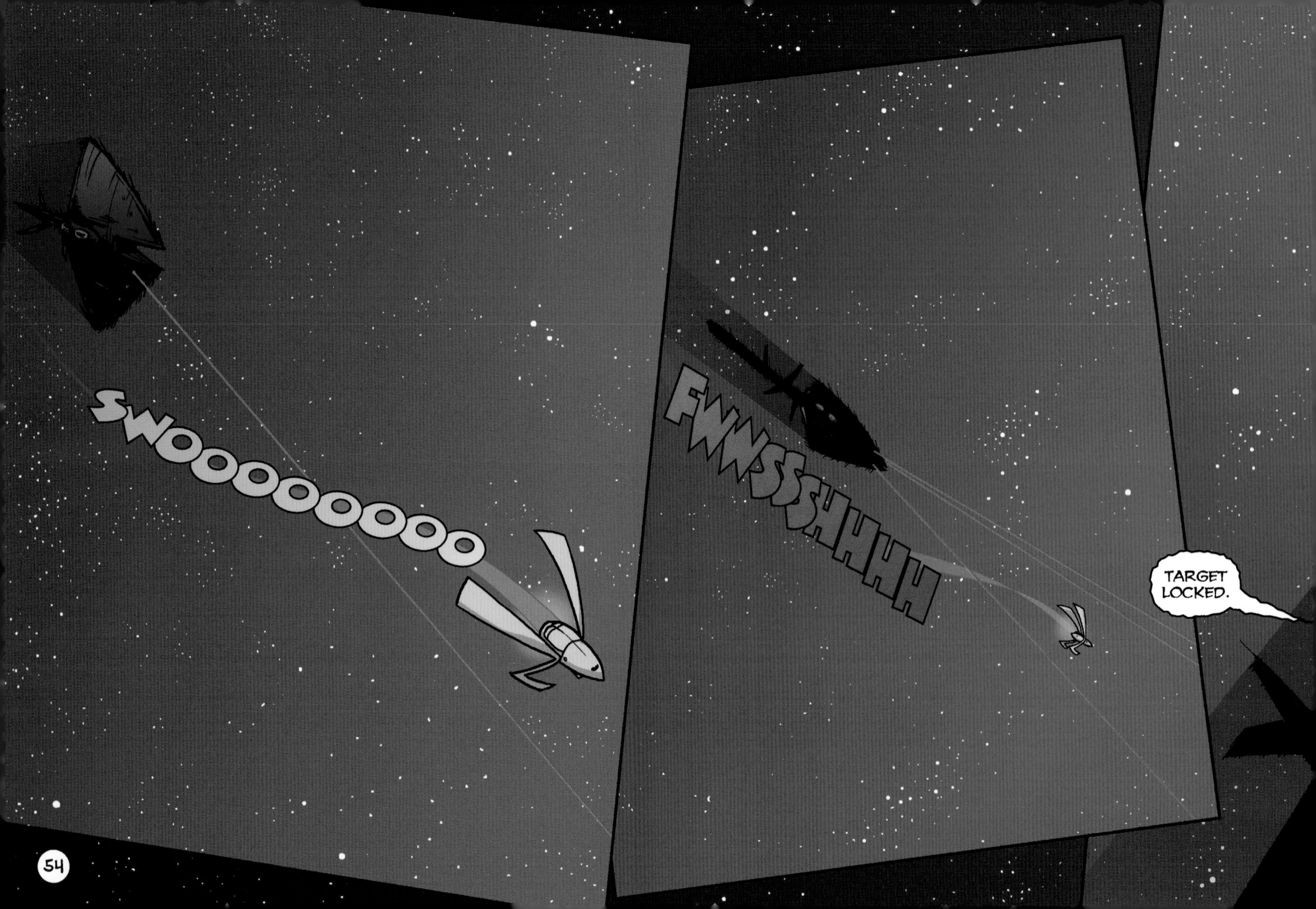
SWOOOOOOOOO
FWNSSSHHHH
TARGET LOCKED.

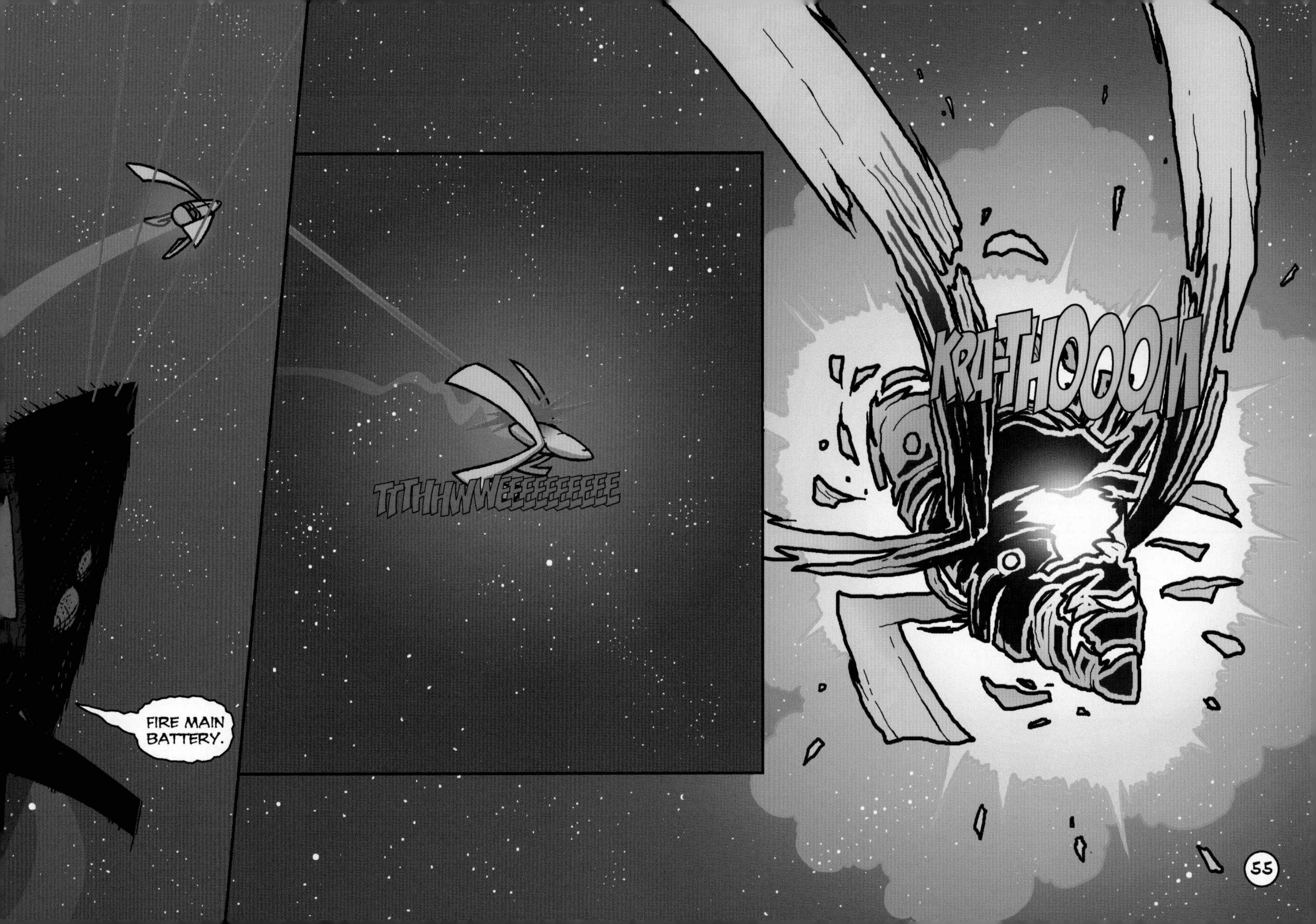
FIRE MAIN BATTERY.
TTTHHWWEEEEEEEEEE
KRA-THOOOM

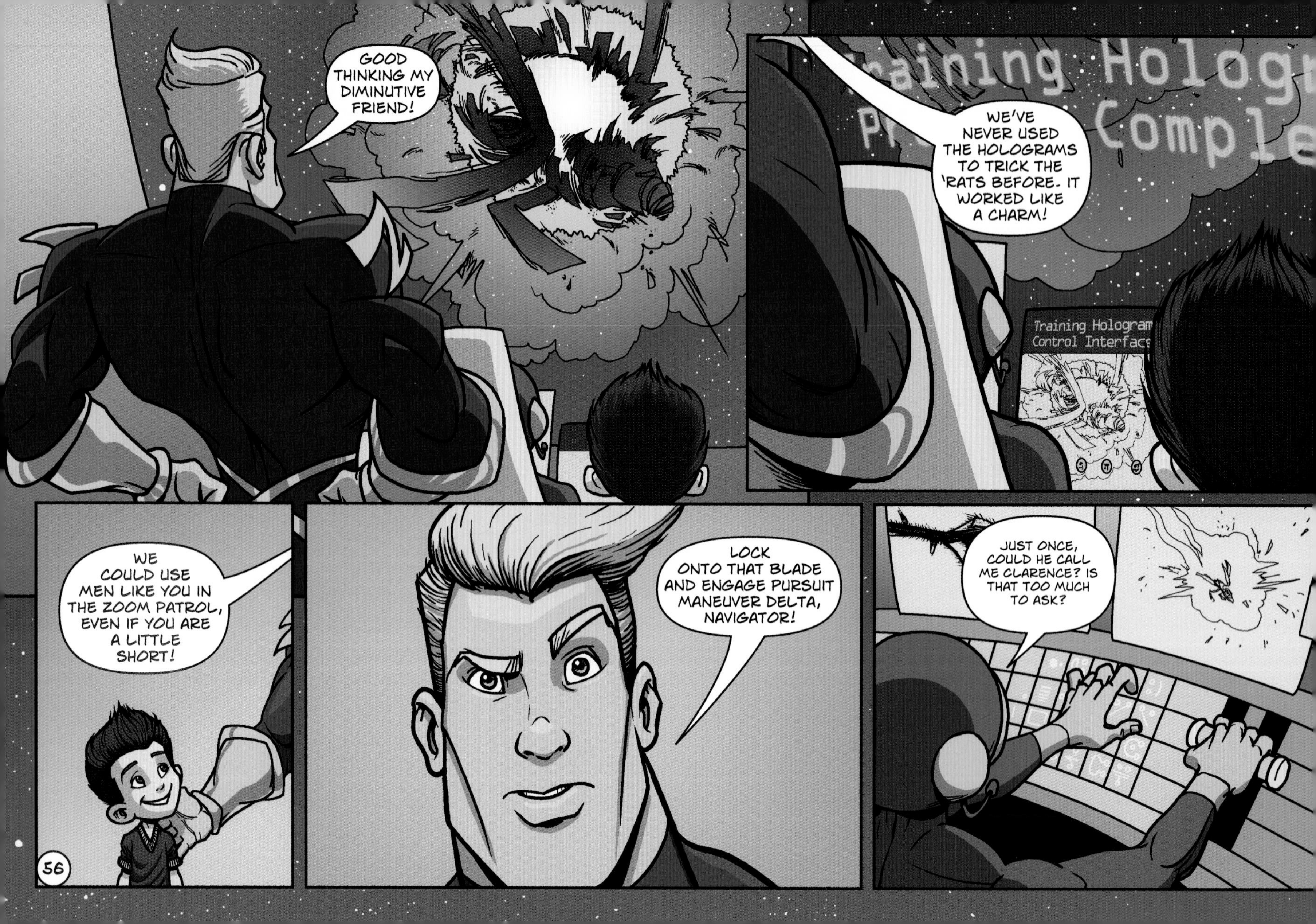
GOOD THINKING MY DIMINUTIVE FRIEND!
Training Hologr... Comple...
WE'VE NEVER USED THE HOLOGRAMS TO TRICK THE 'RATS BEFORE. IT WORKED LIKE A CHARM!
Training Hologram Control Interface
WE COULD USE MEN LIKE YOU IN THE ZOOM PATROL, EVEN IF YOU ARE A LITTLE SHORT!
LOCK ONTO THAT BLADE AND ENGAGE PURSUIT MANEUVER DELTA, NAVIGATOR!
JUST ONCE, COULD HE CALL ME CLARENCE? IS THAT TOO MUCH TO ASK?

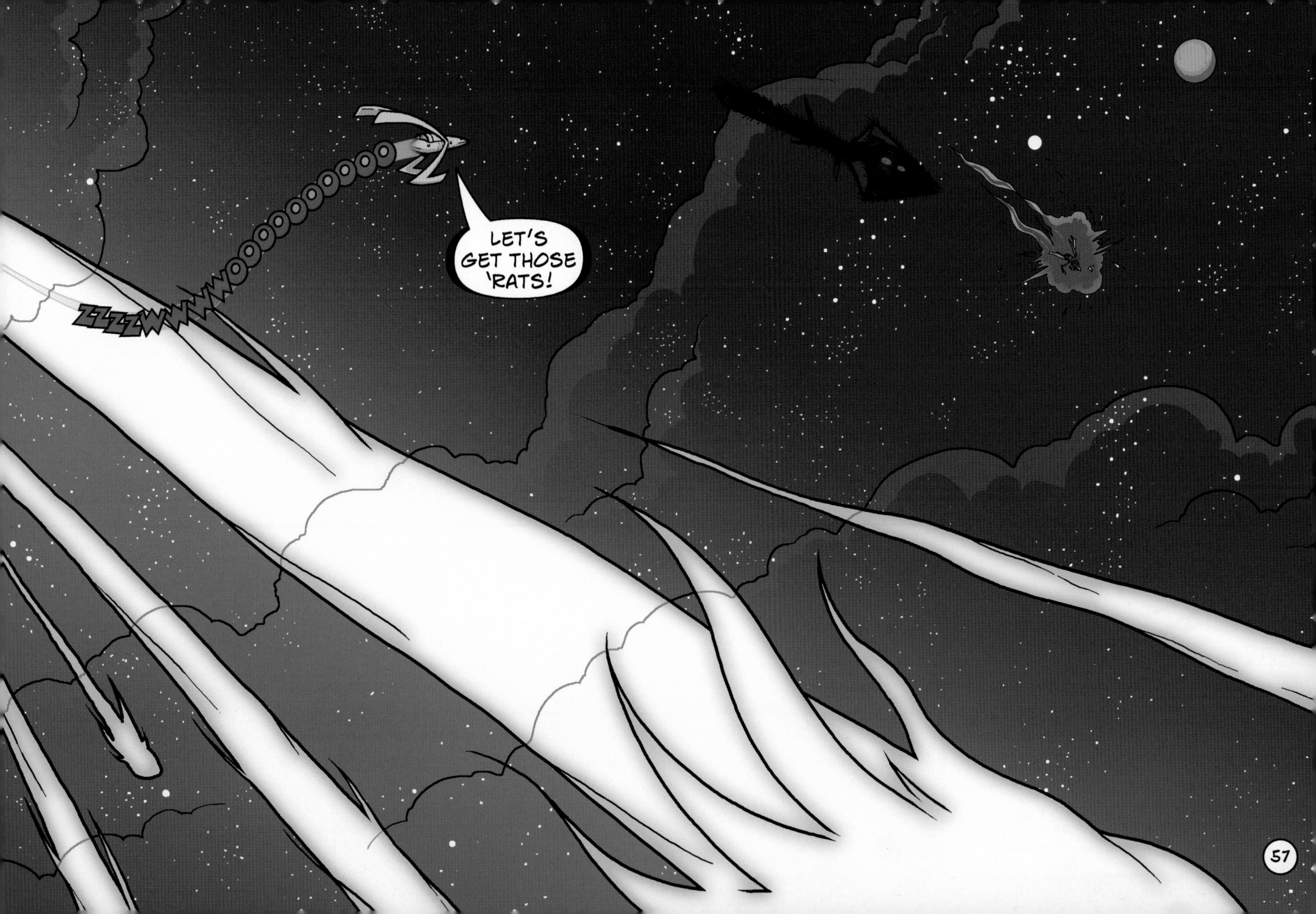
ZZZZWWWWWWOOOOOOOOOOOOO
LET'S GET THOSE 'RATS!

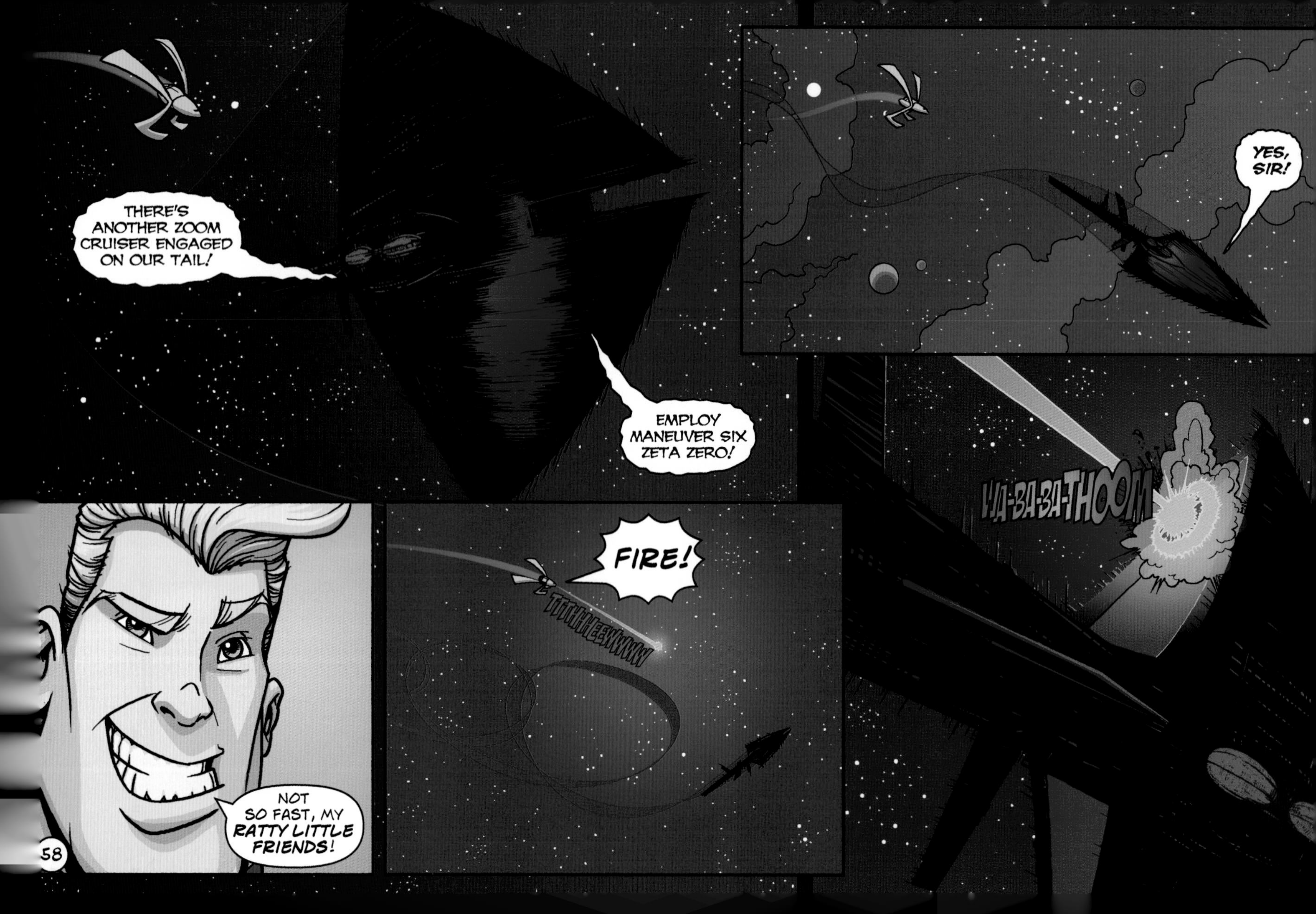
THERE'S ANOTHER ZOOM CRUISER ENGAGED ON OUR TAIL!
EMPLOY MANEUVER SIX ZETA ZERO!
YES, SIR!
NOT SO FAST, MY RATTY LITTLE FRIENDS!
FIRE!
TTTTHHEEWWWW
WA-BA-BA-THOOM

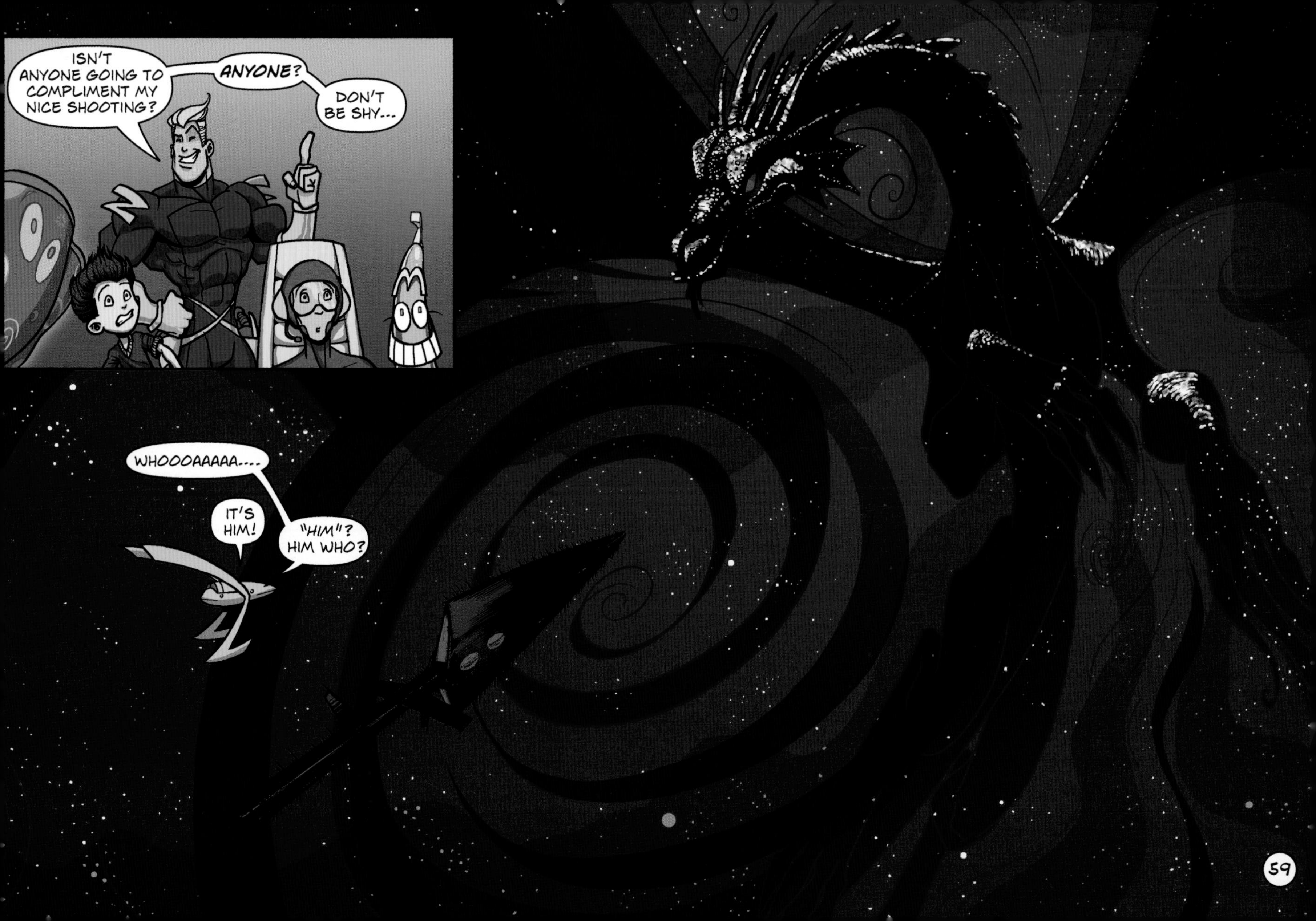

ISN'T ANYONE GOING TO COMPLIMENT MY NICE SHOOTING?
ANYONE?
DON'T BE SHY...
WHOOOAAAAA....
IT'S HIM!
"HIM"? HIM WHO?

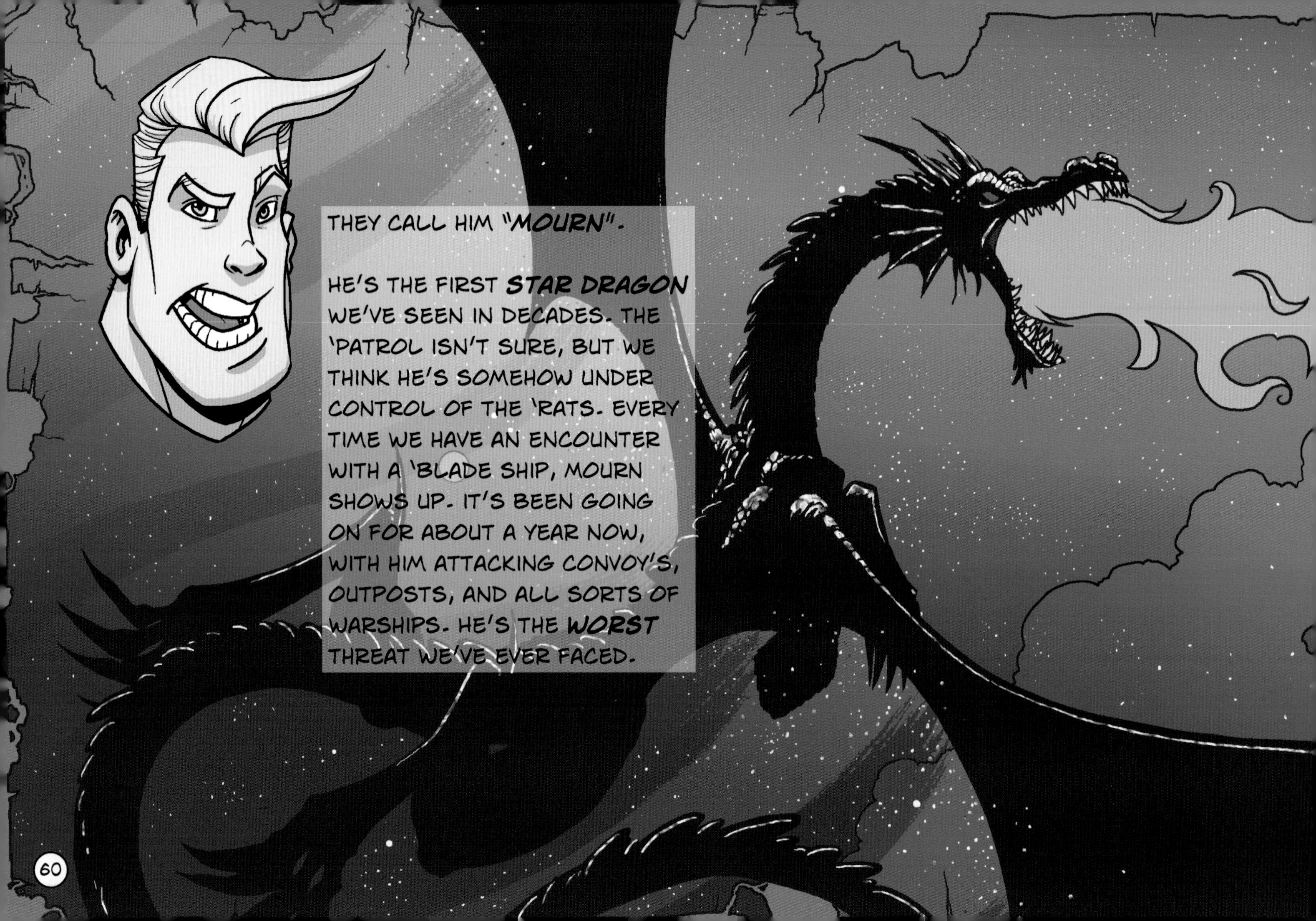
THEY CALL HIM "MOURN".
HE'S THE FIRST STAR DRAGON WE'VE SEEN IN DECADES. THE 'PATROL ISN'T SURE, BUT WE THINK HE'S SOMEHOW UNDER CONTROL OF THE 'RATS. EVERY TIME WE HAVE AN ENCOUNTER WITH A 'BLADE SHIP, MOURN SHOWS UP. IT'S BEEN GOING ON FOR ABOUT A YEAR NOW, WITH HIM ATTACKING CONVOY'S, OUTPOSTS, AND ALL SORTS OF WARSHIPS. HE'S THE WORST THREAT WE'VE EVER FACED.

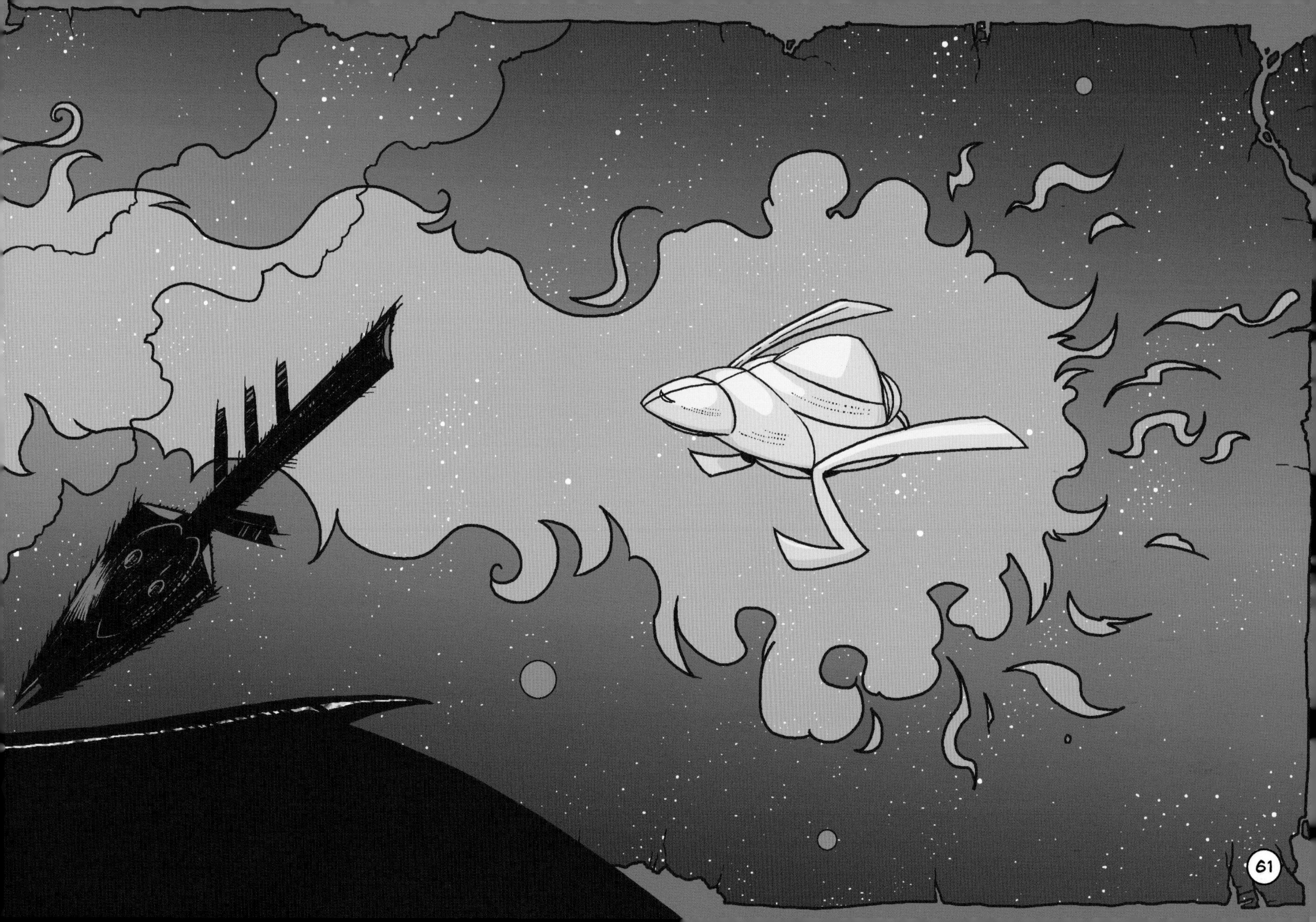

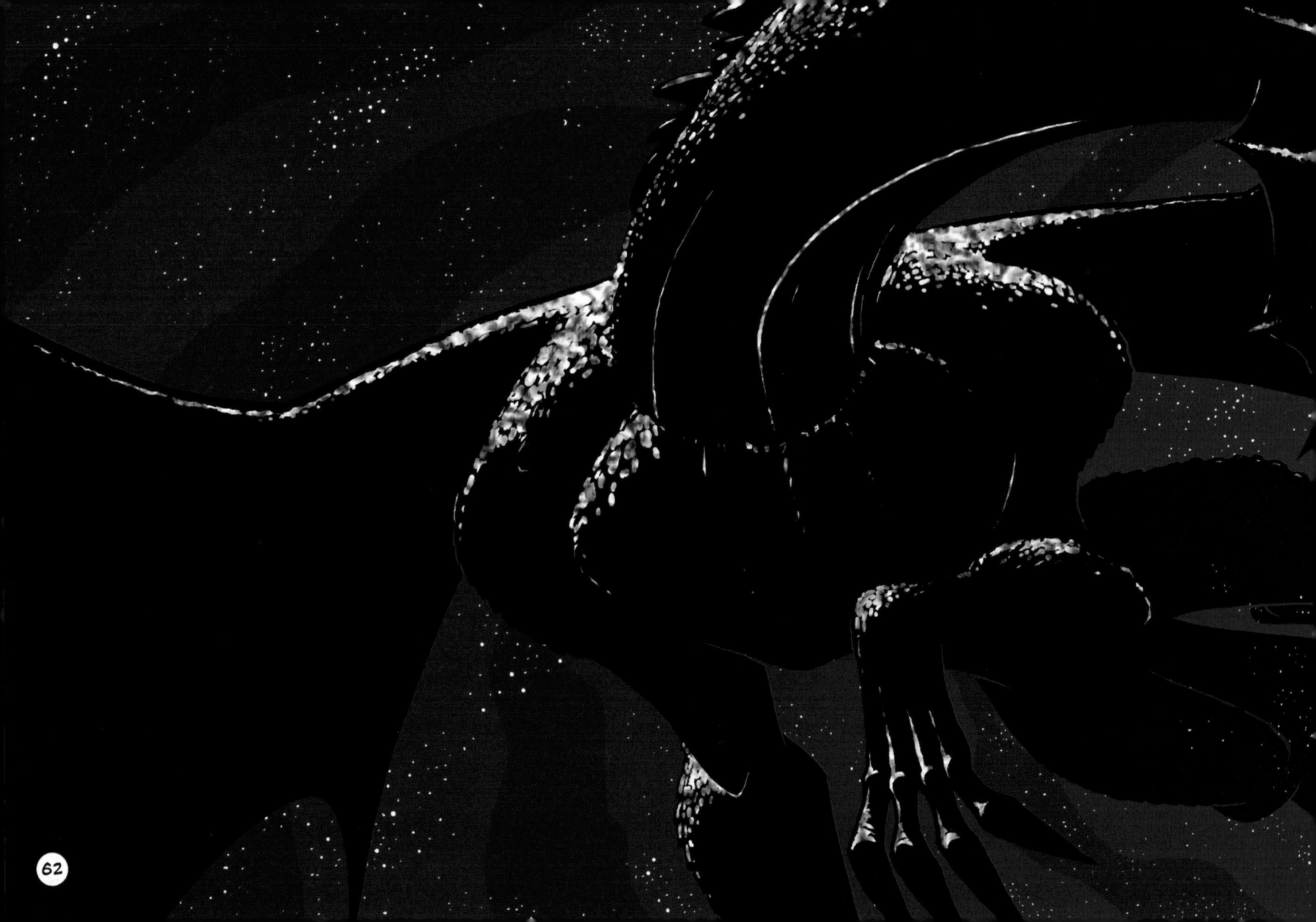

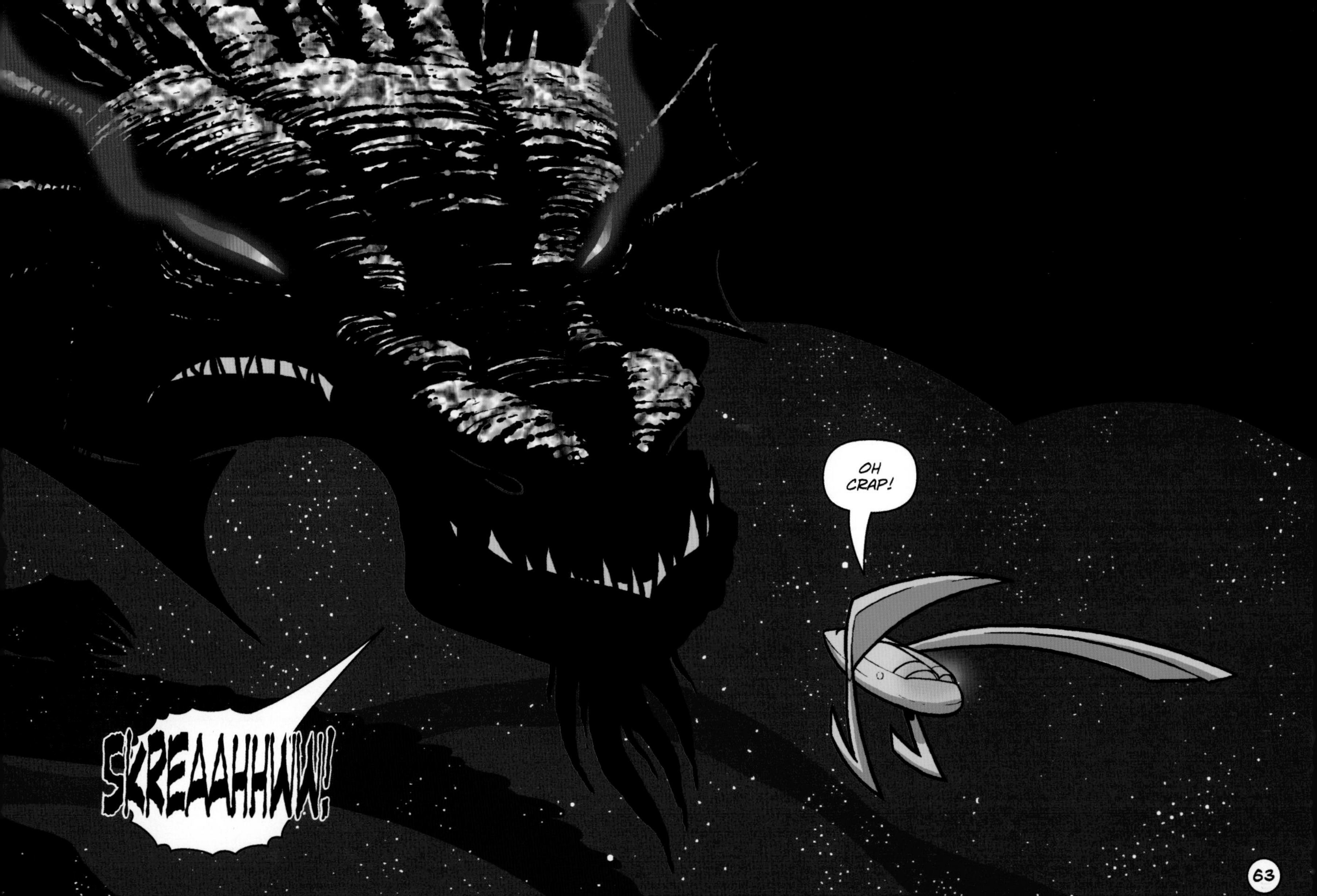
SKREAAHHWW!
OH CRAP!

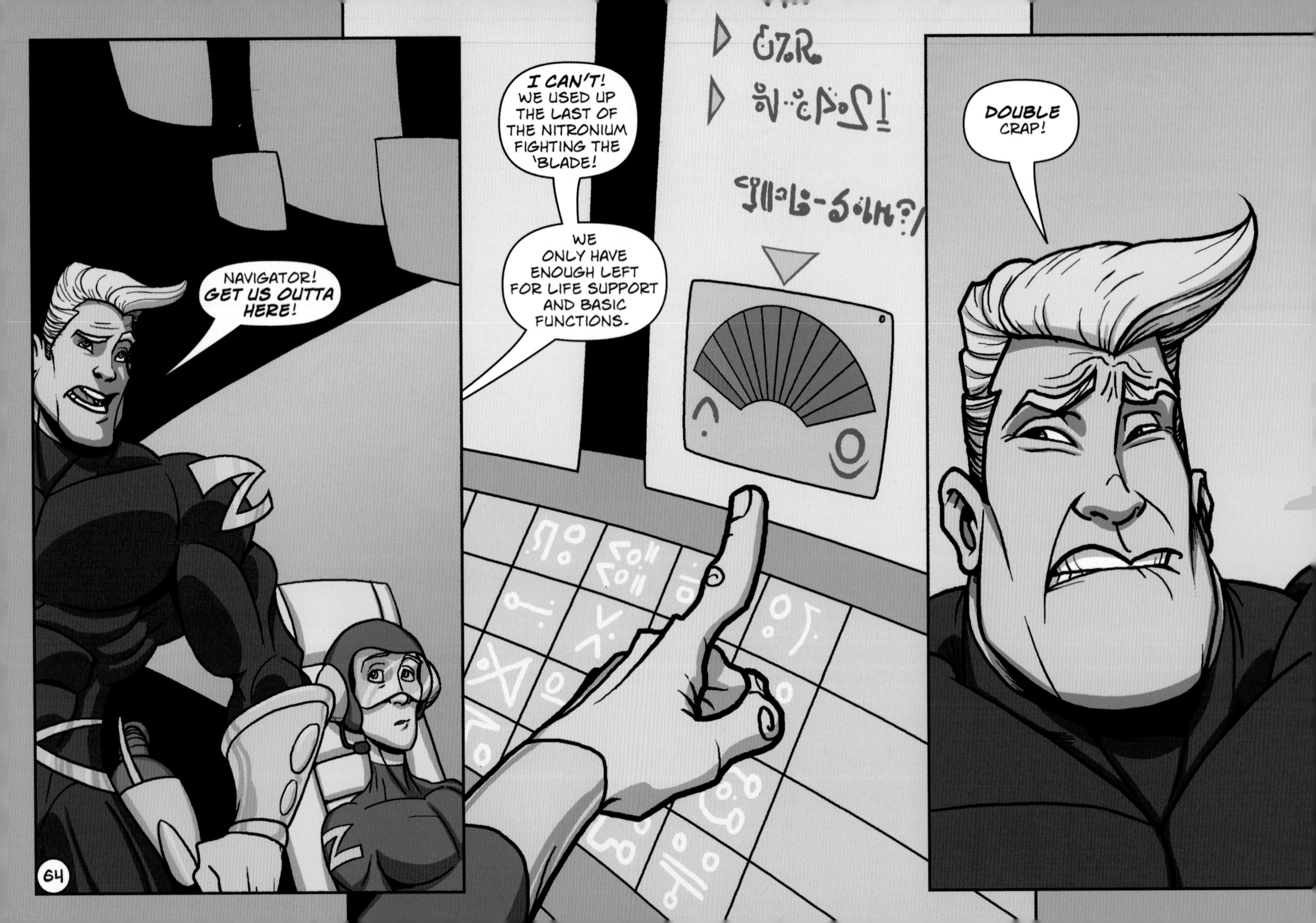

NAVIGATOR! GET US OUTTA HERE!
I CAN'T! WE USED UP THE LAST OF THE NITRONIUM FIGHTING THE 'BLADE!
WE ONLY HAVE ENOUGH LEFT FOR LIFE SUPPORT AND BASIC FUNCTIONS.
DOUBLE CRAP!

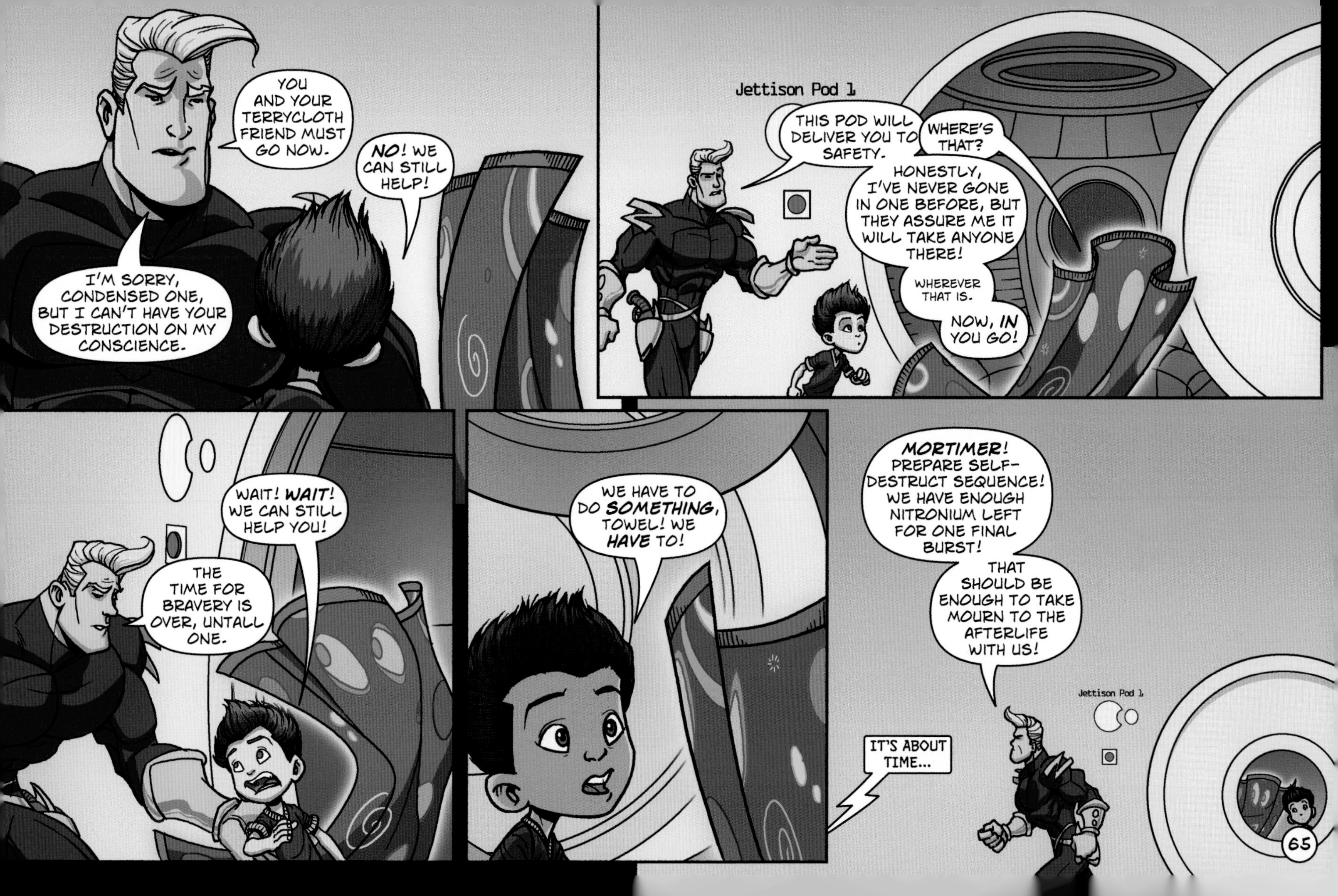

YOU AND YOUR TERRYCLOTH FRIEND MUST GO NOW.
NO! WE CAN STILL HELP!
I'M SORRY, CONDENSED ONE, BUT I CAN'T HAVE YOUR DESTRUCTION ON MY CONSCIENCE.
Jettison Pod 1
THIS POD WILL DELIVER YOU TO SAFETY.
WHERE'S THAT?
HONESTLY, I'VE NEVER GONE IN ONE BEFORE, BUT THEY ASSURE ME IT WILL TAKE ANYONE THERE!
WHEREVER THAT IS.
NOW, IN YOU GO!
WAIT! WAIT! WE CAN STILL HELP YOU!
THE TIME FOR BRAVERY IS OVER, UNTALL ONE.
WE HAVE TO DO SOMETHING, TOWEL! WE HAVE TO!
MORTIMER! PREPARE SELF-DESTRUCT SEQUENCE! WE HAVE ENOUGH NITRONIUM LEFT FOR ONE FINAL BURST!
THAT SHOULD BE ENOUGH TO TAKE MOURN TO THE AFTERLIFE WITH US!
IT'S ABOUT TIME...
Jettison Pod 1

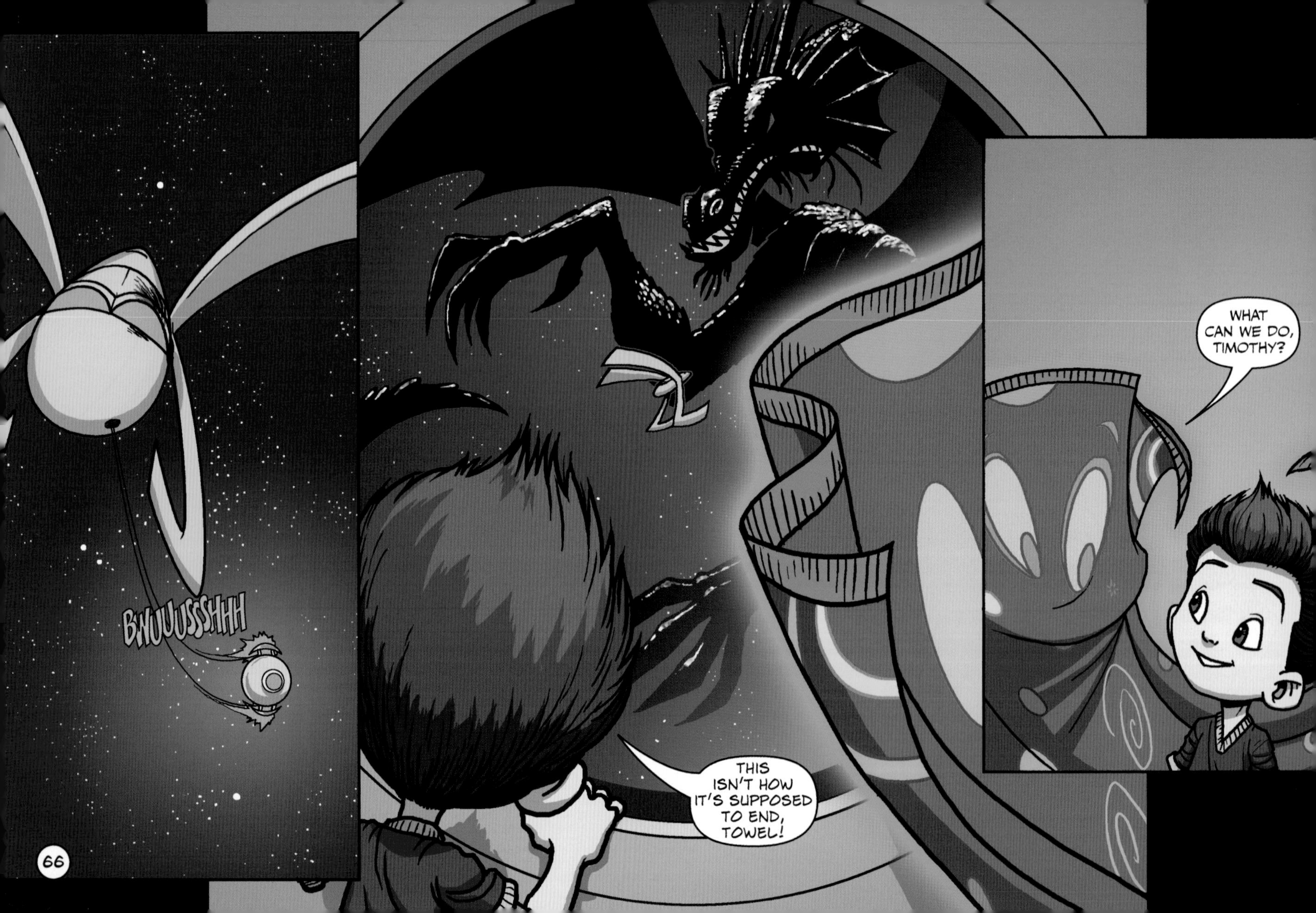
BWUUUSSSHHH
THIS ISN'T HOW IT'S SUPPOSED TO END, TOWEL!
WHAT CAN WE DO, TIMOTHY?

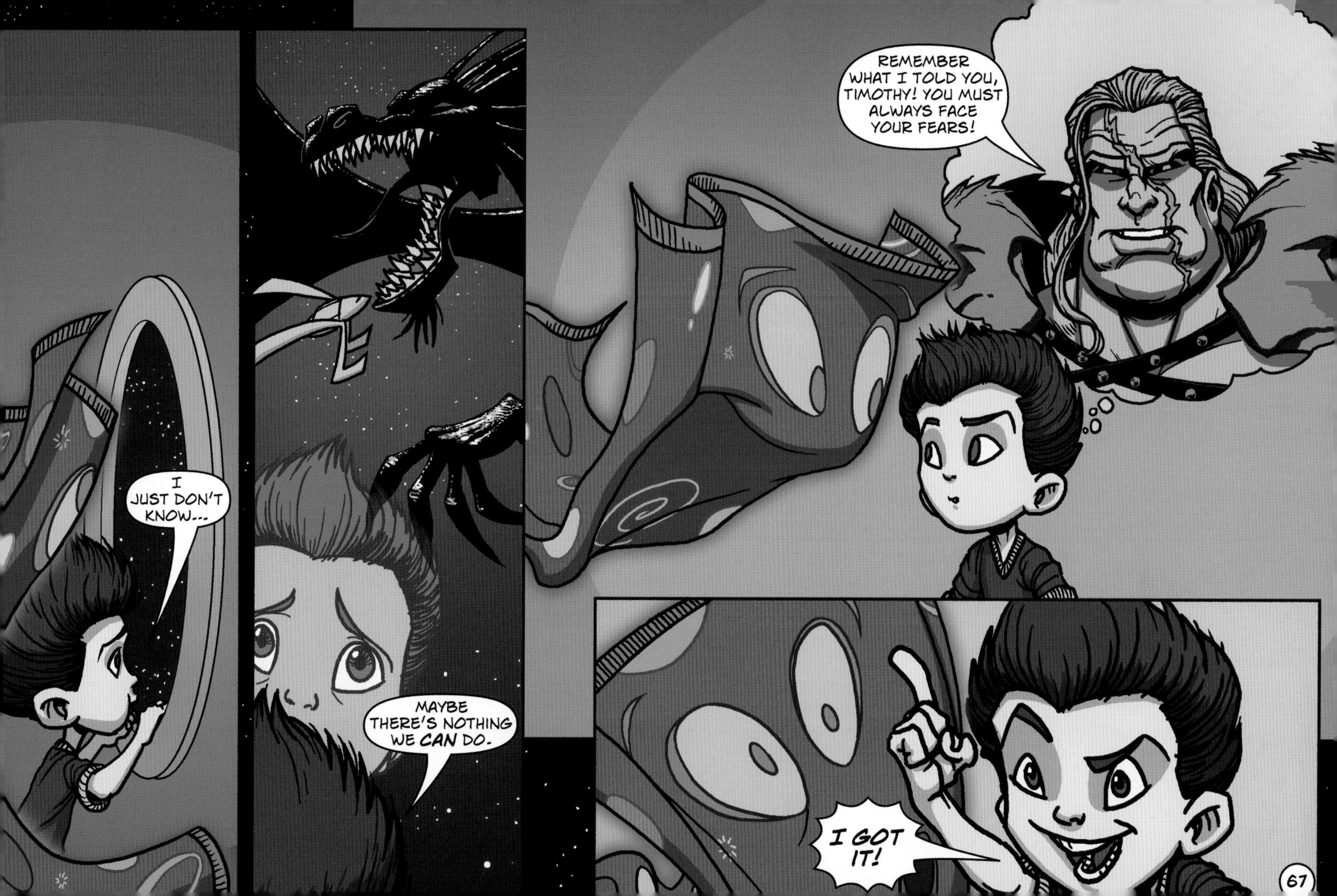
I JUST DON'T KNOW...
MAYBE THERE'S NOTHING WE CAN DO.
REMEMBER WHAT I TOLD YOU, TIMOTHY! YOU MUST ALWAYS FACE YOUR FEARS!
I GOT IT!

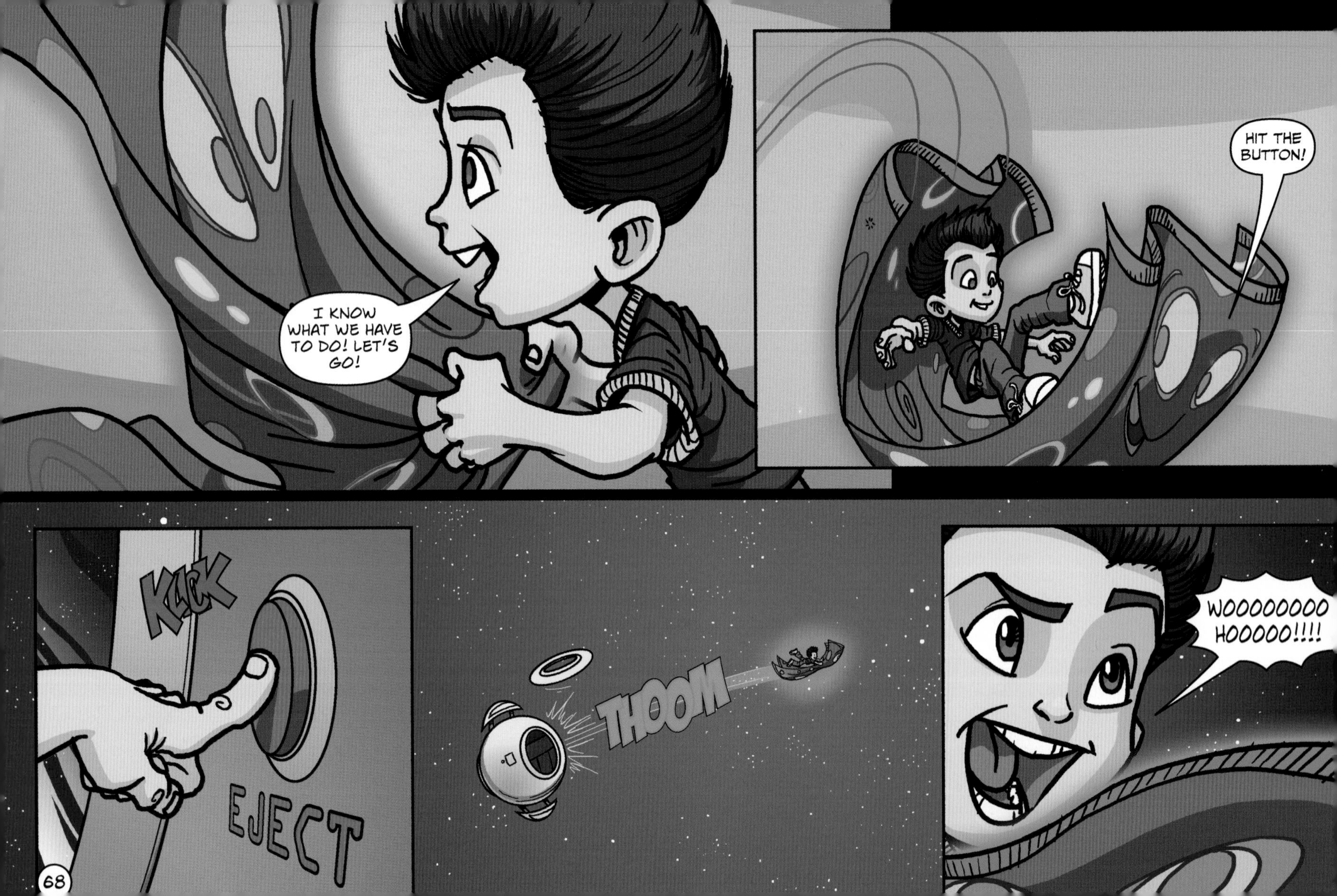
I KNOW WHAT WE HAVE TO DO! LET'S GO!
HIT THE BUTTON!
KLICK
EJECT
THOOM
WOOOOOOOO HOOOOO!!!!

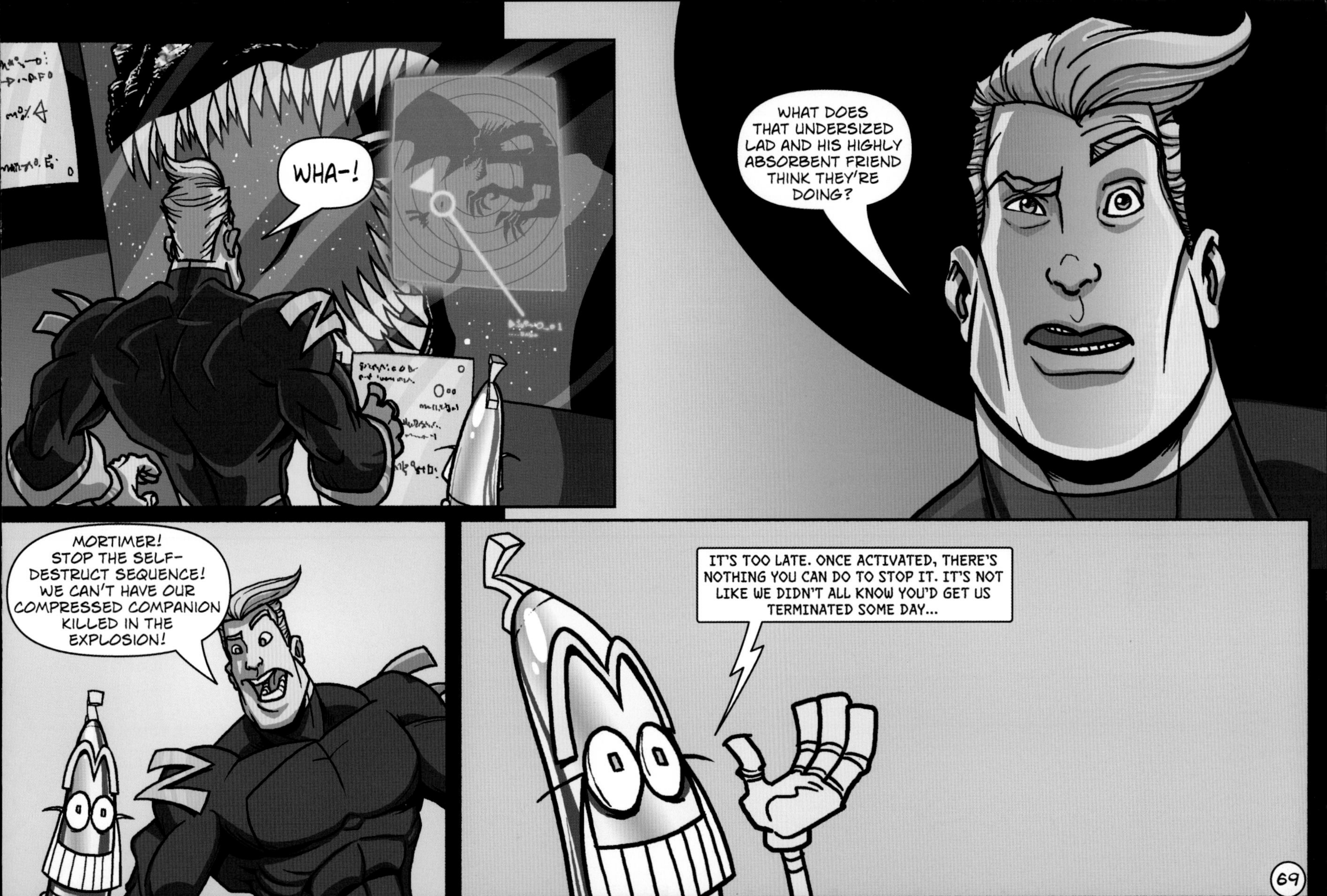
WHA-!
WHAT DOES THAT UNDERSIZED LAD AND HIS HIGHLY ABSORBENT FRIEND THINK THEY'RE DOING?
MORTIMER! STOP THE SELF-DESTRUCT SEQUENCE! WE CAN'T HAVE OUR COMPRESSED COMPANION KILLED IN THE EXPLOSION!
IT'S TOO LATE. ONCE ACTIVATED, THERE'S NOTHING YOU CAN DO TO STOP IT. IT'S NOT LIKE WE DIDN'T ALL KNOW YOU'D GET US TERMINATED SOME DAY...

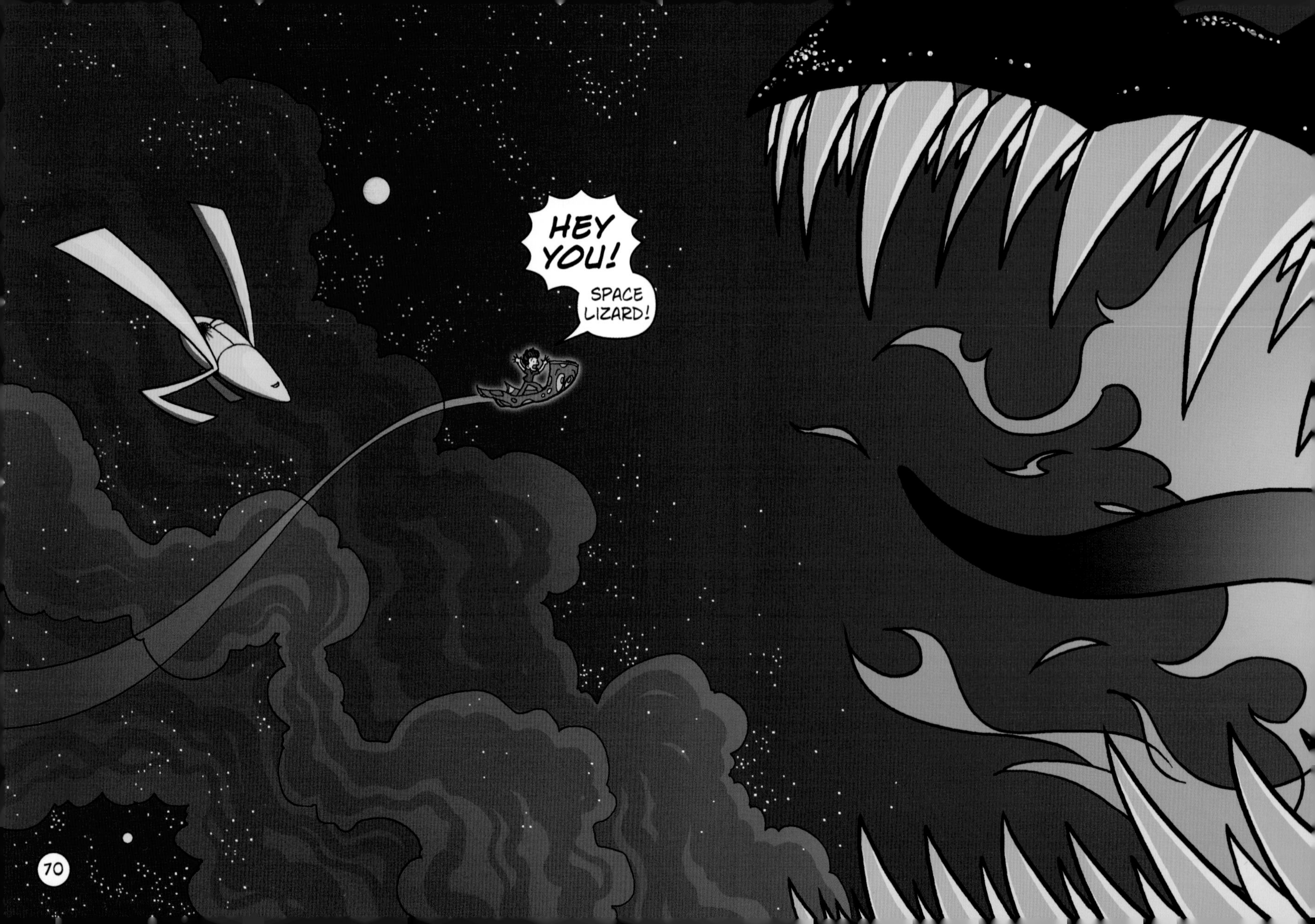
HEY YOU!
SPACE LIZARD!

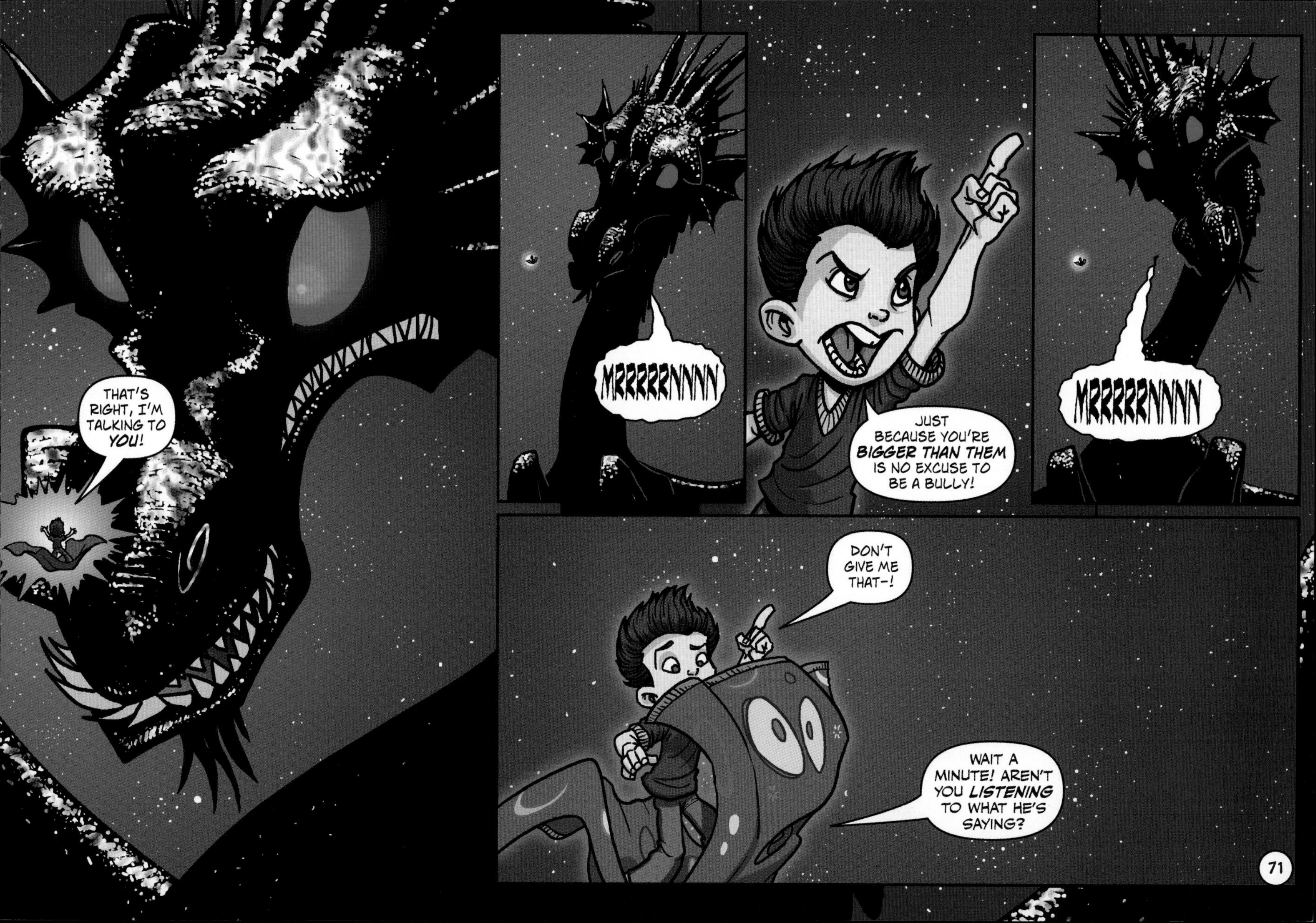
THAT'S RIGHT, I'M TALKING TO *YOU!*
MRRRRRNNNN
JUST BECAUSE YOU'RE ***BIGGER THAN THEM*** IS NO EXCUSE TO BE A BULLY!
MRRRRRNNNN
DON'T GIVE ME THAT-!
WAIT A MINUTE! AREN'T YOU ***LISTENING*** TO WHAT HE'S SAYING?

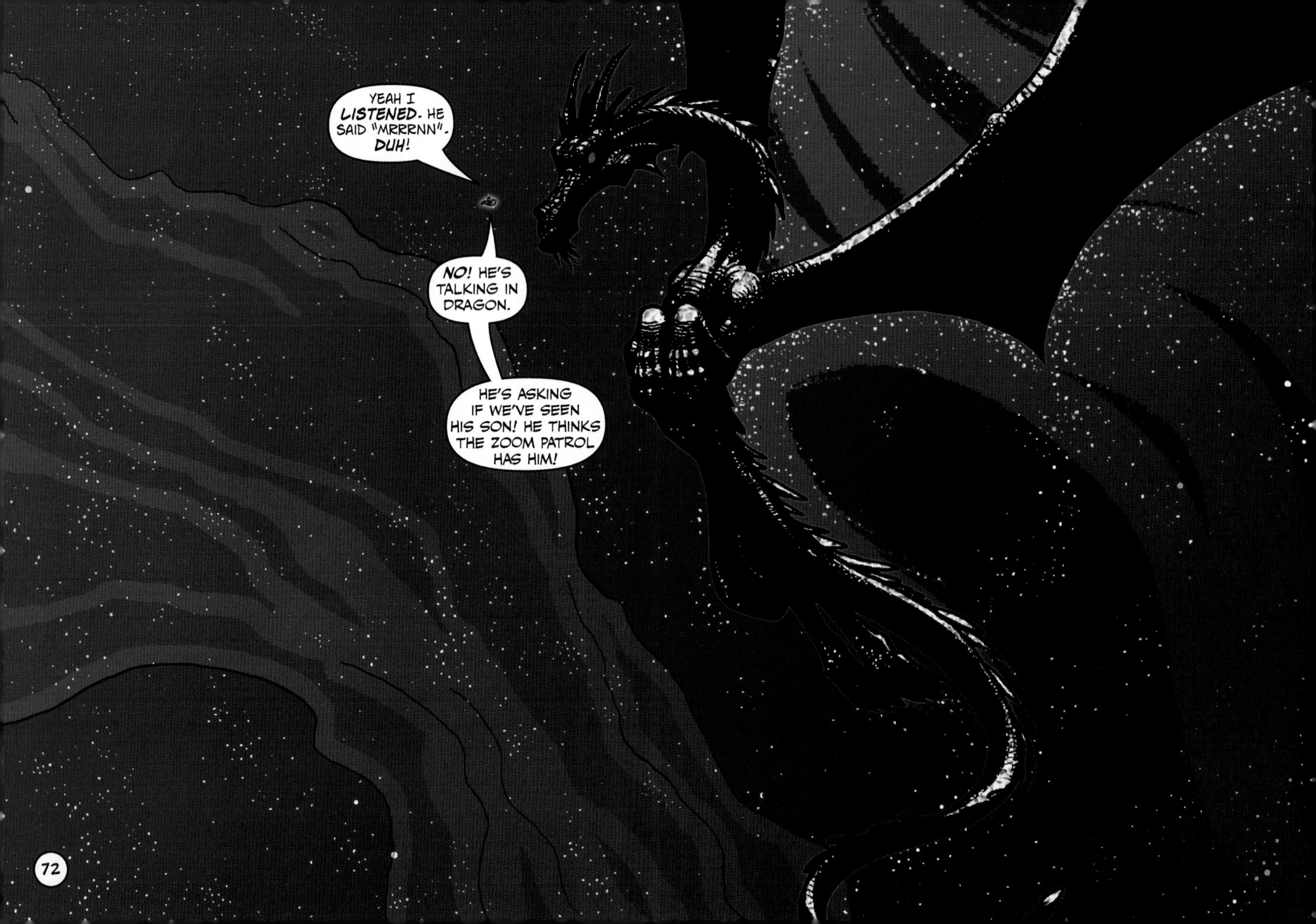
YEAH I LISTENED. HE SAID "MRRRNN". DUH!
NO! HE'S TALKING IN DRAGON.
HE'S ASKING IF WE'VE SEEN HIS SON! HE THINKS THE ZOOM PATROL HAS HIM!

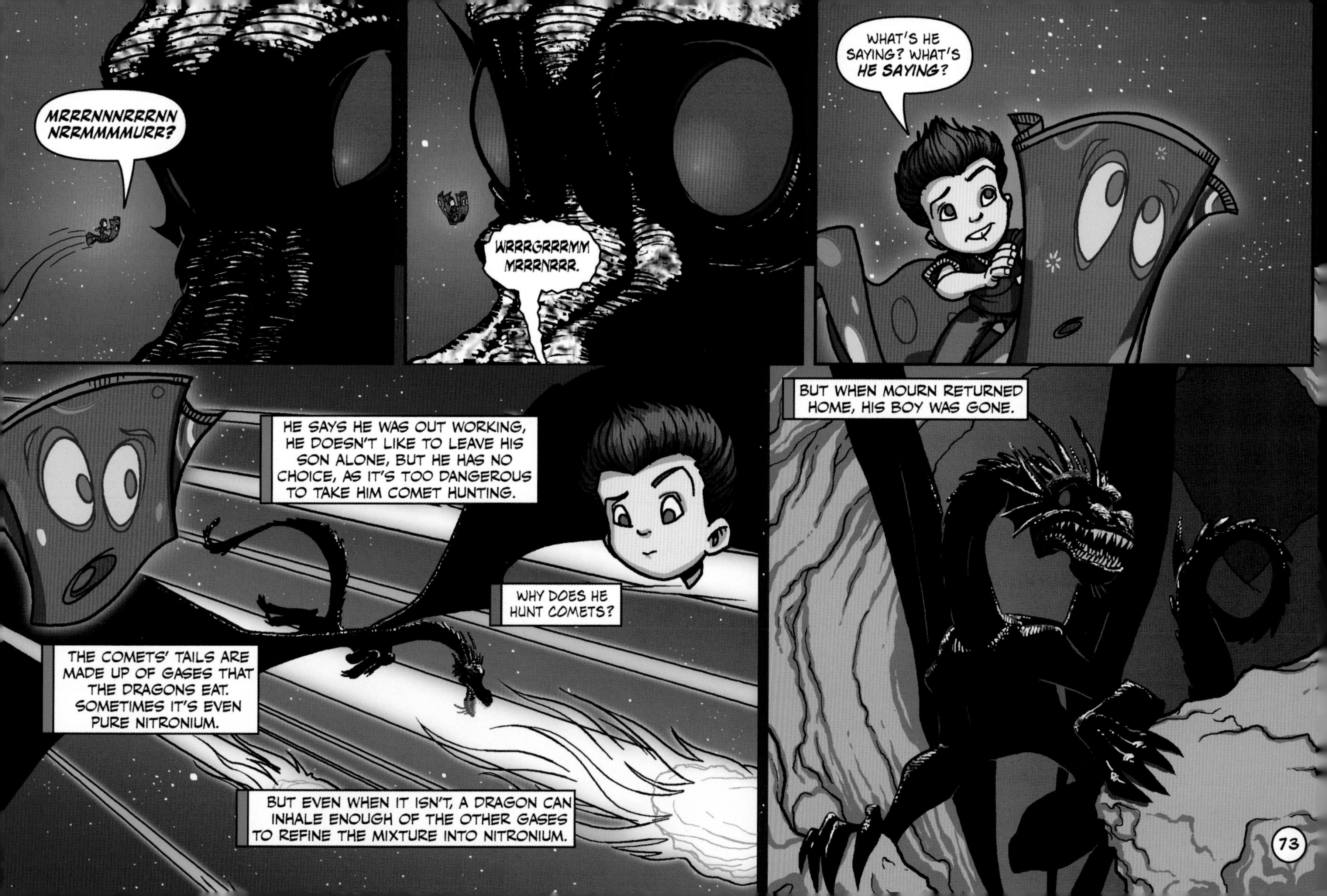

MRRRNNNRRRNN NRRMMMMURR?
WRRRGRRRMM MRRRNRRR.
WHAT'S HE SAYING? WHAT'S HE SAYING?
HE SAYS HE WAS OUT WORKING, HE DOESN'T LIKE TO LEAVE HIS SON ALONE, BUT HE HAS NO CHOICE, AS IT'S TOO DANGEROUS TO TAKE HIM COMET HUNTING.
WHY DOES HE HUNT COMETS?
THE COMETS' TAILS ARE MADE UP OF GASES THAT THE DRAGONS EAT. SOMETIMES IT'S EVEN PURE NITRONIUM.
BUT EVEN WHEN IT ISN'T, A DRAGON CAN INHALE ENOUGH OF THE OTHER GASES TO REFINE THE MIXTURE INTO NITRONIUM.
BUT WHEN MOURN RETURNED HOME, HIS BOY WAS GONE.

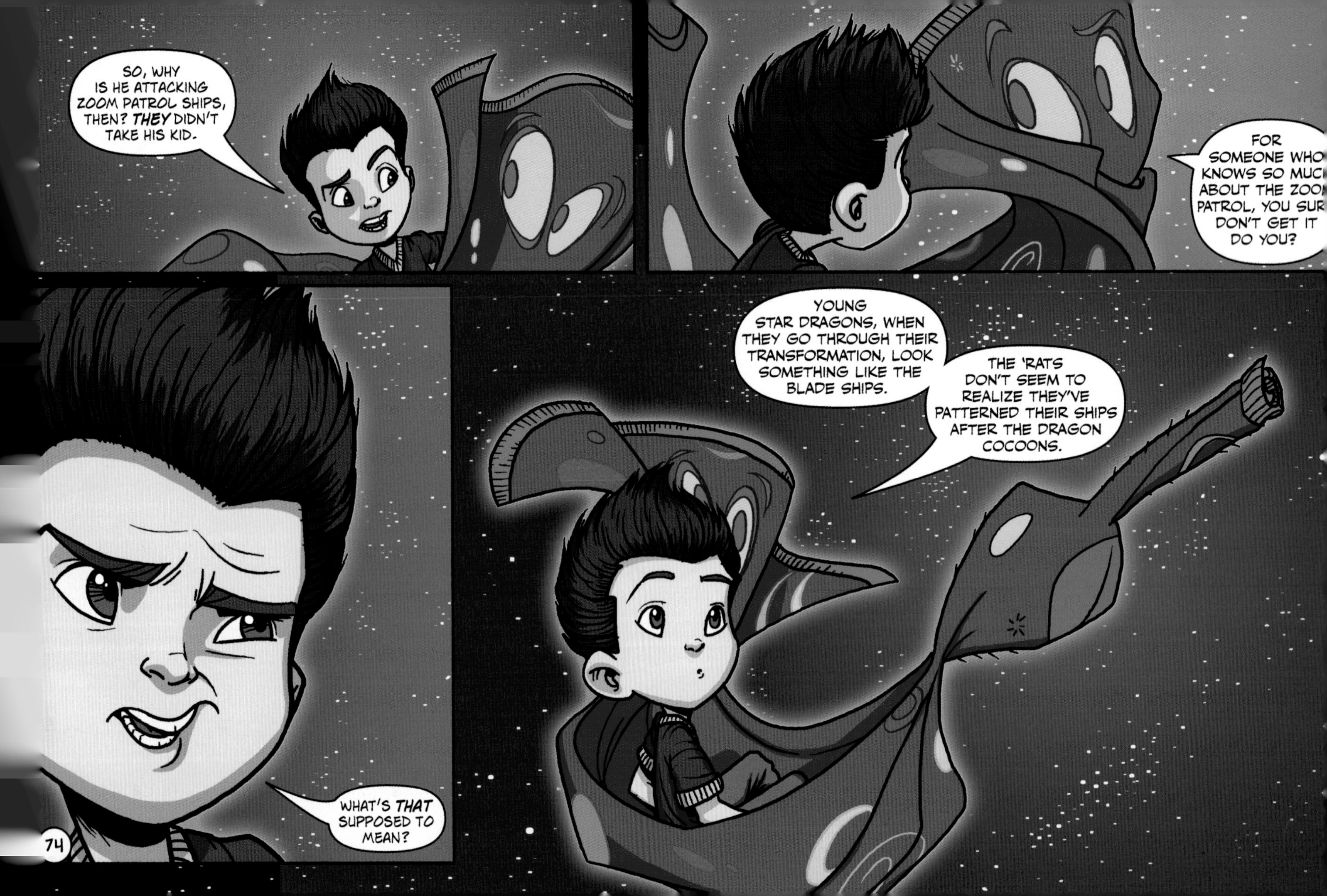
SO, WHY IS HE ATTACKING ZOOM PATROL SHIPS, THEN? ***THEY*** DIDN'T TAKE HIS KID.
FOR SOMEONE WHO KNOWS SO MUC ABOUT THE ZOO PATROL, YOU SUR DON'T GET IT DO YOU?
WHAT'S ***THAT*** SUPPOSED TO MEAN?
YOUNG STAR DRAGONS, WHEN THEY GO THROUGH THEIR TRANSFORMATION, LOOK SOMETHING LIKE THE BLADE SHIPS.
THE 'RATS DON'T SEEM TO REALIZE THEY'VE PATTERNED THEIR SHIPS AFTER THE DRAGON COCOONS.

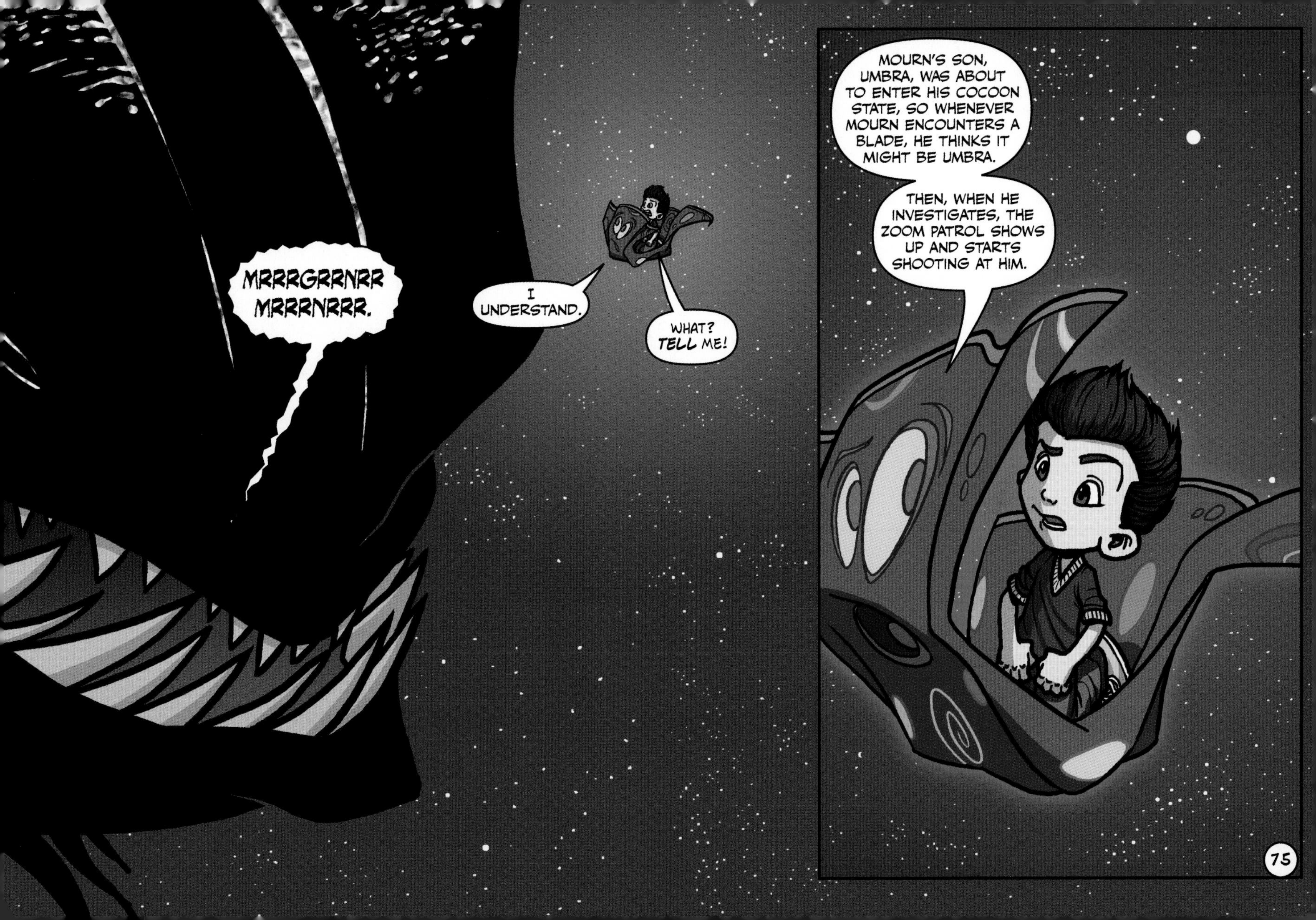
MRRRGRRNRR MRRRNRRR.
I UNDERSTAND.
WHAT? TELL ME!
MOURN'S SON, UMBRA, WAS ABOUT TO ENTER HIS COCOON STATE, SO WHENEVER MOURN ENCOUNTERS A BLADE, HE THINKS IT MIGHT BE UMBRA.
THEN, WHEN HE INVESTIGATES, THE ZOOM PATROL SHOWS UP AND STARTS SHOOTING AT HIM.

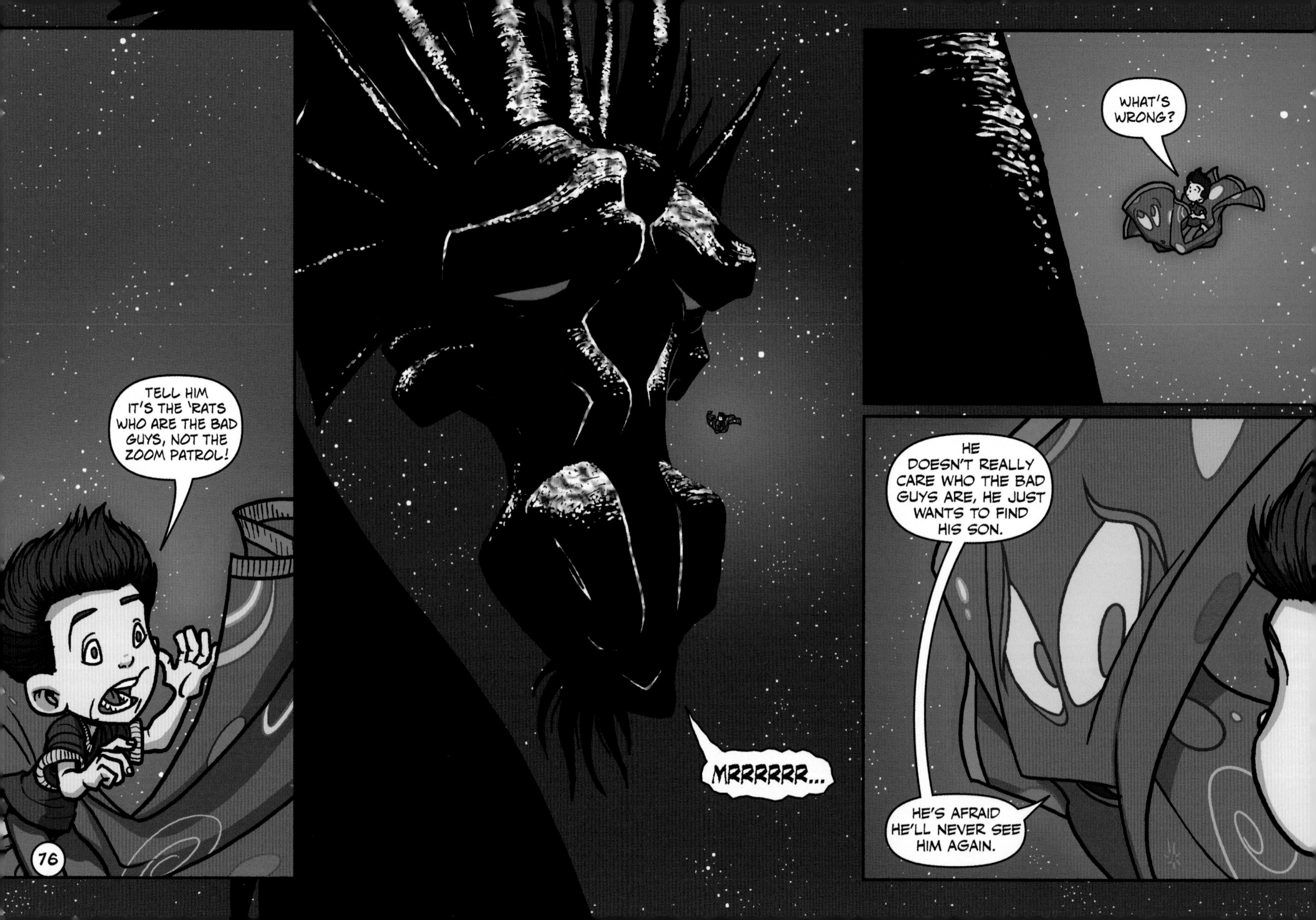
TELL HIM IT'S THE 'RATS WHO ARE THE BAD GUYS, NOT THE ZOOM PATROL!
MRRRRRR...
WHAT'S WRONG?
HE DOESN'T REALLY CARE WHO THE BAD GUYS ARE, HE JUST WANTS TO FIND HIS SON.
HE'S AFRAID HE'LL NEVER SEE HIM AGAIN.

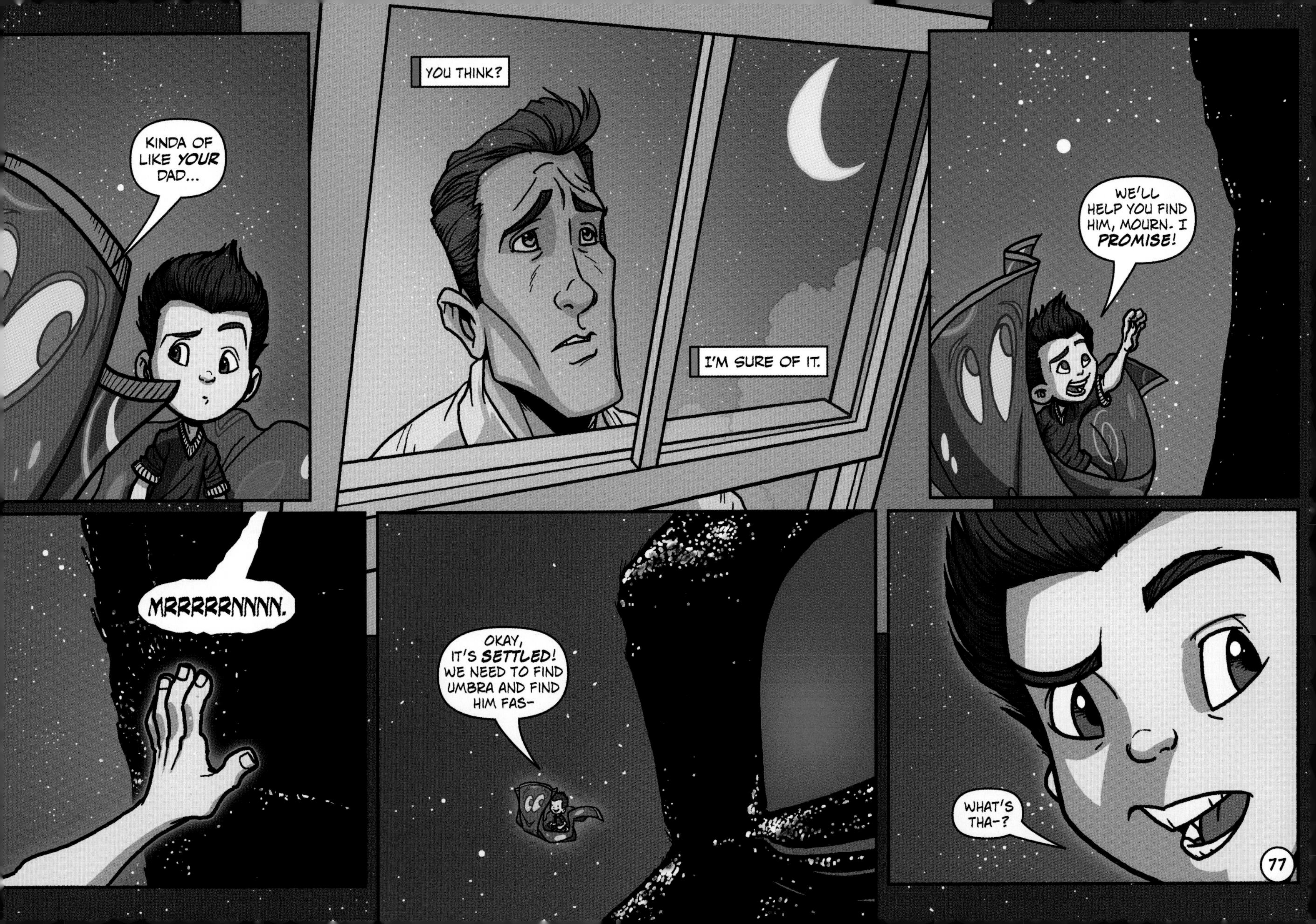
KINDA OF LIKE YOUR DAD...
YOU THINK?
I'M SURE OF IT.
WE'LL HELP YOU FIND HIM, MOURN. I PROMISE!
MRRRRRNNNN.
OKAY, IT'S SETTLED! WE NEED TO FIND UMBRA AND FIND HIM FAS-
WHAT'S THA-?

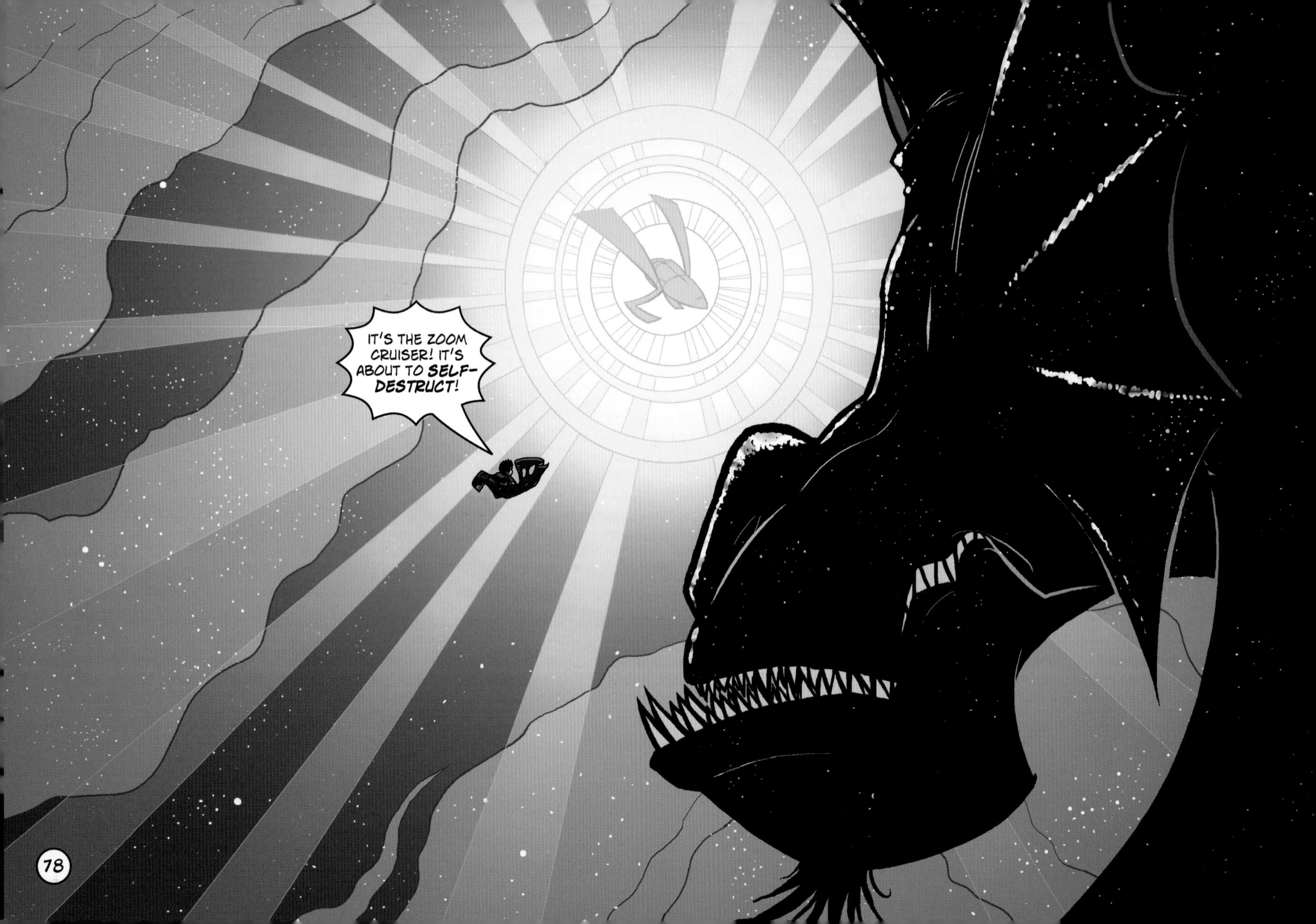
IT'S THE ZOOM CRUISER! IT'S ABOUT TO **SELF-DESTRUCT!**

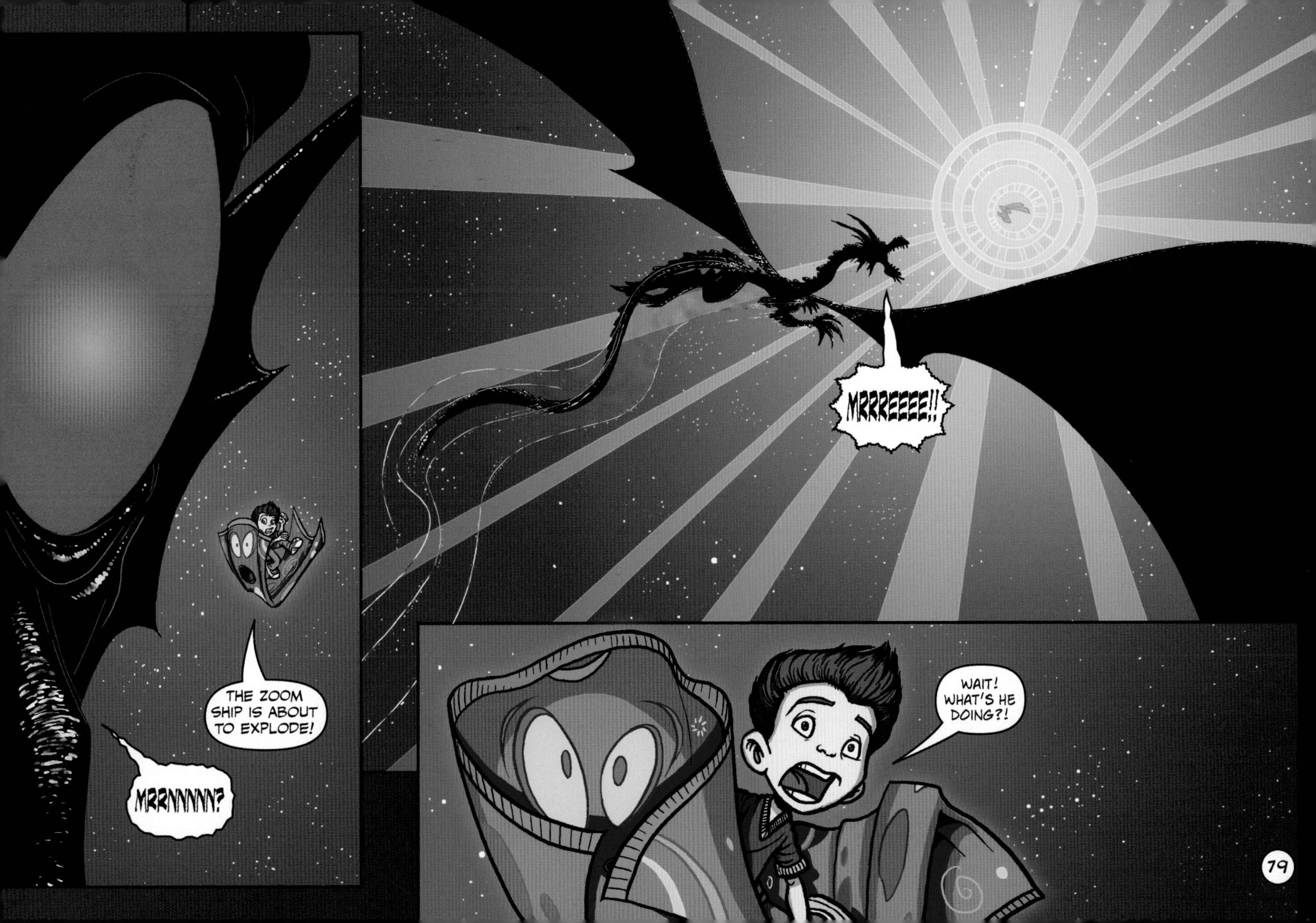
MRRREEEE!!
THE ZOOM SHIP IS ABOUT TO EXPLODE!
MRRNNNNN?
WAIT! WHAT'S HE DOING?!

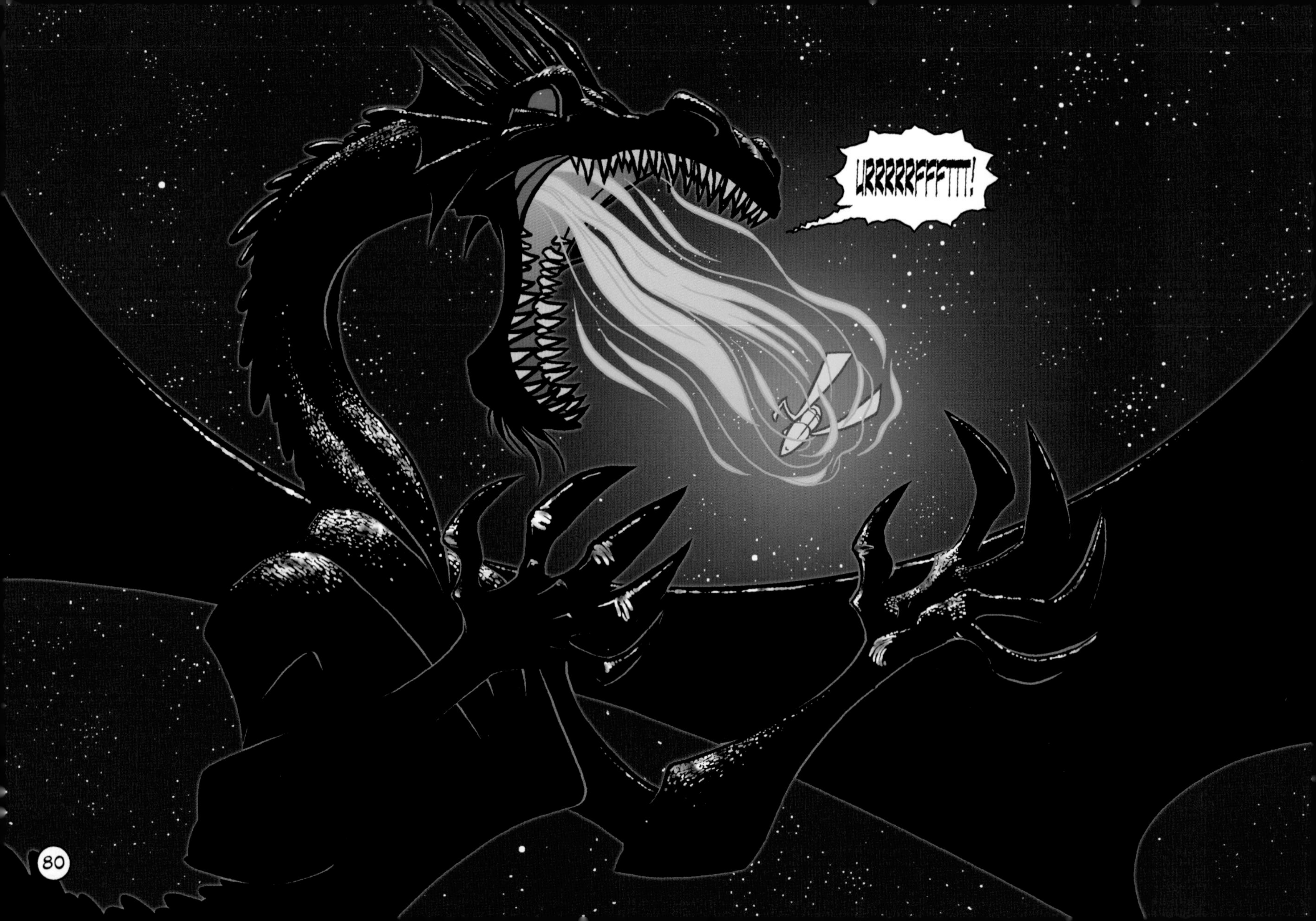
URRRRRFFFTTT!

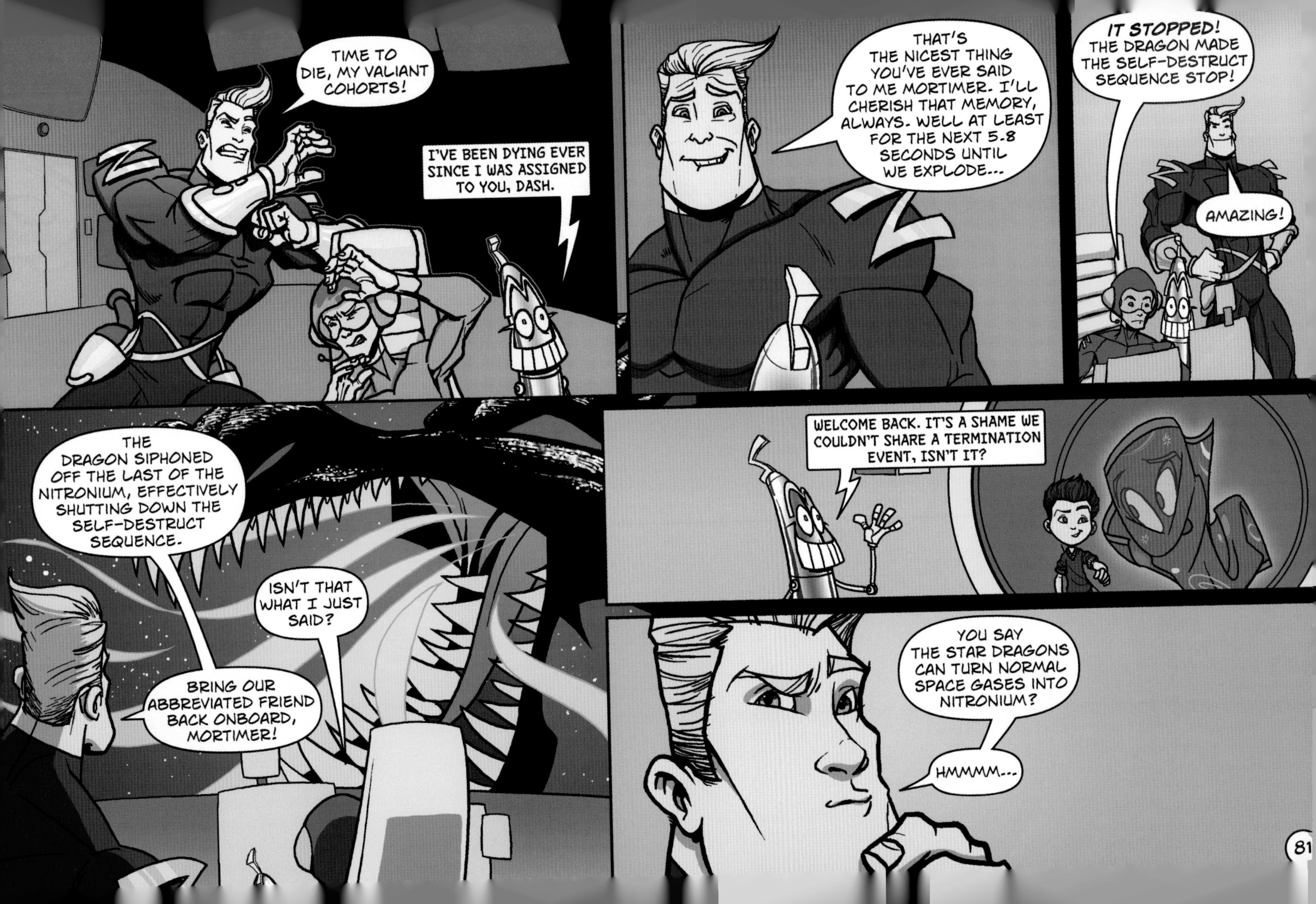
TIME TO DIE, MY VALIANT COHORTS!
I'VE BEEN DYING EVER SINCE I WAS ASSIGNED TO YOU, DASH.
THAT'S THE NICEST THING YOU'VE EVER SAID TO ME MORTIMER. I'LL CHERISH THAT MEMORY, ALWAYS. WELL AT LEAST FOR THE NEXT 5.8 SECONDS UNTIL WE EXPLODE...
IT STOPPED! THE DRAGON MADE THE SELF-DESTRUCT SEQUENCE STOP!
AMAZING!
THE DRAGON SIPHONED OFF THE LAST OF THE NITRONIUM, EFFECTIVELY SHUTTING DOWN THE SELF-DESTRUCT SEQUENCE.
ISN'T THAT WHAT I JUST SAID?
BRING OUR ABBREVIATED FRIEND BACK ONBOARD, MORTIMER!
WELCOME BACK. IT'S A SHAME WE COULDN'T SHARE A TERMINATION EVENT, ISN'T IT?
YOU SAY THE STAR DRAGONS CAN TURN NORMAL SPACE GASES INTO NITRONIUM?
HMMMM...

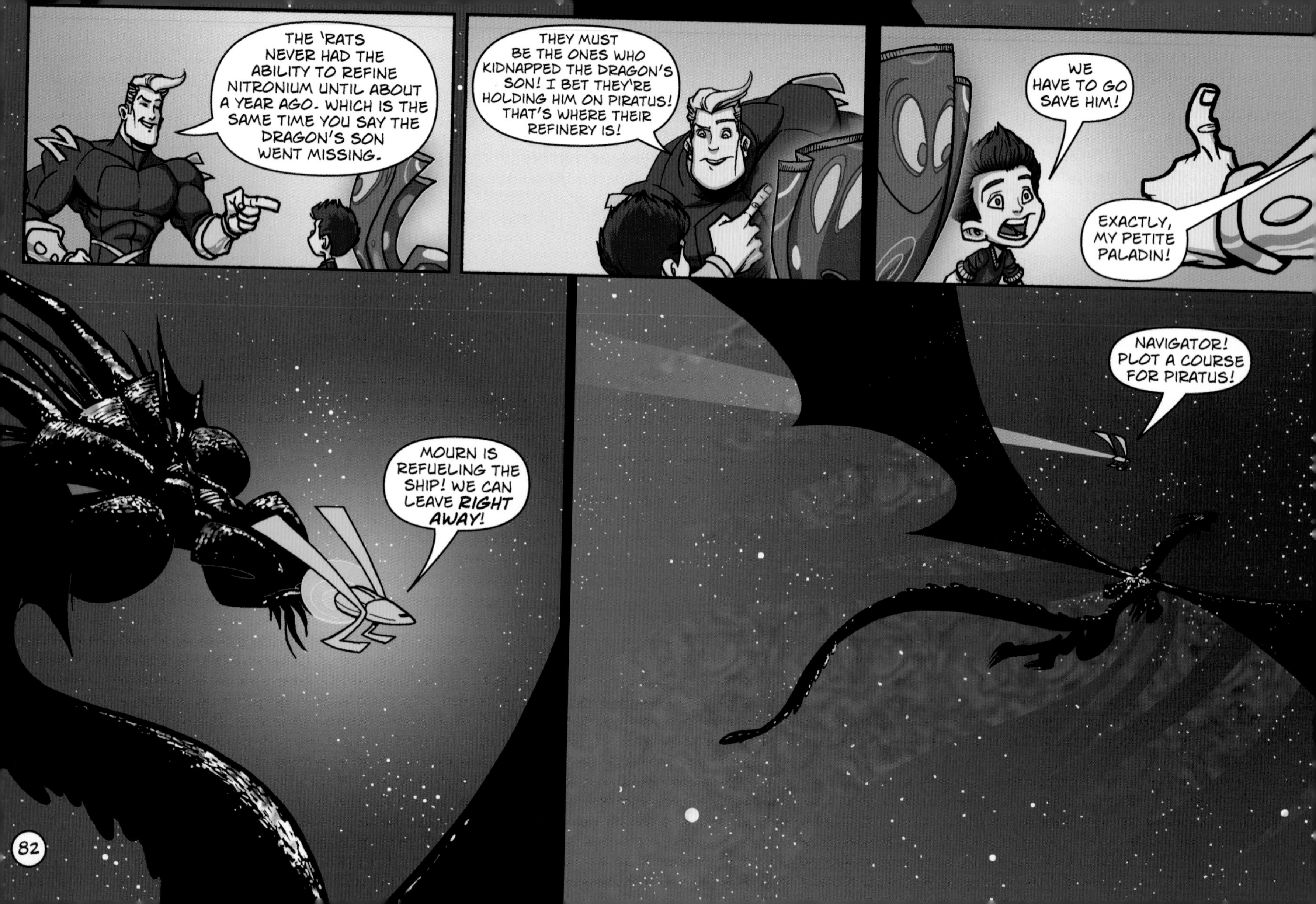
THE 'RATS NEVER HAD THE ABILITY TO REFINE NITRONIUM UNTIL ABOUT A YEAR AGO. WHICH IS THE SAME TIME YOU SAY THE DRAGON'S SON WENT MISSING.
THEY MUST BE THE ONES WHO KIDNAPPED THE DRAGON'S SON! I BET THEY'RE HOLDING HIM ON PIRATUS! THAT'S WHERE THEIR REFINERY IS!
WE HAVE TO GO SAVE HIM!
EXACTLY, MY PETITE PALADIN!
MOURN IS REFUELING THE SHIP! WE CAN LEAVE **RIGHT AWAY!**
NAVIGATOR! PLOT A COURSE FOR PIRATUS!

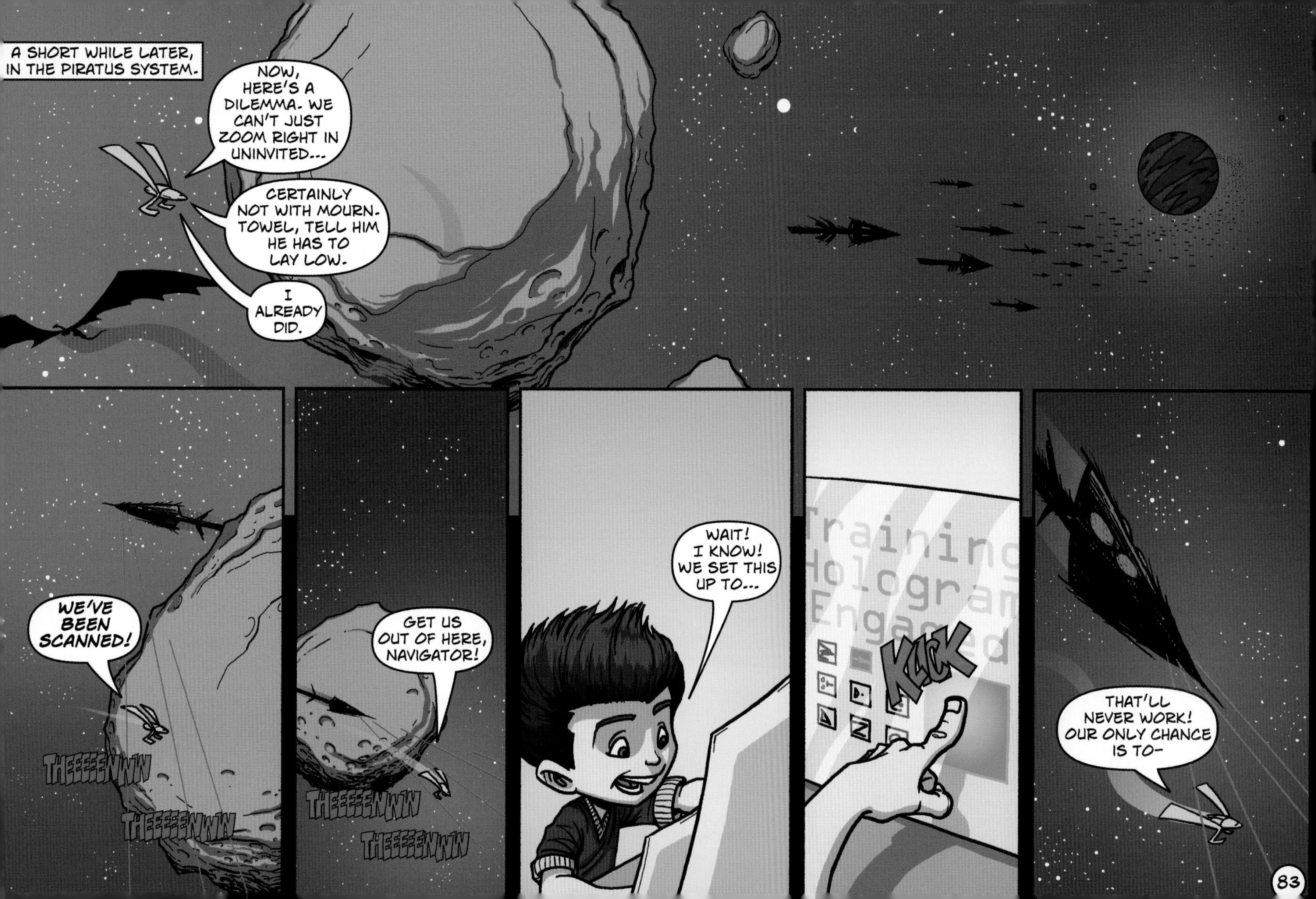
A SHORT WHILE LATER, IN THE PIRATUS SYSTEM.
NOW, HERE'S A DILEMMA. WE CAN'T JUST ZOOM RIGHT IN UNINVITED...
CERTAINLY NOT WITH MOURN-TOWEL, TELL HIM HE HAS TO LAY LOW.
I ALREADY DID.
WE'VE BEEN SCANNED!
THEEEEENNN
THEEEEENNN
GET US OUT OF HERE, NAVIGATOR!
THEEEEENNN
THEEEEENNN
WAIT! I KNOW! WE SET THIS UP TO...
Training Hologram Engaged
KLICK
THAT'LL NEVER WORK! OUR ONLY CHANCE IS TO-

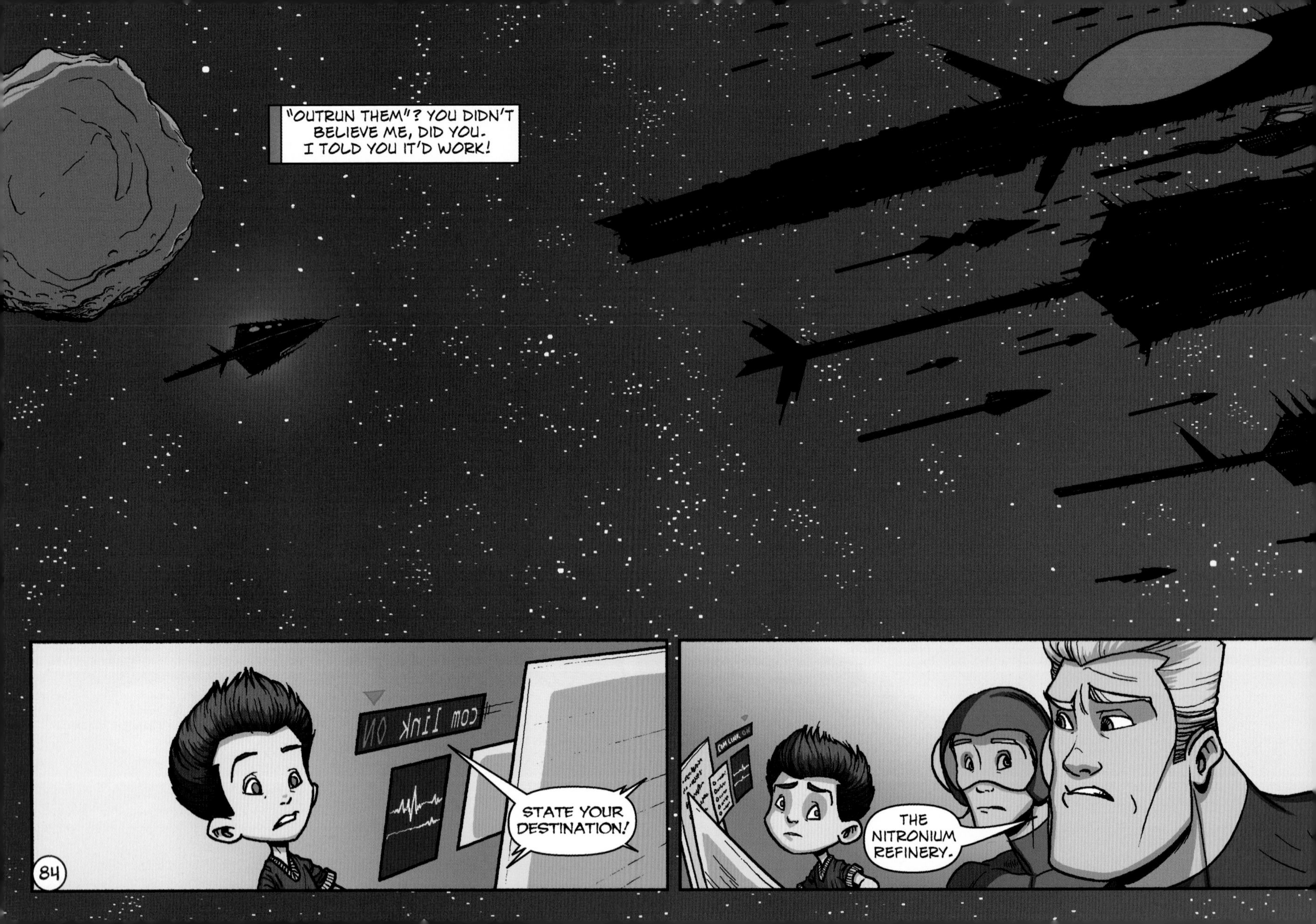
"OUTRUN THEM"? YOU DIDN'T BELIEVE ME, DID YOU. I TOLD YOU IT'D WORK!
STATE YOUR DESTINATION!
THE NITRONIUM REFINERY.

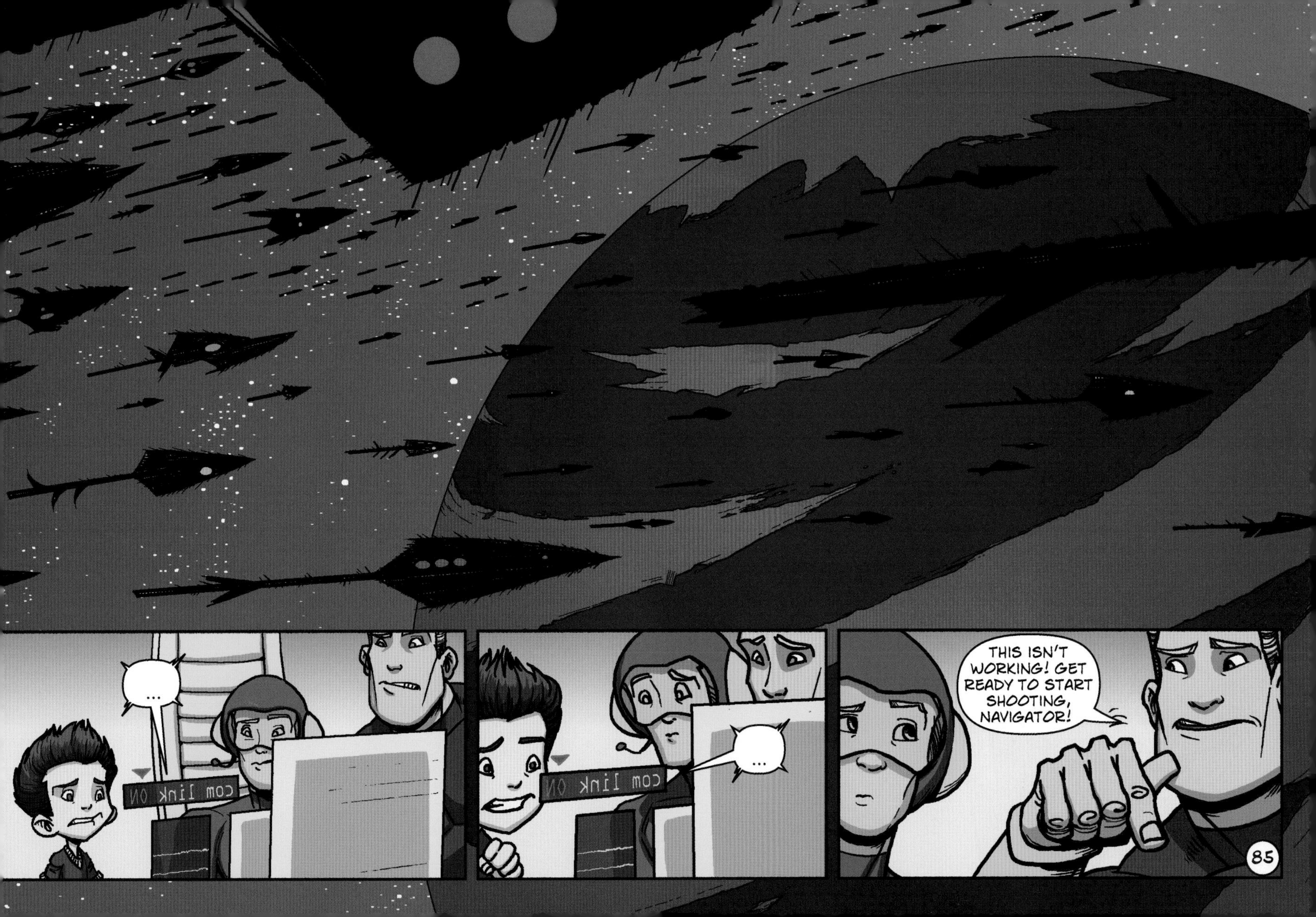
...
...
THIS ISN'T WORKING! GET READY TO START SHOOTING, NAVIGATOR!

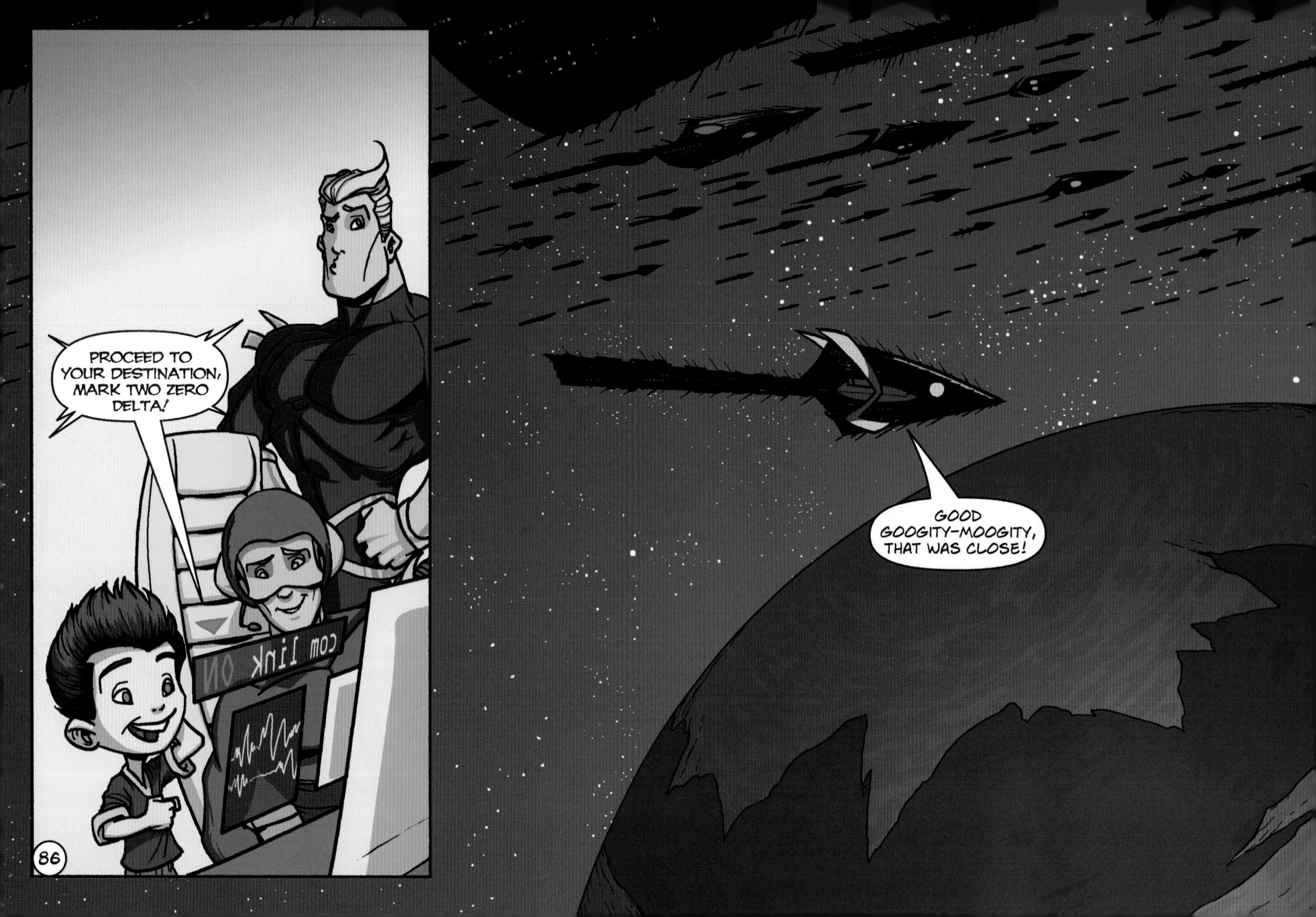
PROCEED TO YOUR DESTINATION, MARK TWO ZERO DELTA!
GOOD GOOGITY-MOOGITY, THAT WAS CLOSE!

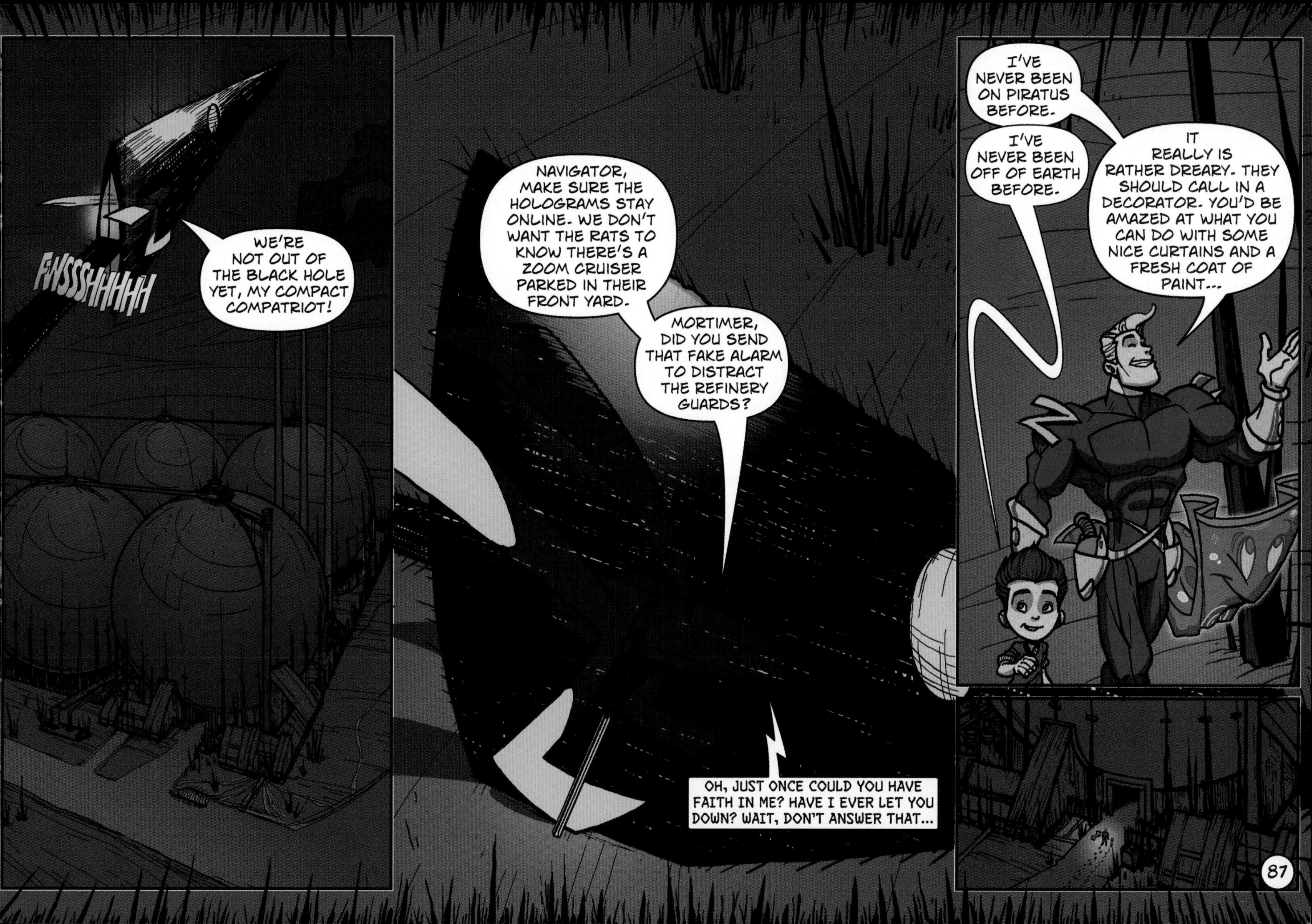
FWSSSHHHHH
WE'RE NOT OUT OF THE BLACK HOLE YET, MY COMPACT COMPATRIOT!
NAVIGATOR, MAKE SURE THE HOLOGRAMS STAY ONLINE. WE DON'T WANT THE RATS TO KNOW THERE'S A ZOOM CRUISER PARKED IN THEIR FRONT YARD.
MORTIMER, DID YOU SEND THAT FAKE ALARM TO DISTRACT THE REFINERY GUARDS?
OH, JUST ONCE COULD YOU HAVE FAITH IN ME? HAVE I EVER LET YOU DOWN? WAIT, DON'T ANSWER THAT...
I'VE NEVER BEEN ON PIRATUS BEFORE.
I'VE NEVER BEEN OFF OF EARTH BEFORE.
IT REALLY IS RATHER DREARY. THEY SHOULD CALL IN A DECORATOR. YOU'D BE AMAZED AT WHAT YOU CAN DO WITH SOME NICE CURTAINS AND A FRESH COAT OF PAINT...

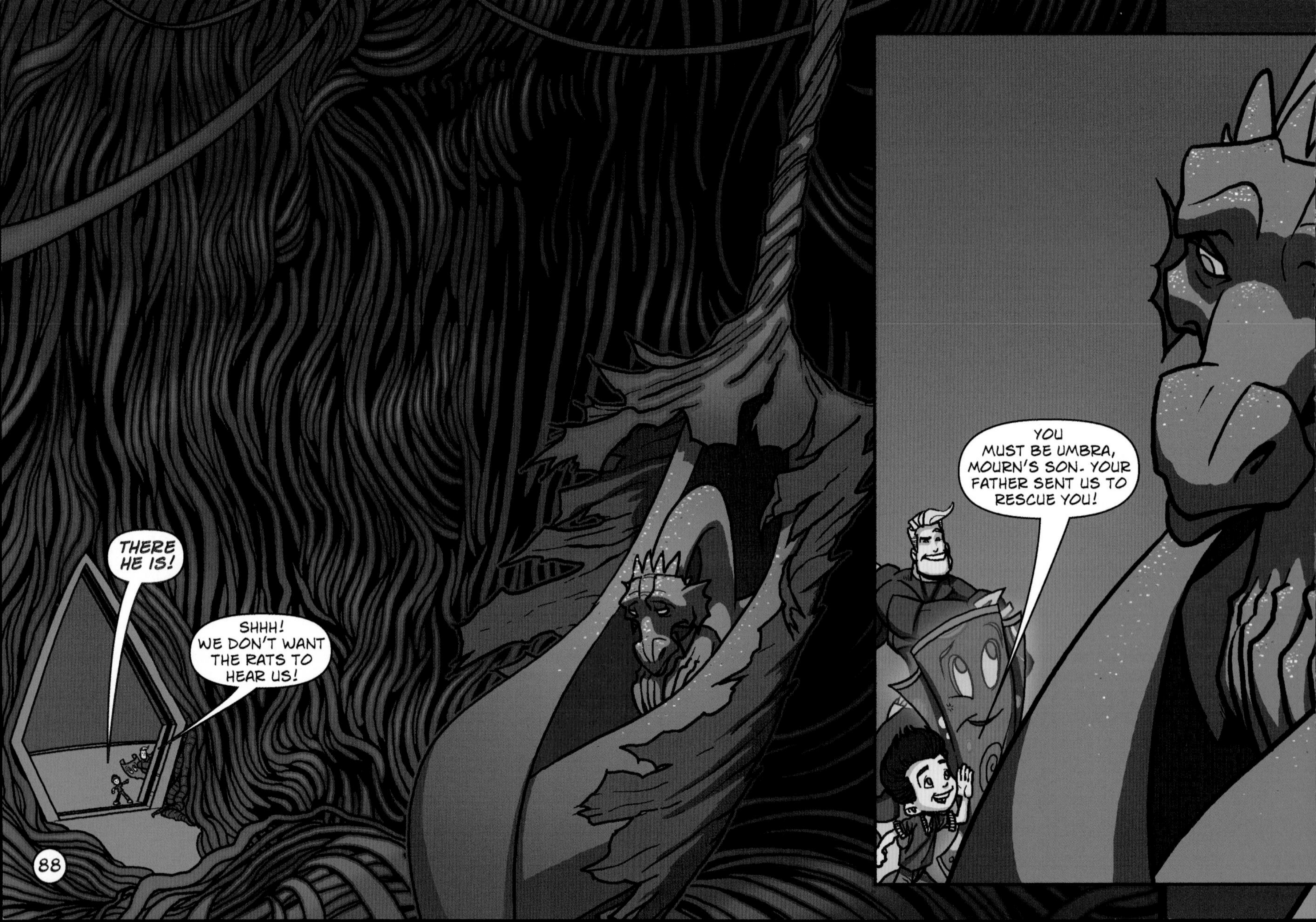
THERE HE IS!
SHHH! WE DON'T WANT THE RATS TO HEAR US!
YOU MUST BE UMBRA, MOURN'S SON. YOUR FATHER SENT US TO RESCUE YOU!

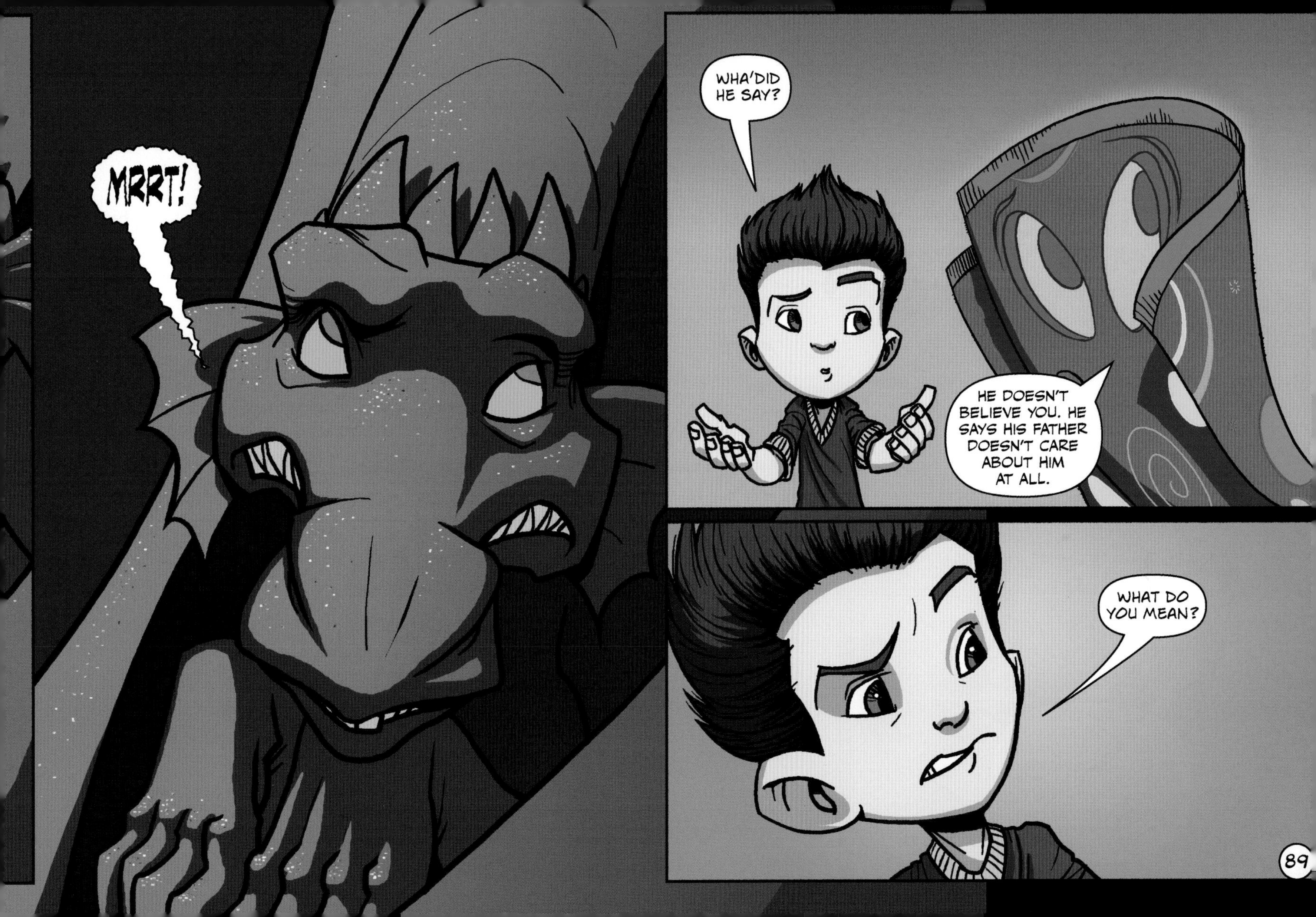
MRRT!
WHA'DID HE SAY?
HE DOESN'T BELIEVE YOU. HE SAYS HIS FATHER DOESN'T CARE ABOUT HIM AT ALL.
WHAT DO YOU MEAN?

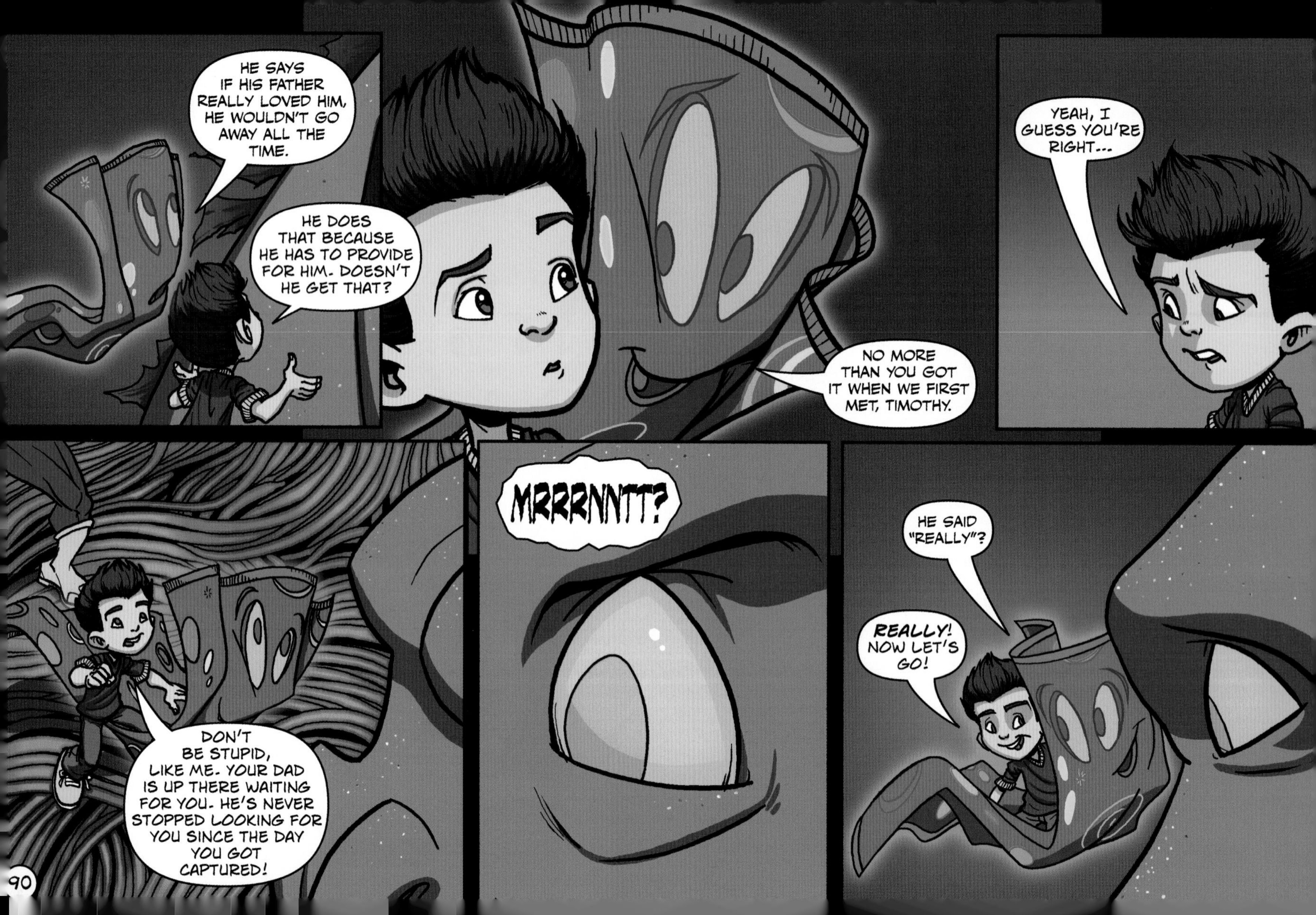
HE SAYS IF HIS FATHER REALLY LOVED HIM, HE WOULDN'T GO AWAY ALL THE TIME.
HE DOES THAT BECAUSE HE HAS TO PROVIDE FOR HIM. DOESN'T HE GET THAT?
NO MORE THAN YOU GOT IT WHEN WE FIRST MET, TIMOTHY.
YEAH, I GUESS YOU'RE RIGHT...
DON'T BE STUPID, LIKE ME. YOUR DAD IS UP THERE WAITING FOR YOU. HE'S NEVER STOPPED LOOKING FOR YOU SINCE THE DAY YOU GOT CAPTURED!
MRRRNNTT?
HE SAID "REALLY"?
REALLY! NOW LET'S GO!

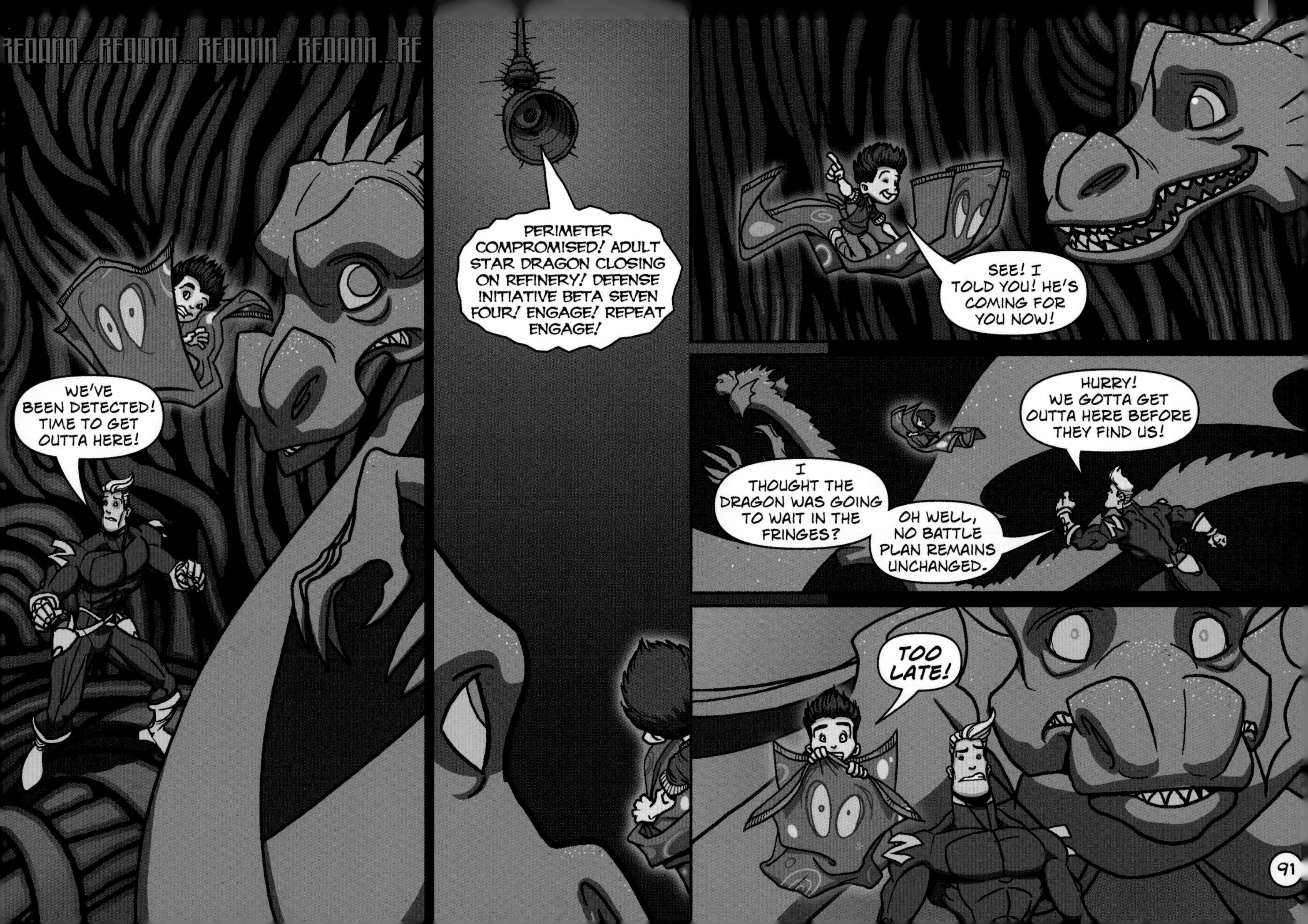

REAAAN...REAAAN...REAAAN...REAAAN...RE
WE'VE BEEN DETECTED! TIME TO GET OUTTA HERE!
PERIMETER COMPROMISED! ADULT STAR DRAGON CLOSING ON REFINERY! DEFENSE INITIATIVE BETA SEVEN FOUR! ENGAGE! REPEAT ENGAGE!
SEE! I TOLD YOU! HE'S COMING FOR YOU NOW!
HURRY! WE GOTTA GET OUTTA HERE BEFORE THEY FIND US!
I THOUGHT THE DRAGON WAS GOING TO WAIT IN THE FRINGES?
OH WELL, NO BATTLE PLAN REMAINS UNCHANGED.
TOO LATE!

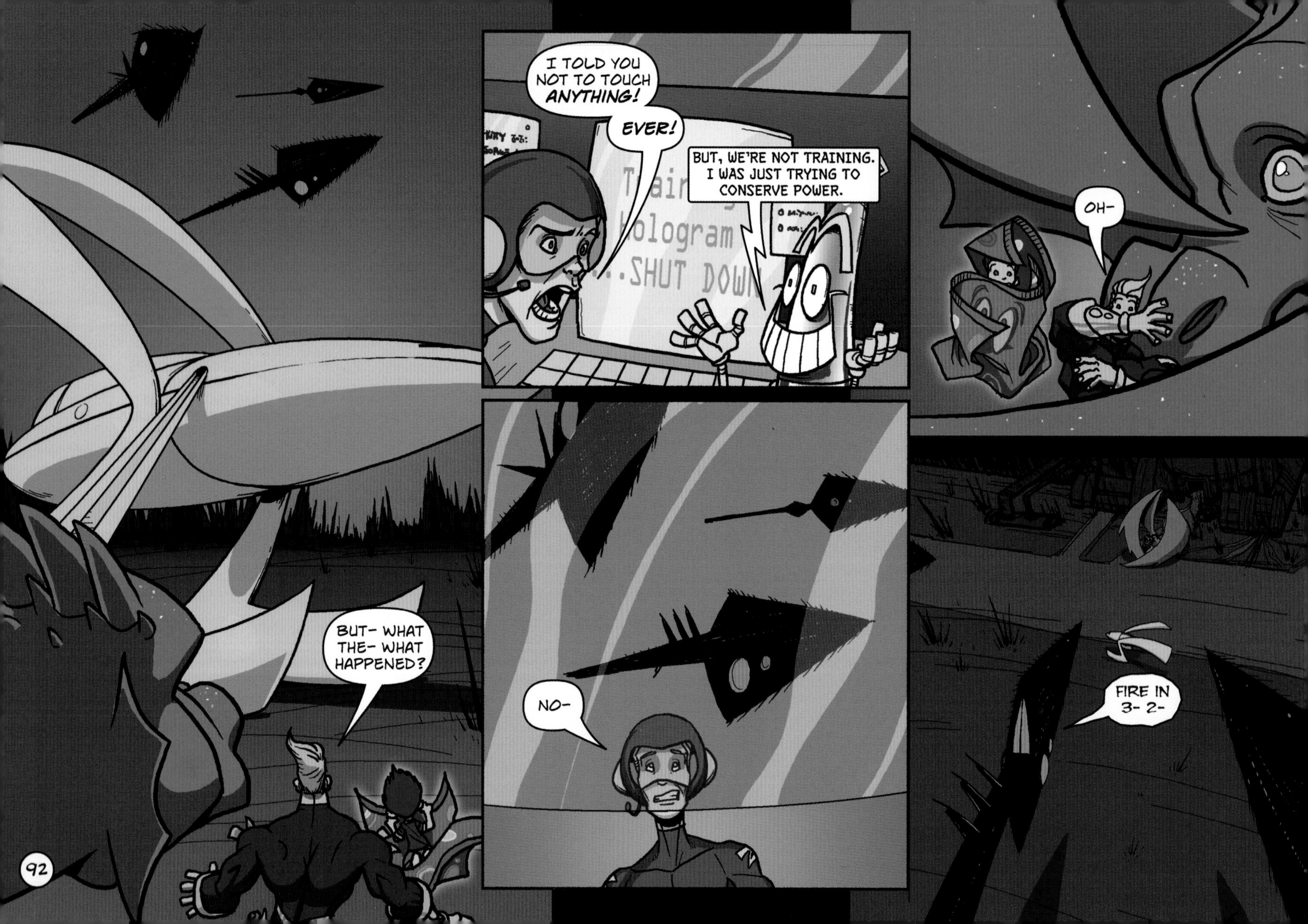
BUT- WHAT THE- WHAT HAPPENED?
I TOLD YOU NOT TO TOUCH ANYTHING!
EVER!
BUT, WE'RE NOT TRAINING. I WAS JUST TRYING TO CONSERVE POWER.
Training Hologram ...SHUT DOWN
NO-
OH-
FIRE IN 3- 2-

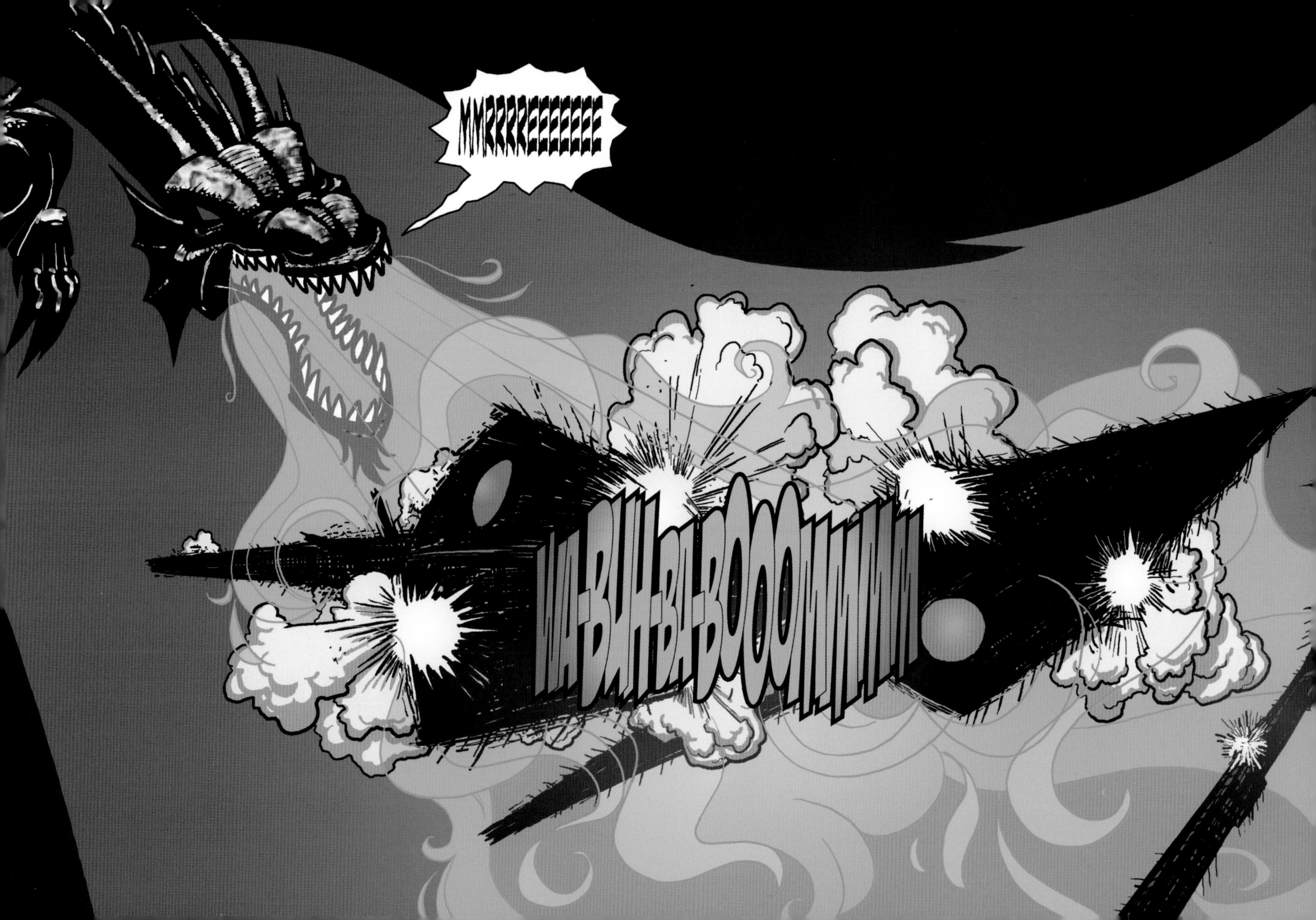
MMRRRREEEEEEE
KA-BUH-BA-BOOOMMMM

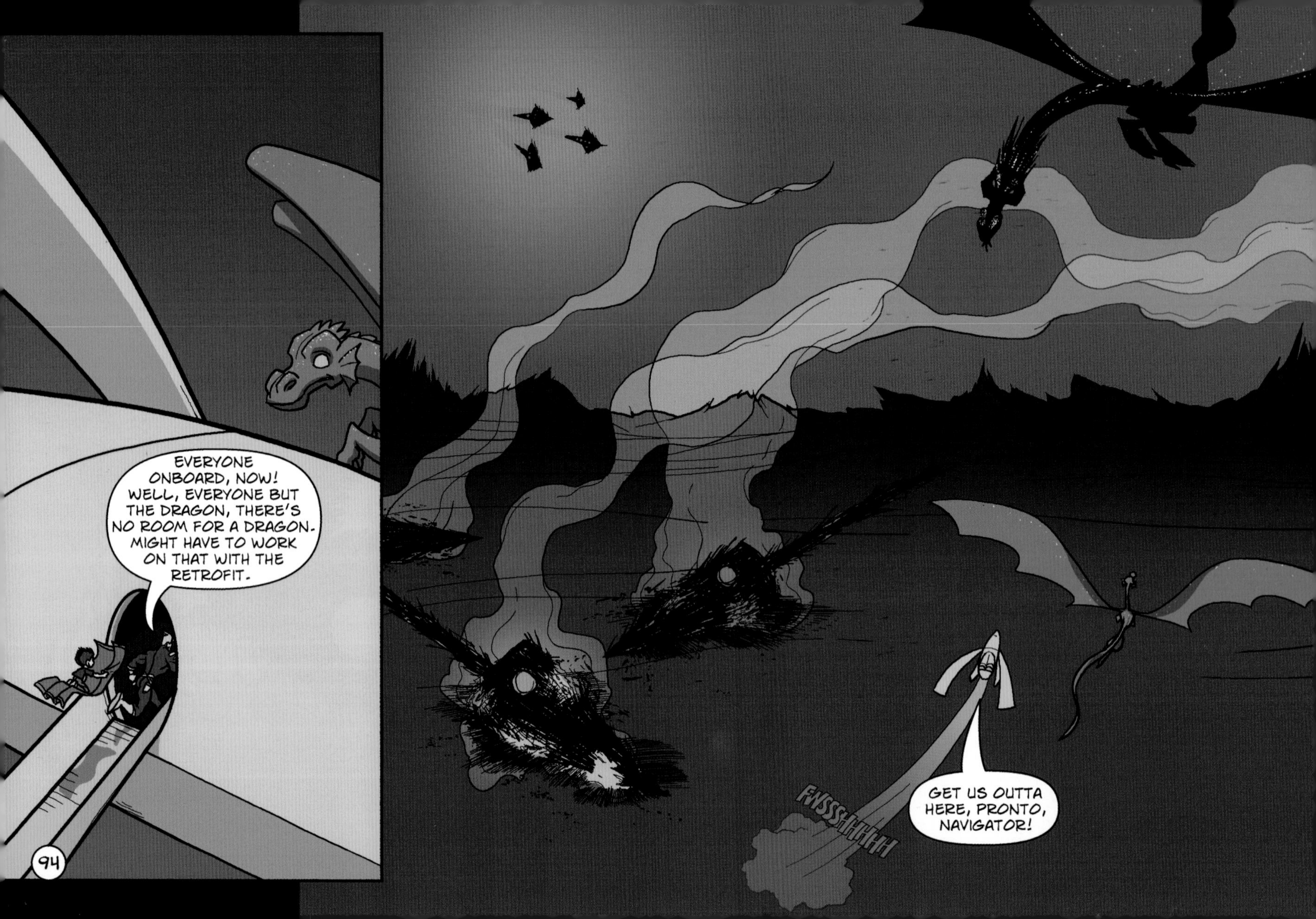
EVERYONE ONBOARD, NOW! WELL, EVERYONE BUT THE DRAGON, THERE'S NO ROOM FOR A DRAGON. MIGHT HAVE TO WORK ON THAT WITH THE RETROFIT.
FWSSSHHHHH
GET US OUTTA HERE, PRONTO, NAVIGATOR!

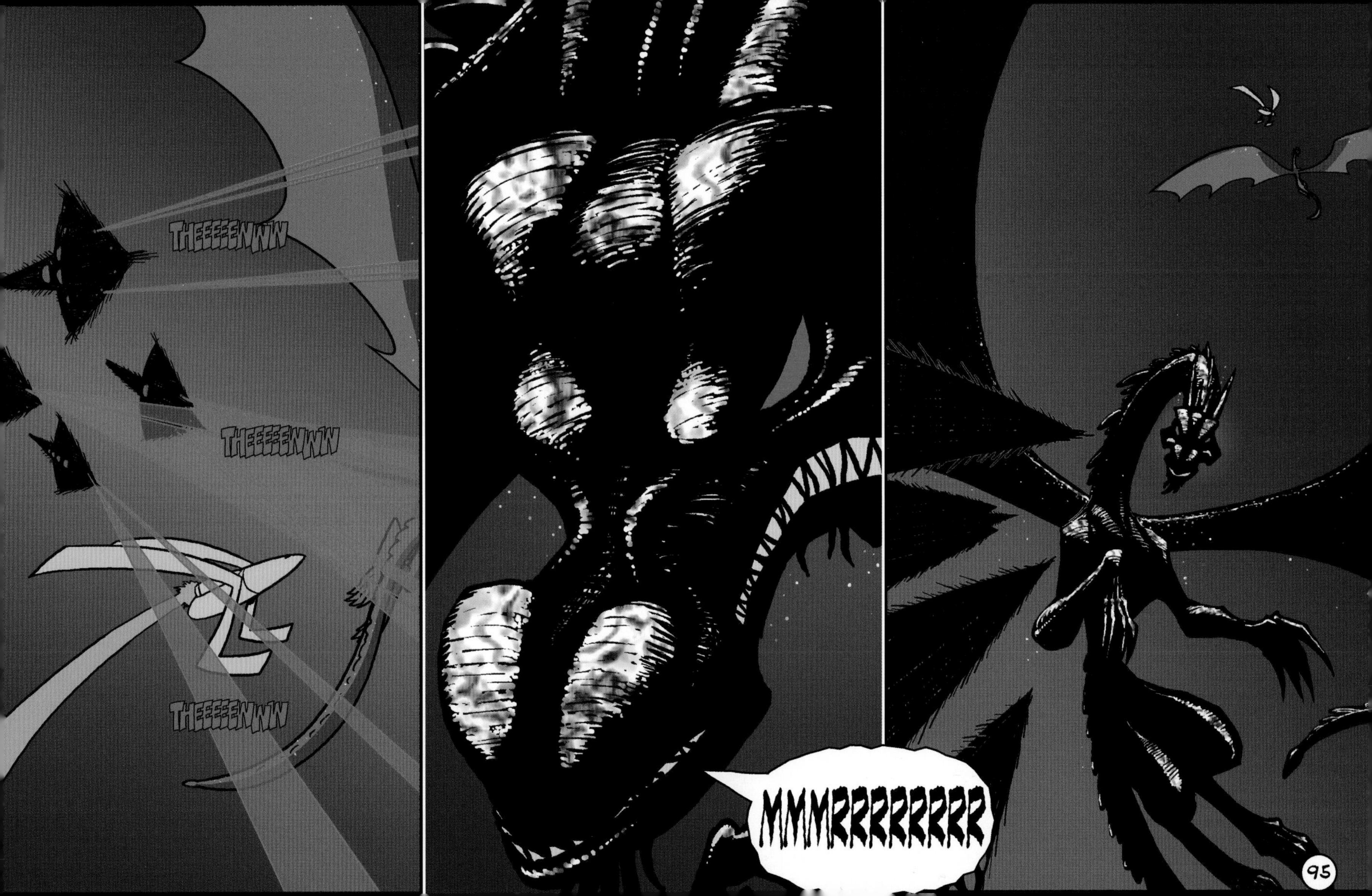
THEEEEENWN
THEEEEENWN
THEEEEENWN
MMMRRRRRRRR

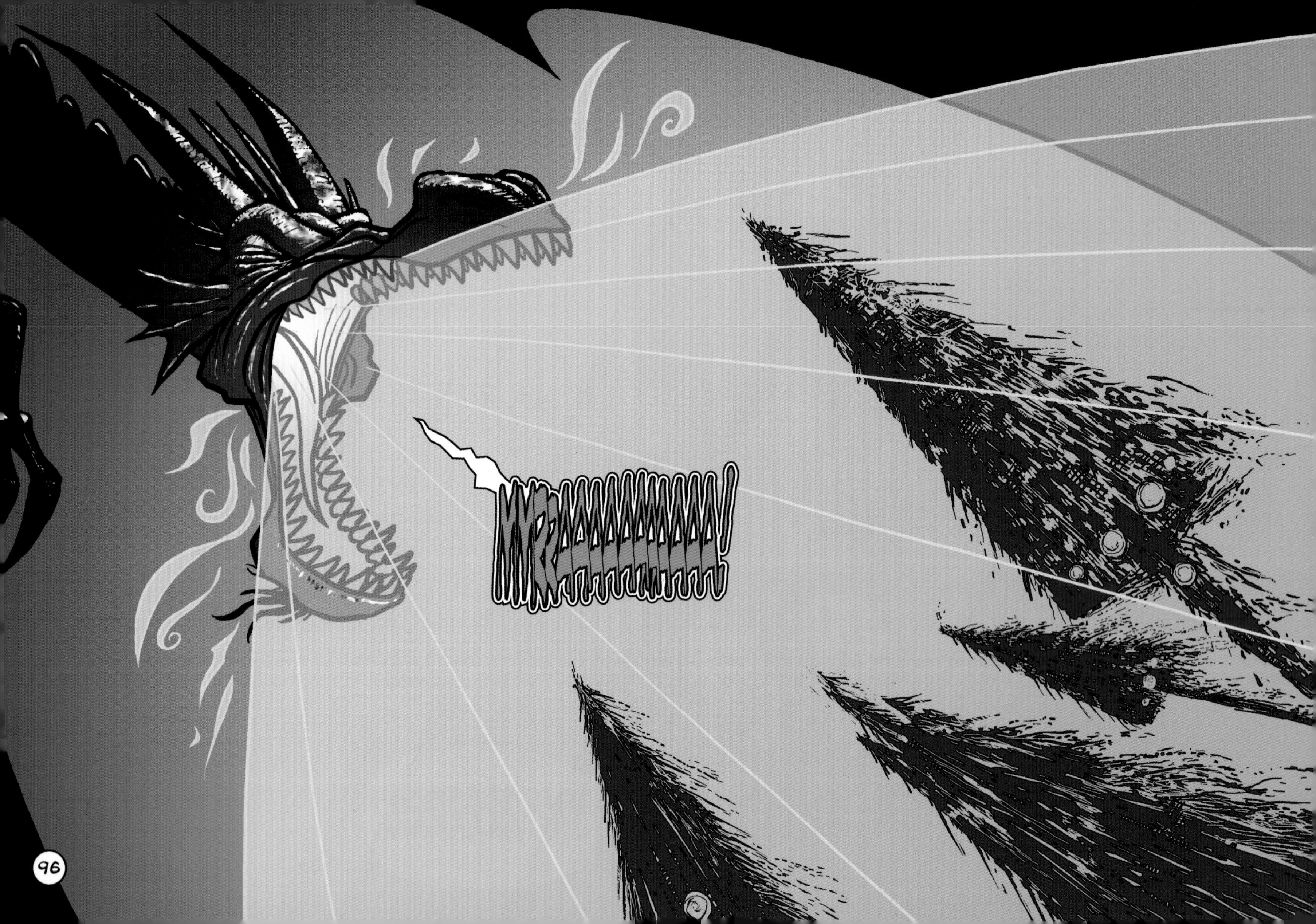
MYRRAAAAAAAAAAA!

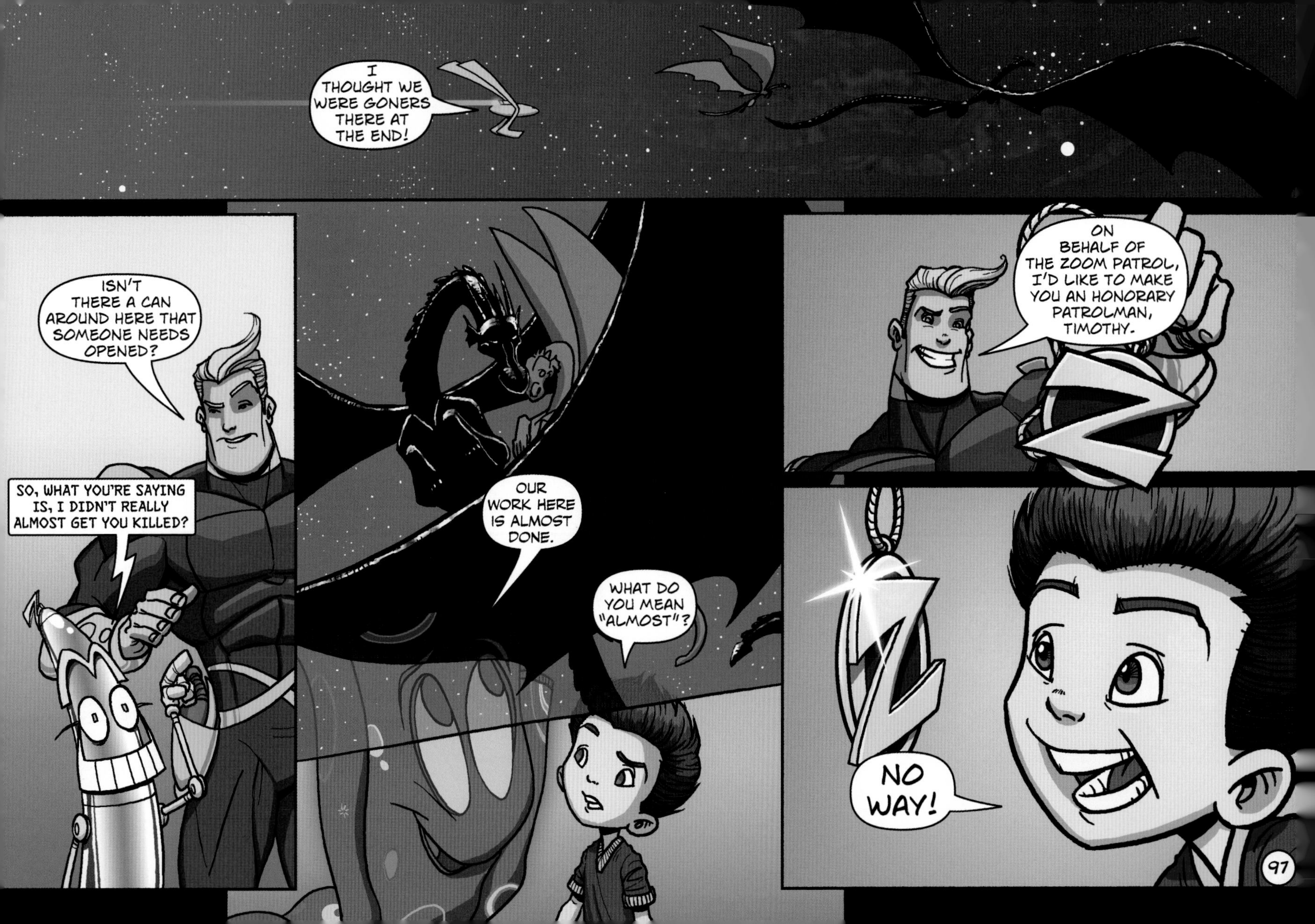

I THOUGHT WE WERE GONERS THERE AT THE END!
ISN'T THERE A CAN AROUND HERE THAT SOMEONE NEEDS OPENED?
SO, WHAT YOU'RE SAYING IS, I DIDN'T REALLY ALMOST GET YOU KILLED?
OUR WORK HERE IS ALMOST DONE.
WHAT DO YOU MEAN "ALMOST"?
ON BEHALF OF THE ZOOM PATROL, I'D LIKE TO MAKE YOU AN HONORARY PATROLMAN, TIMOTHY.
NO WAY!

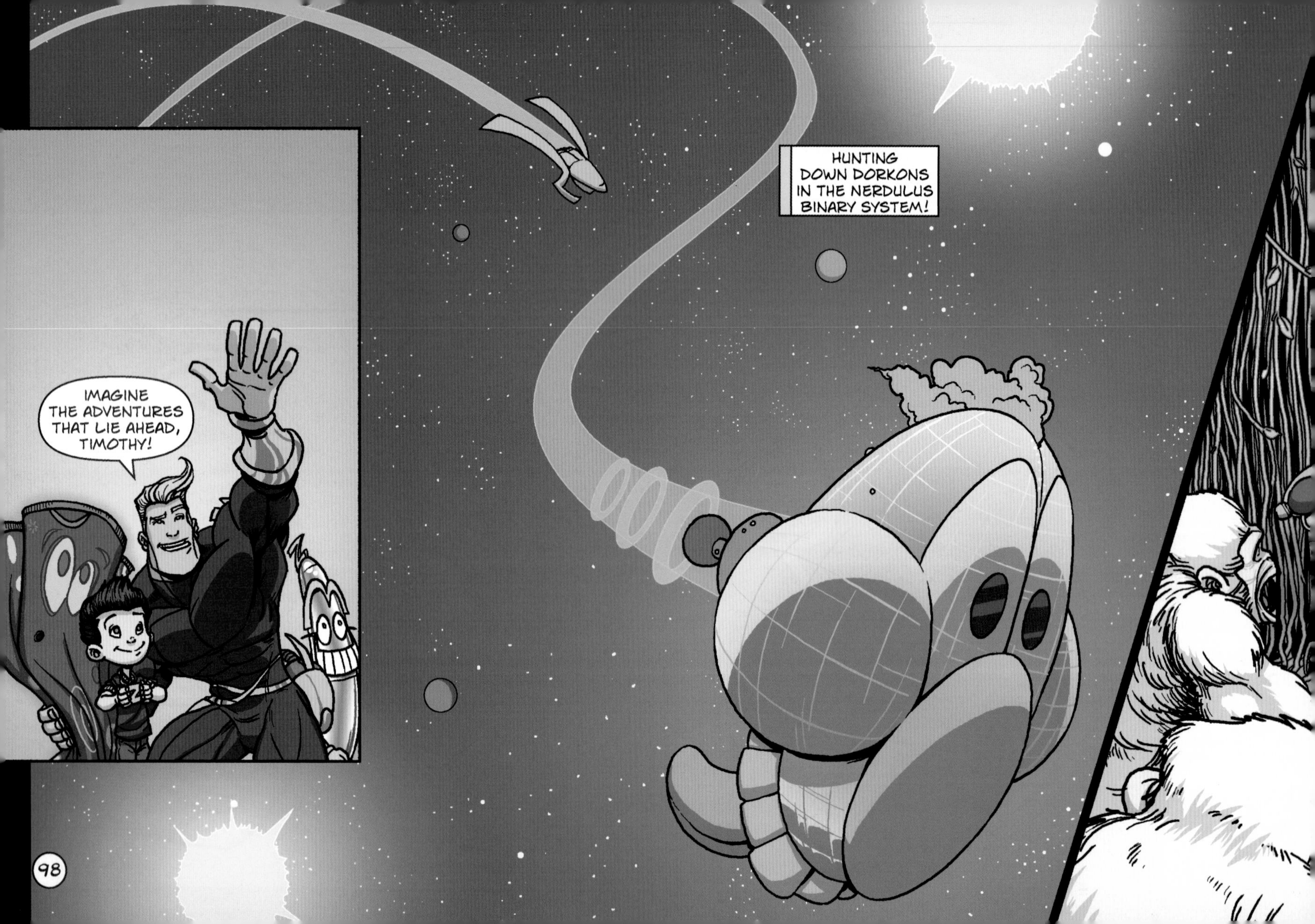
IMAGINE THE ADVENTURES THAT LIE AHEAD, TIMOTHY!
HUNTING DOWN DORKONS IN THE NERDULUS BINARY SYSTEM!

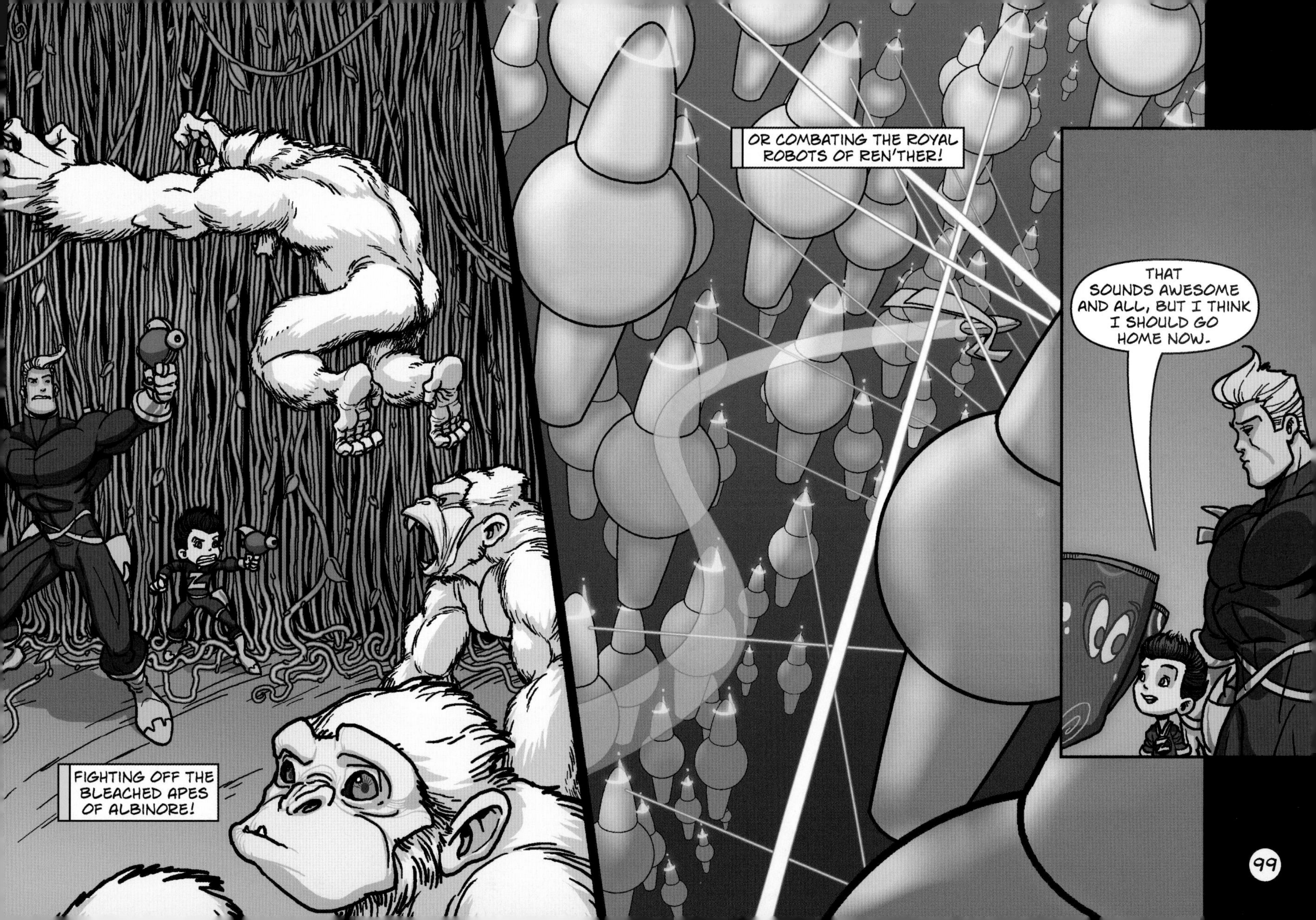
FIGHTING OFF THE BLEACHED APES OF ALBINORE!
OR COMBATING THE ROYAL ROBOTS OF REN'THER!
THAT SOUNDS AWESOME AND ALL, BUT I THINK I SHOULD GO HOME NOW.

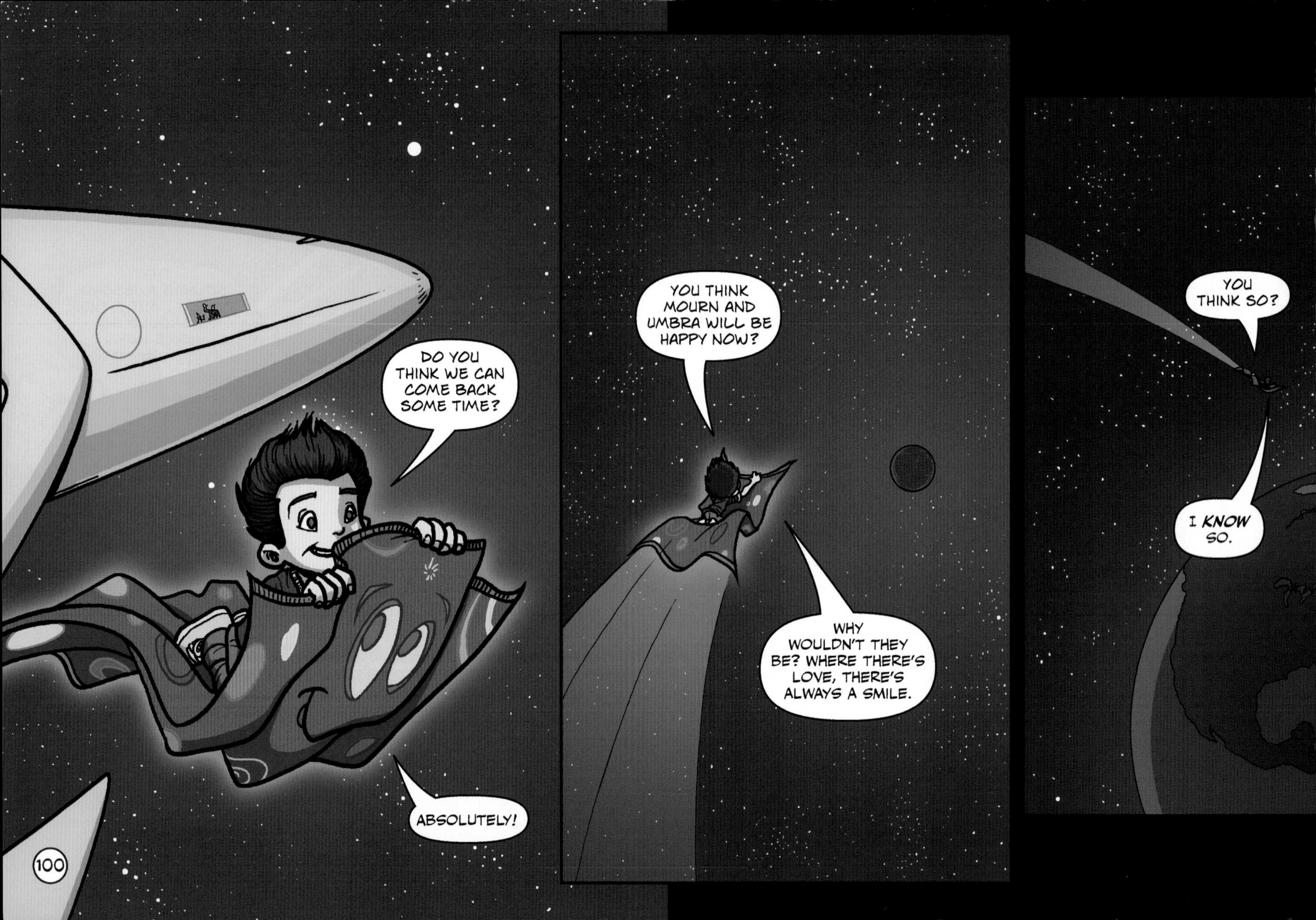
DO YOU THINK WE CAN COME BACK SOME TIME?
ABSOLUTELY!
YOU THINK MOURN AND UMBRA WILL BE HAPPY NOW?
WHY WOULDN'T THEY BE? WHERE THERE'S LOVE, THERE'S ALWAYS A SMILE.
YOU THINK SO?
I *KNOW* SO.

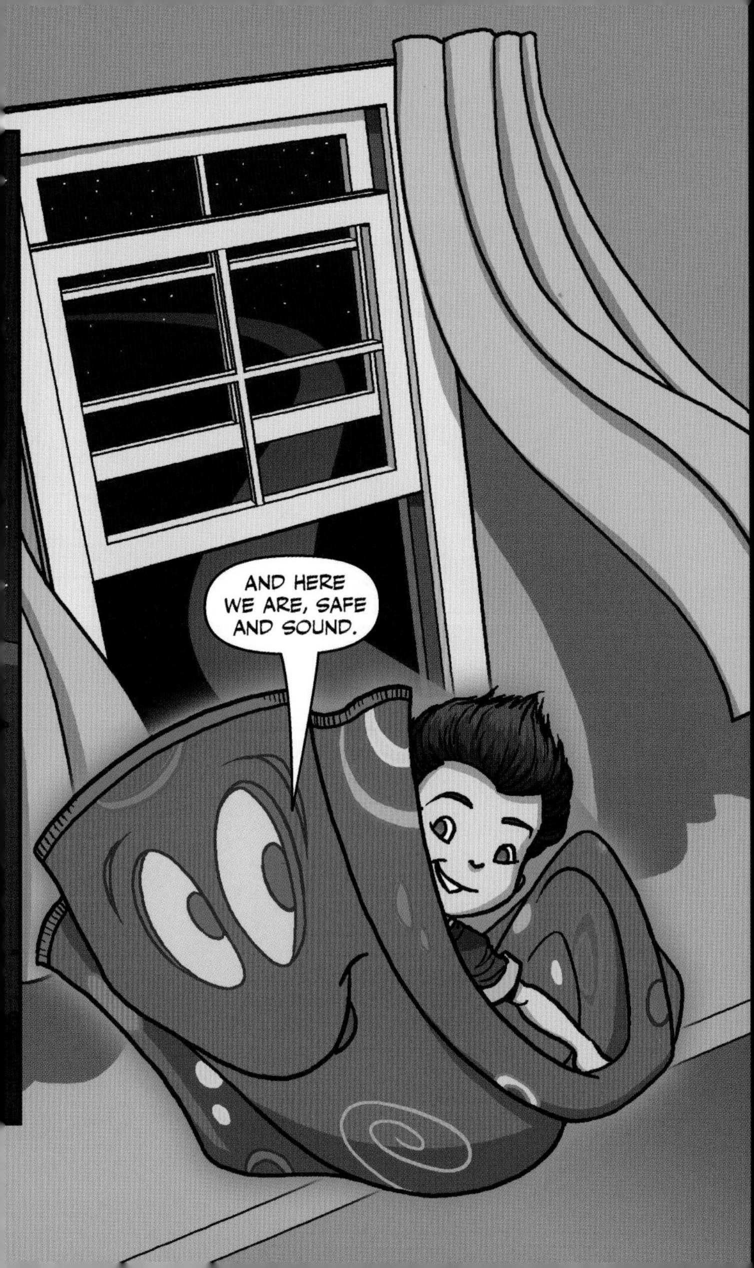
AND HERE WE ARE, SAFE AND SOUND.

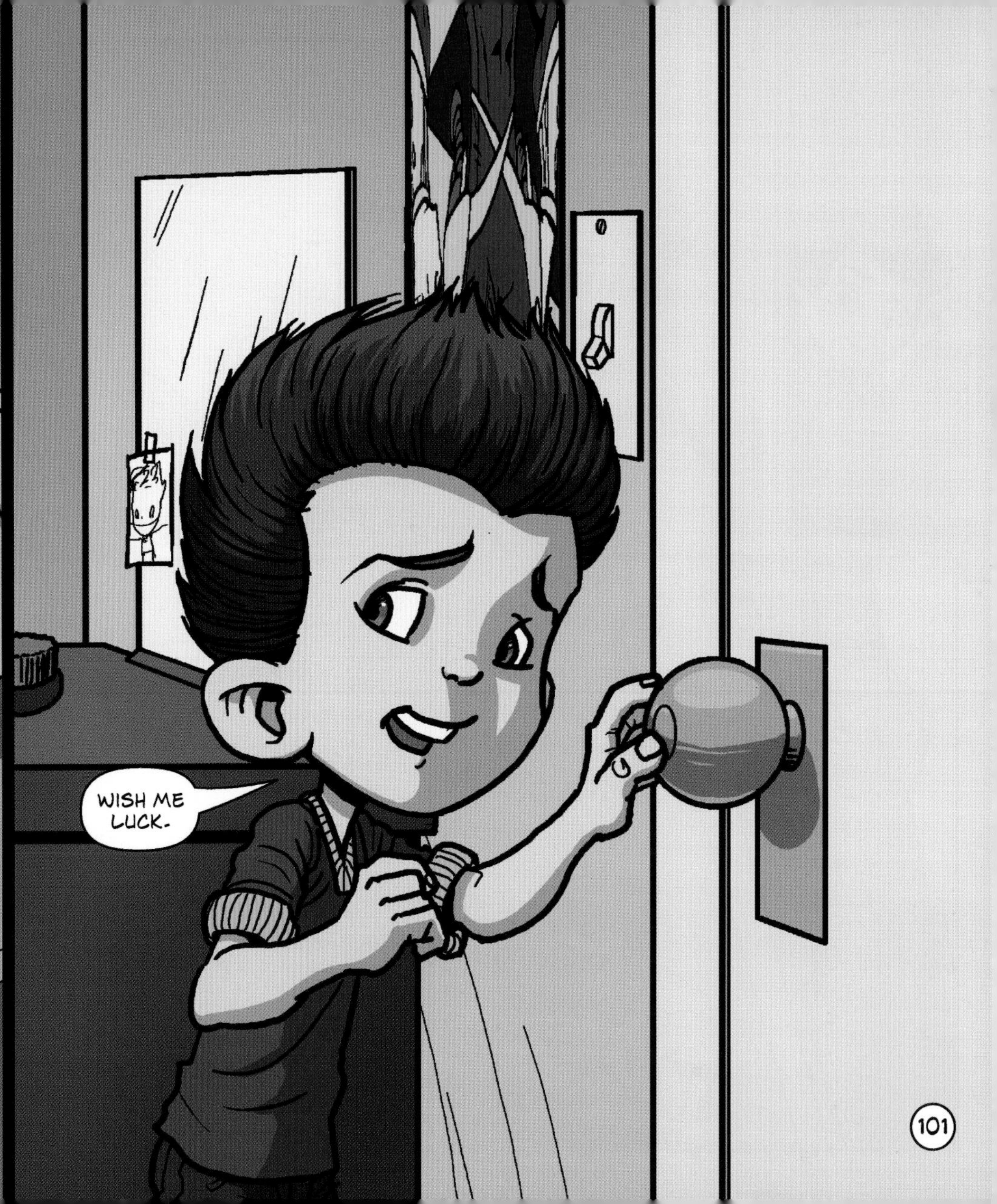
WISH ME LUCK.

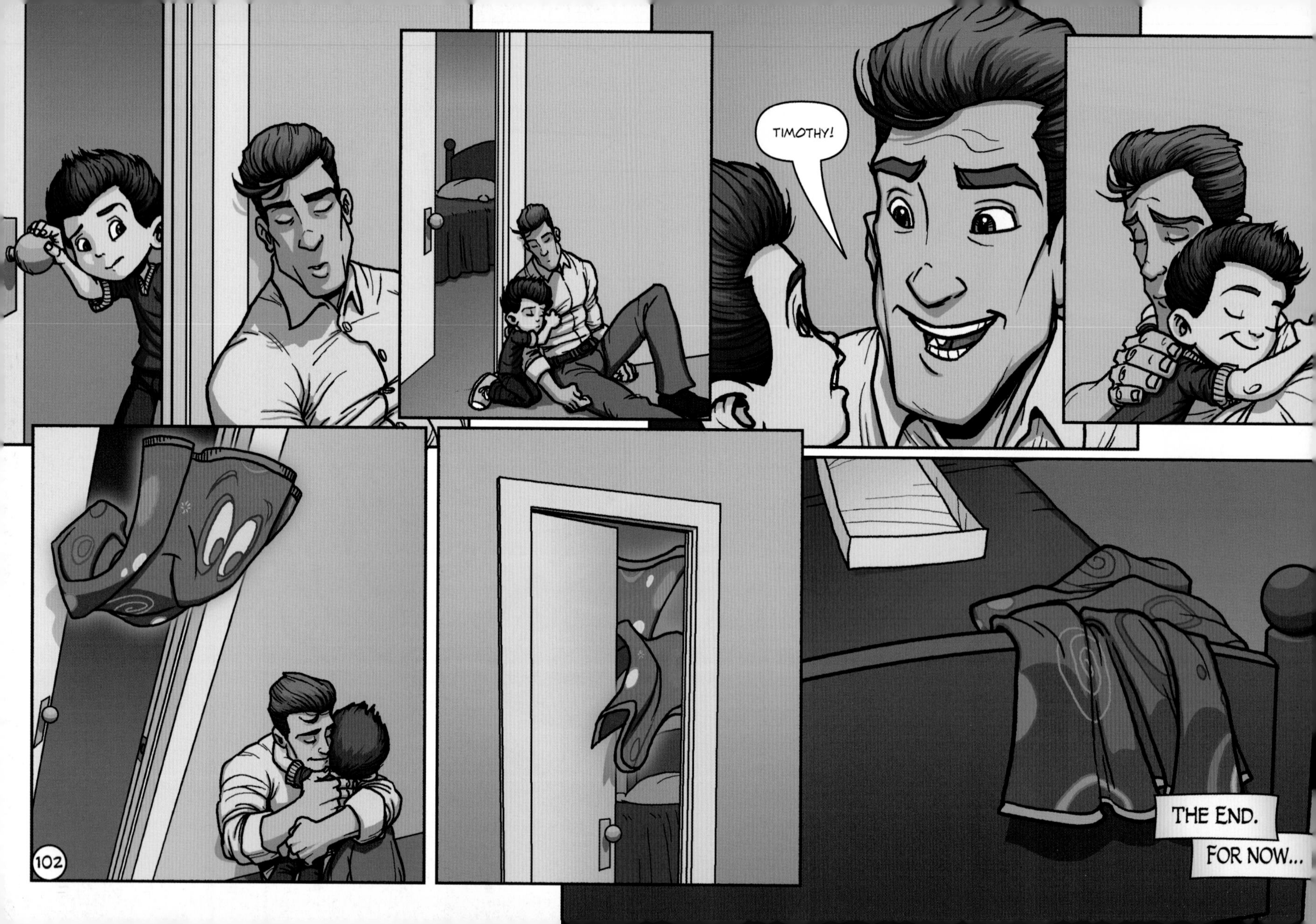
TIMOTHY!
THE END.
FOR NOW...

Other Silverline Books you and your family will enjoy...

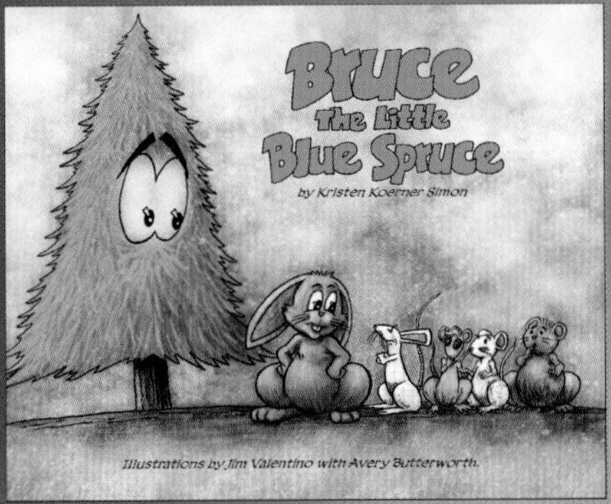
Bruce
The Little
Blue Spruce
by Kristen Koerner Simon
Illustrations by Jim Valentino with Avery Butterworth.

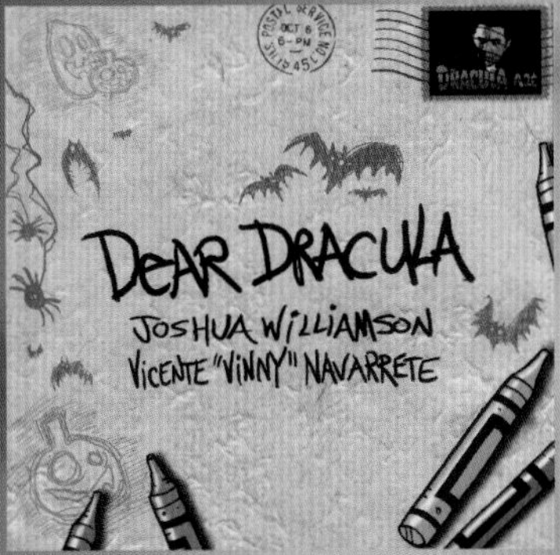
DEAR DRACULA
JOSHUA WILLIAMSON
VICENTE "VINNY" NAVARRETE

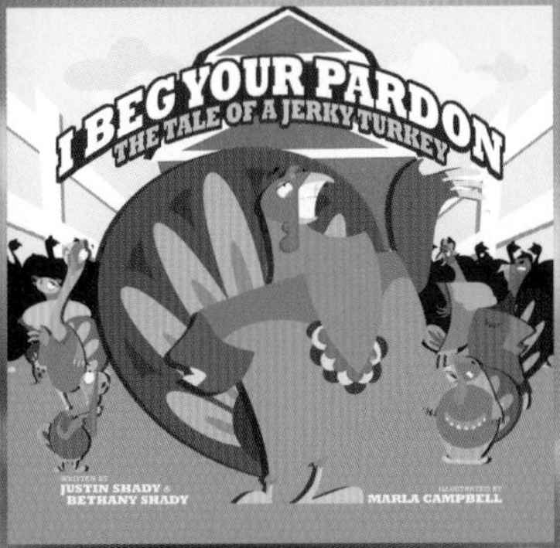
I BEG YOUR PARDON
THE TALE OF A JERKY TURKEY
JUSTIN SHADY & BETHANY SHADY
MARLA CAMPBELL

Ages 4-8:

Bruce: The Little Blue Spruce
32 pages Hardcover $9.99
ISBN: 978-1-60706-008-6

Dear Dracula
48 pages Hardcover $7.99
ISBN: 978-1-58240-970-2

I Beg Your Pardon
32 pages Hardcover $12.99
ISBN: 978-1-60706-136-6

The Lava Is A Floor!
32 pages Hardcover $12.99
ISBN: 978-1-60706-123-6

Night of the Bedbugs
32 pages Hardcover $12.99
ISBN: 978-1-60706-145-8

T. Runt
40 pages Hardcover $12.99
ISBN: 978-1-60706-074-1

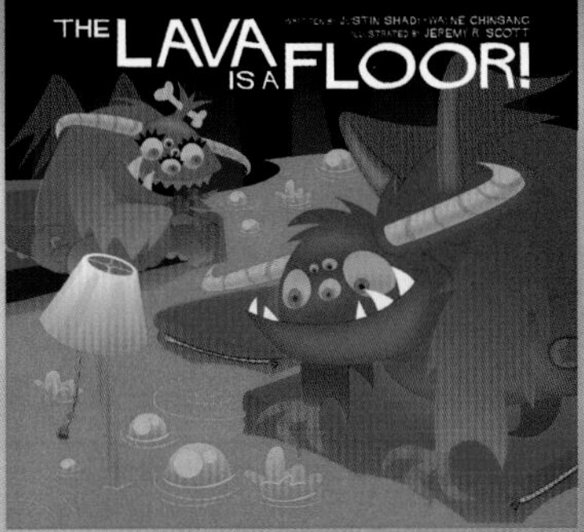
THE LAVA IS A FLOOR!

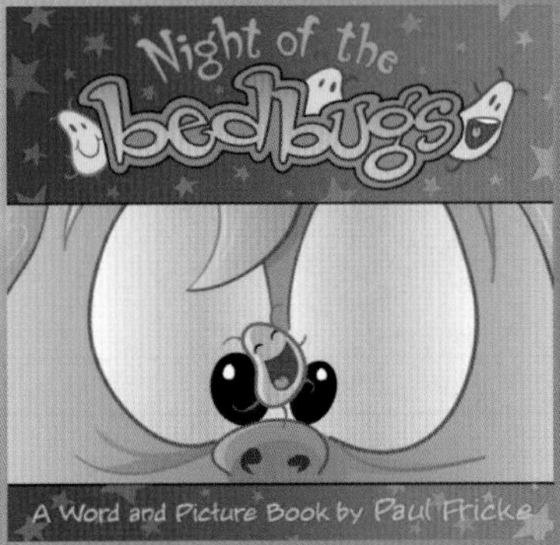
Night of the bedbugs
A Word and Picture Book by Paul Fricke

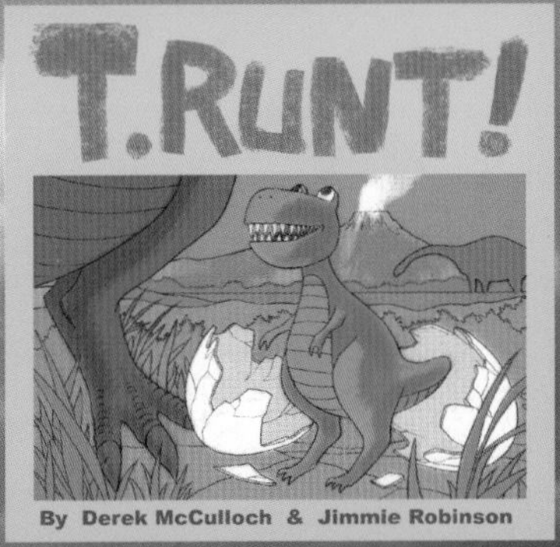
T.RUNT!
By Derek McCulloch & Jimmie Robinson

Please visit us at: **www.silverlinebooks.com**
for activity pages, mazes and other fun stuff!

EVIL & MALICE
SAVE THE WORLD!

The Surreal Adventures of
Edgar Allan Poo
Silverline Books

MISSING the BOAT

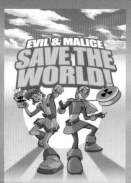

Ages 9-12

Timothy and the Transgalactic Towel
112 pages Softcover $16.99
ISBN: 978-1-60706-021-5

Evil and Malice Save the World!
128 pages Softcover $14.99
ISBN: 978-1-60706-091-8

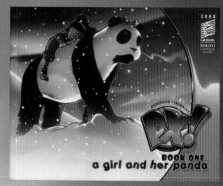

Ages 12 and up

Missing the Boat
96 pages Hardcover $18.99
ISBN: 978-1-58240-015-4

PX! Book One: A Girl and Her Panda
168 pages Softcover $16.99
ISBN: 978-1-58240-820-0

PX! Book Two: In Service To the Queen
152 pages Softcover $16.99
ISBN: 978-1-58240-018-5

The Surreal Adventures of Edgar Allan Poo
96 pages Softcover $9.99
ISBN: 978-1-58240-816-3

The Surreal Adventures of Edgar Allan Poo Book Two
96 pages Softcover $12.99
ISBN: 978-1-58240-975-7

Coming Soon

Tiffany's Epiphany (Ages 4-8)
32 pages Hardcover $12.99
ISBN: 978-1-60706-110-6

2008
ANDERSON • TREMBLEY
PX!
BOOK ONE:
a girl and her panda

ANDERSON • TREMBLEY
PX!
BOOK TWO:
In the Service of the Queen

TIFFANY'S EPIPHANY
by Kristen Koerner Simon & Jim Valentino
Book Two of the Blue Forest Series

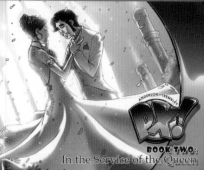

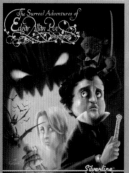

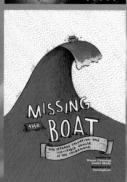

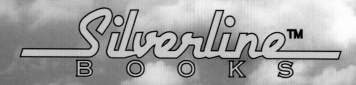

Silverline™ BOOKS

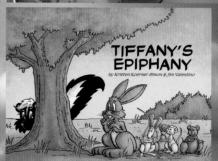

Available wherever finer books are sold!